THE POWER OF KETCHUP

Sarah Hauer

The story, names, characters, and incidents portrayed in this production are fictitious. No identification with actual persons, living or deceased, are intended or should be inferred.

Edited by Claire Steakley and Jonah Nelson
Content editing by Lana Nelson and Elizabeth Kilian
Copyright 2021

For Sherlock,
Always, Sunshine

For J, J, and Y

1

In The Beginning, There Was Ketchup...

There is something about the splat of dropped ketchup onto the dusty ground in front of the bleachers of a softball field that sends an ant colony into a frenzy. The vibration of it reverberates throughout the community causing each individual to set itself on a course of discovery almost uncontrollable as it connects itself to its more heavenly desires. It is manna from heaven, a reward for behavior above and beyond the call of duty.

Ketchup from the late morning breakfast hotdog of one Maggie Johnson is exactly what set this adventurous day alight for the entire town of Pennington's Corner, MN on Sunday, July 4th, 1982. Maggie took a bite of her hotdog inadvertently sending a splat of ketchup down miraculously missing the bleachers entirely and landing on the ground just barely in front of her. It sent an immediate mania throughout the colony below ground. The ant workers felt the vibration and sensed the sweetness of the heavenly gift. One worker had already arrived before the splat had fully settled into the dust, depositing its ant pheromones in a trail for other workers to follow. Another arrived, and another, and then a dozen before a creature of a higher order had the opportunity to acknowledge the existence of the ketchup. The line for sustenance to be observed, analyzed, and processed for colonial benefit began, and production proceeded with haste. In a most efficient manner, particles of ketchup were divided up, defined for their meaning and usefulness for the community at large, and the individuals got down to the business of bringing that meaning to life. They went about their work undaunted until a giant, black, wet nose entered the scene.

Caring nothing for the hard work the ants had already done analyzing, defining, and sorting, Charlie blew away many of the individuals with one blast of his nostrils and lapped up the ketchup splat in one sweep of his tongue before Maggie tugged at his leash wondering what the golden retriever puppy was up to with his nose so interested in terrestrial events.

"Charlie, what are you doing there? Is that food? Don't eat food off the ground, dear. That's gross." Maggie gave another tug after the first failed to get the pup's attention as the ants became a fascinating display for him. They scattered wondering why the manna from heaven disappeared.

Six year old Daisy could not help herself. She had to pet Charlie. Trying to be a good little girl, she gently posed the question. That level of cuteness demanded attention. "Mrs. Johnson? May I pet Charlie?"

"Sure, go ahead," Maggie responded, not paying any real attention to the child. Her eyes fixated on the softball game. Her mouth filled with another bite of hotdog. "My God, Marty looks better every year," she said to no one, not realizing the words had come out of her mouth.

"Who looks better every year?" asked Lori, Maggie's employee at the salon and Daisy's mother sitting a few feet away. *God, can I never get away from this woman?* Lori thought to herself.

"Oh! Ah, I was talking about Daisy, dear. I said, 'My! Doesn't she look prettier every year? Growing so fast.'" Maggie said in an attempt to fix the near conversational disaster.

Because of her history with Lori's mother, Sharon Greenfield, Maggie didn't care for Lori. Maggie and Sharon were in high school together and competed in everything, including boys. They were sworn enemies until Sharon died in a one vehicle drunk driving accident in 1978. However, she didn't want to lose Lori from the salon either. She was talented at getting frizzy bangs to sit high up off the forehead in the latest 80s trend.

Maggie's mind traveled four years earlier to the memorial for Sharon at the funeral home. The mourners were sparse and mostly male. Pete, Maggie's husband, held the door wide open for her with a smile.

"For heaven's sake, Pete!" scolded Maggie. "This is a funeral, not a softball game. Wipe that grin off your face."

Pete attempted to look serious. "Oh, right. Sorry." He closed the door and breezed past Maggie and went in search of the grieving daughter and her two children, Michael and Daisy. Pete found them in the front by the casket. Eight year old Michael was trying so hard to see the body of his dead grandmother that he was on the verge of tipping it over. Two year old Daisy was at her mother's side trying to get her attention in the swarm of men offering their sympathies to the beautiful, young, mother.

Pete approached first until Maggie grabbed his arm and pulled him back to make a point. "Can you believe how those men are flocking to that poor child? My God! You'd think they'd have some decency. She just lost her mother, and now has no help to raise those children, not that Sharon was much of a help anyways. I wonder which one of them is the father?" She looked lovingly at Pete whose grin was now gone. "I'm so glad you aren't that kind of man, Pete. That I can count on you and trust you."

"Yeah. Of course, you can," he responded quietly.

"I heard she is nearly done with classes to be a hair stylist. If the rumors are true that she has real talent for hair, I'm going to hire her. Someone should try and give her a hand with the money it takes to raise children. I don't see how she can do it on her own. I know Sharon didn't teach her anything. That woman was a waste of human flesh. Sharon spent more energy sleeping around than raising her child. Maybe Lori is too. Who knows?"

Everyone in town knew, except Maggie.

Maggie's mind was brought back to the softball game by Daisy petting Charlie who was still on the hunt for more ketchup even though his tender nose was under attack from the ant colony. They wanted their gift from their benevolent God returned. She looked up to see the last of Maggie's hotdog entering the older woman's mouth and realized she was hungry too.

"Mommy, can I have a hotdog?"

Lori Greenfield was too engrossed in watching Marty's muscular features along with Maggie as he pitched in the third inning of the biggest game of the year to pay any attention to her daughter. The score was tied at zero to zero. Individual players had made it to first and some to second base, but no one had gotten all the way around yet. Besides, Pete, who was sitting on the other side of Maggie and slightly up and behind her level to Lori, was doing his best to flirt with Daisy's mother. The flirting could not be ignored. She got lots of bonuses from the male half of her employers that Maggie Johnson did not know about. Lori had a lifestyle to keep up and children to raise. Not that she raised them. She left them pretty much to themselves and the community at large.

"Mommy, I'm hungry," Daisy insisted.

Lori continued to ignore her daughter who hadn't had breakfast yet even though it was past 10 AM. She was too busy making eyes at Pete wondering if she could suck him well enough to get a car out of the owner of the only dealership in town.

"Mommy!"

"Michael!" Lori called out to her older child whom she was certain was around somewhere. "Michael!" she called out again not taking her eyes off Pete. *Good Lord,* she thought to herself. *Can I stand the taste of him well enough to get a car? He smells.*

"Yes, Mom?" 12 year old Michael appeared out of nowhere. Often out and about with his friends doing things he shouldn't be doing, he typically waited around until he could discern what kind of day his mother was having. It looked like he would be released soon.

Lori dug around in her purse for a couple of dollars. "Take your sister to the concession stand and get her some food."

"Okay." He didn't want to do it. But why not? Then he could be off and running for hours. Besides, he knew from this point on she would be busy with men until tomorrow morning leaving him free and clear to do as he pleased. "Come on!"

Even though Daisy was hungry, Michael felt the need to give her a pull to get her away from the fluffy goodness that was Charlie. "I'm coming," she said to her brother.

"A hit to center field leads to a catch, and that is three outs," spouted Larry, the owner and DJ on KPCN, the only local radio station. He sat in the booth above the concession stand where he could watch his paramour, Lori, flirting with other men during what was probably his most popular broadcast of the entire year. Everyone who couldn't attend wanted to know how this game was going. It was half the town versus the other half of the town, Catholic versus Lutheran, friend versus friend, where old scores sometimes got settled. "We are in the bottom of the third inning with a score still at zero-zero, one out."

Michael continued to pull Daisy over to the concession stand as fast as he could. The sooner he got her food, the sooner he could disappear for the day. "What do you want?"

"I don't know."

"Well?" Michael asked Daisy trying to get her to hurry up deciding. "Make up your mind or I will make it up for you."

Daisy pulled a little strand of blonde hair from her face as she contemplated her choices. Did she want a hotdog? Mrs. Johnson was eating a hotdog when she decided she was hungry. Maybe her tummy wanted a hotdog too. "Hotdog."

"One hotdog please and one Snickers."

"I don't want a Snickers."

"That's for me, stupid."

"Oh."

"Here you go, kid," said Sean, the teenager behind the counter. "If you want anything on it, stuff is over there."

"I know that," said Michael, irritated that anyone would dare give him directions. He walked over to where the condiments were stationed and automatically put mustard on the hotdog.

"No! Not mustard. I don't like mustard. I want ketchup!"

"Okay! Sorry! Geez! Don't get your panties in a wad! "

He took a napkin and half-heartedly tried to wipe away the mustard, only getting about half. Then he put on a line of ketchup.

"No," said Daisy. "I still see mustard. I don't like mustard."

"Okay, okay." Michael loaded the ketchup on the dog so no mustard could be seen. "There." He handed it to her with a finality she knew she did not want to challenge. "There's your breakfast. See ya." He disappeared before she could think of a response. She examined her hotdog carefully. As she gave it a little squeeze, some of the ketchup and mustard underneath began to mix together, slightly changing the color of the ketchup making it a bit brighter in appearance. She took her first bite, was satisfied with her breakfast of champions, and wandered off.

Next to the concession stand was a table set up with bottles of beer, plastic cups, and a couple of large silver barrels. There, smiling, was the bar owner, Craig, a friend to Daisy and her family.

"Hello, Daisy. Are you enjoying your hotdog?"

She simply nodded as bite number two made its way into her mouth. Ketchup continued to ooze around her mouth and over her fingers clutching it tight.

"Hmmm...I bet it's quite tasty with all that ketchup."

Daisy simply nodded again in agreement and smiled politely keeping her mouth closed as she ate.

Craig knew from this innocent conversation that if Daisy was roaming around on her own, then Lori must be at it again. He glanced around. His smile disappeared. Sure enough, there she was heading across the street toward some storage sheds with Pete Johnson trailing not far behind. Why Pete bothered to hide his exploits with Lori, no one understood. Everyone over the age of 10 knew what he was doing.

Craig felt the burn of anger deep inside himself. He didn't know why or where it came from. He had no hold over Lori or what she did. Never mind he had been in love with her since forever. He told her once in the fourth grade.

It was a warm March day in 1964, out on the playground during the school lunch break, Craig was in his usual spot sitting in the bushes alone where he could watch the girls play.

"Hey, Craig. What are you up to?" asked TJ, a classmate and fellow loner who didn't care for getting hurt in the playground football ritual either.

"I'm just sitting here."

"Can I watch the girls with you?"

"I'm not watching the girls!"

"I am." TJ settled in next to Craig.

They couldn't tell what the girls were doing. They seemed to be sitting in a half circle. Sometimes they giggled. Sometimes they seemed serious. After a while, the girls got up as one large group and started challenging each other to cartwheels. Lori Greenfield remained sitting on the grass. She pulled her skirt tighter around her.

Their louder voices started to carry across the playground.

"Come on, Lori!" taunted Perry, the most popular girl in the fourth grade. "I know you can do a cartwheel. I've seen you."

"I can't," Lori replied. "I'm wearing a dress."

"Why should that stop you?" Easy for Perry to say in her green corduroy pants and striped shirt.

The other girls joined in the taunts.

Craig watched Lori succumb to the peer pressure. She looked around determining where all the boys were on the playground. She glared at the football game. They were preoccupied with their own doings. She took a step back preparing to do the cartwheel.

"She's going to do it!" TJ expressed his own excitement while Craig kept his within.

The girls started to cheer, "Lori! Lori! Lori!"

She continued to eye the boys playing football. Just as she was about to do it, she took one more wide view. She locked eyes with Craig and froze.

"She sees us!" TJ could hardly contain his excitement.

Inside, Craig had conflicting emotions. On the one hand, he hoped she would stand up for herself and tell them no. On the other hand, he wanted to see her underpants as much as TJ.

She smiled at Craig. A slight smile of shyness and resignation. She did the cartwheel.

Her pink underpants were exposed. To Craig, they were magnificent!

"She did it!" yelled TJ.

She stopped and looked in Craig's direction again. She was still smiling, this time from embarrassment. He was flush with excitement and smiled back. Both their smiles faded when a cheer came up from the football game. All the boys from grades four through six stopped to observe the show.

Lori's cheeks turned red. She curtsied for the boys and walked back into the school. Lori was determined to appear confident. Inside, she was mortified.

After school, Craig caught up with her as she was walking home.

"Hi," he ventured.

"Hi," she responded shyly.

"Um. I just wanted to say I'm sorry about what happened on the playground."

"Oh..."

"I didn't think it was right that the guys all cheered like that."

"Yeah..."

There was a long pause as they walked along towards her home in the exact opposite of his. Craig was trying to be careful about what to say.

"But," he pressed, "I did like it myself."

"Really?"

"Yeah. I...I thought it was kinda brave of you. I mean you were wearing a dress today. Who does a cartwheel while wearing a dress? I think it was brave."

"Yeah...who does do something like that." It wasn't a question.

"I thought your panties were pretty."

"Okay."

"Lori?"

"Yes..."

"Can I kiss you?"

Lori stopped abruptly. A blank look came over her face. "You want to kiss me?"

"May I?"

"I suppose so."

Craig planted a quick little kiss on her lips. She somewhat kissed back, but not really.

"I love you, Lori Greenfield! Bye!" He turned the other way and started running home feeling on top of the world.

Tears ran down Lori's face as she finished her walk to an empty house.

A tug on his pants pulled Craig back to reality. He looked down at Daisy looking as pretty as her mother did as a child. She was pointing to a can of pop. "I'm sorry, Daisy. What can I do for you?" He felt oddly responsible for the neglect in her life. "You want a coke? Here you are." He handed her a can, and she trotted on.

"Top of the fourth. Pitcher for St. Paul's back on the mound." Larry's voice reverberated around the field.

Noises drew Daisy to the dugout of St. Paul's Lutheran Church's team. Daisy liked Pastor James. He always said hi to her when he passed her by. He didn't ignore her like a lot of other people did. She poked her head in as most players emptied the dugout headed to their positions not seeing her at all.

"All I'm saying is I don't understand why we have to have this game every year."

"Because, Pastor James," a player chided, "It's tradition."

"Now you sound like a Catholic," replied the Pastor, Bible in hand, using it to point out the Catholics in the other dug-out. "And I understand it's good exercise. But you guys get way too competitive with people who are supposedly your life-long friends. Why is it that on this same day every year, you want to beat each other's brains out?"

"Cause it's fun," another player retorted as he headed out to his position on the field.

Pastor James slumped down on the bench shaking his head. He wasn't getting anywhere with this bunch. Year after year, he failed to make them see how this game was not an appropriate way for Lutherans and Catholics to be interacting. It should be in a calm, respectful manner with distance between them. After all, they were Catholics. Catholics didn't like Lutherans. Catholics believed all other Christians who were not Catholic were going to hell. Pastor James missed the point. This annual game was a tradition that spanned almost a hundred years and kept civil disputes out of the courts.

Daisy tried to get Pastor James's attention by waving her hand holding the hotdog. She had to be extra careful with the oozing ketchup, so she kept her movements small. He didn't see her. She gave up and trotted off.

She decided if she could look into one dugout, she may as well look into the other one. She skipped over to the opposing team. In similar fashion, she poked her head in to find this dugout crawling with people.

"Hey, Daisy!" Marty rarely noticed her but did today. She smiled as he breezed past her with his bat to the batter's box, and that little bit of attention made her happy. She squeezed her hotdog a little bit more. She peeked further in to see what was going on with the other players.

"Come on, Lord," prayed Fr. Andrew through stern lips. "We have to show these Lutherans what we're made of. Hit it out of the park, Marty!"

Other players were either busy talking or were spitting out sunflower seeds. One player spit out something really gross near Daisy's feet that seemed so icky that she pulled herself right back out of the dugout. "Yuck!" she complained. A tiny yellowish moth caught her eye, and she followed it barely remembering she was carrying her hotdog.

Maggie watched her go. She looked around to see if Lori was paying attention to her own daughter. Not seeing Lori around, Maggie muttered out loud, "Of course she isn't," to Pete. She didn't notice Pete wasn't there to hear her either. When no response came from him, she looked over her other shoulder. "Now where has he gotten off to?" She shrugged her shoulders and went back to appreciating Marty's physique at bat.

"A hit to right field!" yelled Larry into the microphone. "A base hit. St. John's has a runner on first." A little cheer came up from about half the crowd. The other half groaned.

Pete and Lori were still across the street between sheds of a storage facility for a local agricultural business on a hidden bench. His mouth slobbering all over her completely exposed breasts and his fingers well up in her vagina, Lori started the conversation delicately.

"Pete, my love?" Lori said in between her fake moans and irritated eye rolls.

"Hm?"

"Are you (moan) enjoying this?"

"Oh, yes."

"That's good." She looked quite bored, but got her moans perfectly timed and appropriately pitched to keep him believing she was into him and to keep his brain preoccupied. "You know, Pete, (moan) my car hasn't been working very well lately. (moan)"

"It hasn't?" he mumbled with his mouth full of nipple.

"Oh, baby, I just love that. (moan)" Except she didn't love it at all. "No, it hasn't."

"Well, I can probably get Marty to take a look at it."

"Marty already did. (moan) He couldn't find anything (moan) wrong. But it just isn't running right." She got just the right whiny pitch in her tone to produce his pity for her lifestyle.

Pete started to pick up his head and think. Lori could not risk that happening if she was going to get a car out of this encounter. She pushed his head back down and did a slight subject change. "Oh, Pete. I just love what you're doing to me." He got right back to it. She made sure his brain was solidly housed in his penis. "Did you want to come like this, or did you want me to do something else to you?" She felt Pete shutter in excitement. She knew it. She had him right where she wanted him.

He flipped her off the bench and deposited himself on it. She went right to work on him bearing the stench of his body that turned her off immensely. As she felt him getting close to climaxing, she stopped and stroked just long enough to ask in a slow, low tone, "Pete, could you get me a new car?" And then she went all out on him. His eyes rolled back. He started off saying the one word she wanted to hear, "Yes! Yes!" Then he continued with the promise more profoundly than she had expected. "I will get you a new car!" He followed it up with enough noises of intense orgasm that spectators heard from across the street. The only one who looked back in curiosity at the strange animalistic screeches was Maggie. Nobody else was curious enough to question because they already knew what was happening. Women winced, some of the men looked jealous of Pete, other men cowered from their wives in truthful ignorance or feigned innocence.

One person who was not around to give auditory witness to the indiscretion was Michael. He was running around town collecting friends so they could find trouble somewhere, anywhere, where adults were not around. He collected three other boys, making a nice round number for the group. He led them all by bike to the grain elevator along the railroad tracks. They ditched their bikes and started their trek along the tracks heading east of town to the train trestle.

They didn't notice Officer Helen Schafer was observing them from a distance. She stopped her patrol car near where they left their bikes and watched them walk off in the distance. "Stay out of trouble, Michael," she said to the air. "Stay out of trouble." She knew where they were headed. And there was no road near the trestle.

Beaver Creek, so minimal and unimportant that no one remembered the name of it, trickled underneath the train trestle. Graffiti was everywhere on the bridge. People went there periodically to make love, do drugs, or to get away by themselves for a while. It was a quiet spot. The only sound was the wind between the blades of tall grass and the occasional farm dog barking off in the distance.

The boys climbed down the bank of the creek to get below the trestle. Once down there, Michael pulled firecrackers out of his pockets.

"Where'd you get those from?"

"One of my mom's boyfriends."

"I wish my mom had boyfriends."

No, you don't, thought Michael, but he didn't say it out loud.

"What should we blow up?" asked one of them.

"We could get Old Man Larson's dog. His farm is just up a ways."

"Nah. That's too far. Something close by."

"Maybe we can find a toad?"

They all liked that idea. They hunted around. They should have planned their location better. The west side of town was swampier and where toads would be easier to find.

"Nothing," said one kid.

"Let's just set 'em off anyway. That's what we came here for," said another.

"Nah," said Michael. "Let's wait for something more interesting. We'll do 'em later. Let's head back to town. Nothin' to do out here without a toad anyways." They started their trek back.

2

Daisy and Her Hotdog

"Unbelievable!" screamed Larry from the box. "End of the fifth, and the score is now five to one! How did this happen!"

It happened because Marty not only got on base, but ended up being the first and only run for the Catholics at the top of the fifth inning making it one to nothing.

The Lutherans got nervous because the Catholics hadn't won a game in seven long years. During all those losses, the Catholics never scored the first run of the game. The Lutheran team swung into action. Player after player were hitting ground balls off Marty into center field allowing them to make the rounds base by base. One run scored. Then another. And another. By the time they were done with the fifth inning and headed into the sixth, the score was now five to one, the Lutherans in the lead.

"This is looking as bad as the first game ever played," said Fr. Andrew to Marty as the teams exchanged positions.

"No," said Marty. "The way I heard it, that first game was a land dispute that was going to end either with a win or a massacre."

The 4th of July softball game was an annual event of biblical proportions. It transcended social and religious rules of behavior for the entire community of Pennington's Corner regardless of who played, who watched, or who ignored the event.

The games started in 1934 over a land dispute between two farmers, one Catholic and one Lutheran. Neighbors took sides mostly based on religion. As threats of violence increased, Mr.

Pennington, the founder of the community, decided it was time to step in. He held a secret meeting in his home with the priest and the minister. It was decided God would be the best judge by helping one team win a softball game on the 4th of July. Mr. Pennington assigned the management duties to the two pastoral figures. The men brought their best game abilities, and the women brought their best pies. It was a huge success both in terms of dispute settlement and entertainment. The Catholics won.

Over the course of the year until the next game, any personal injury sparked due to some social blunder or misunderstanding and conveniently blamed on religious denomination instead of more appropriately labeled a mistake was allowed to fester over the months without need for attention. No one took revenge or sued for libel because the game itself would decide whom God favored most. Every year on the 4th of July each team in unspoken fashion took on the cause of one person from the church to take up the challenge from the opposing team/church. On the one hand, it helped create peace between the warring factions throughout the year. On the other hand, it made it difficult for the entire community to simply enjoy a 4th of July holiday like normal Americans.

Over time, pies gave way to beer and burgers, and community disputes became more about habitual religious animosities than true acts of insult or injury.

"Hey!" asked Mrs. Peterson to Mr. Horner. "What are we battling over this year? I heard it had something to do with that brawl over at the bar on Valentine's Day. I never heard anything about what started it."

Mr. Horner lied. "Naw, that was nothing. This year it's just a game."

None of the married women heard the true cause of the commotion. The men vowed silence. It did happen the previous Valentine's Day. A fight broke out over who was Lori's official date.

Justin Schneider, Lutheran versus Pat Hollard, Catholic. Neither won the brawl. Lori went home with Dave Allender, Atheist and not from Pennington's Corner.

The top of the sixth inning was led by an extremely loud and venomous Gregorian chant-like prayer from Fr. Andrew that had the Catholics swinging. Almost every other pitch was answered with a crack. Some of them were handily caught. Others hit their mark moving a batter along a base. No one could recall a game with so much action. A switch in the pitching roster did little to change the dynamic of the half inning. By the time Marty was back up to bat, the score was five to four with two men on base, one on third and one on first, with two outs. The heat was on as much for Marty as it had been for Pete earlier when he had returned to his seat under the curious gaze of his wife.

"Where have you been?" asked Maggie.

"Nowhere," Pete replied, preparing himself for the inevitable lie.

"Nowhere took you a very long time."

"I just went to the bathroom. Got myself a hotdog. And then I got a beer. Stood over there and drank it before coming back."

"I would have seen you get the beer."

"I'm telling you I was there."

The spectators could not believe Maggie didn't argue further. One woman leaned down to spill the beans. Her husband dragged her back and indicated no, stay out of it. It was probably best given the circumstances. Lori arrived right at that moment, having gone to clean herself up a bit. Her house was very close by, and Pete had left her a mess.

Maggie did not notice Lori was wearing an entirely different outfit. Mrs. Peterson did. "Lori," she asked loudly. "Is that a new outfit you have on?" Maggie only vaguely glanced at Lori. Her mind was too busy trying to figure out Pete's lie to put two and two together. That was probably a good thing. An altercation between a man and two women with all those spectators cheering the wife on might have turned into a mob. There was enough mob mentality happening in the game.

Jake Keating was new on the team, fresh out of high school. Coach Meir, the coach for the Lutheran team and school principal, made sure Jake graduated even though he did not pass half his classes just so he could play this one summer game. He wanted to stack his pitching roster with a young guy, and high schoolers were not allowed to play.

It didn't work. Marty knew Jake better than Coach Meir understood. Marty looked Jake in the eye draining the poor kid of his mental power. Jake owed Marty a big favor. He purchased beer for the underage kid for his graduation party. It was time for payback.

First pitch did it. Marty hit it over the fence like nobody's business. Three runs in. The score was now seven to five, Catholics in the lead.

Daisy was still walking around the ballpark. She was well on her way to the scoreboard when Sean abandoned the concession stand and ran over to man the board now that some real action was taking place.

The scoreboard was out a little left from center field just behind the chain-link fence, facing the spectators. There was approximately six feet between the fence and the front of the scoreboard. Further along the fence, almost at the center of the entire field, was an opening in the fence. There was a worn path all the way around the outside of the fence, between the fence and the scoreboard, and through the opening onto the field.

Sean did not notice the little girl at all. Her hotdog down to three last bites and her can of pop about half gone, she was more interested in the ketchup on her hand than anything happening with the game. It was turning into a bright red mess. She started licking it off her fingers.

As all this was happening, Mrs. Carol Benson, devout Catholic and a woman of great faith but tiny stature, was in her home across the street from the softball field. The sounds of the annual game wreaked havoc on her aging bones in her arthritic joints. She was a well-respected member of the community due to age and her demands for strict religious adherence even for the Lutherans. Mrs. Benson could hear all the commotion at the game. It was too much for her delicate nature physically and spiritually. She decided she needed to go do something about saving all those people from themselves. In her mind, this game was sacreligious because it reinforced violence as a way to settle disputes. She removed her apron, put on her most sensible shoes, and headed out, rosary in hand.

The women in the bleachers could see Mrs. Benson leave her home from all the way across the softball field. She was more than a block away, but her tiny, bent over frame was recognizable.

"Think that woman will ever die?" asked Mrs. Peterson.

"Nope," was the simple response from Maggie.

Undaunted after being caught for her late morning exploits by everyone but the wife of the other offending party, Lori dared to ask, "Is it true Mrs. Benson was the lover of the guy who started this town?" Everyone but Maggie stared at Lori for her audacity.

"No," answered Maggie thoughtlessly. "I remember my mother talking about that rumor. Mrs. Benson isn't that old."

Mrs. Peterson got curious about the history. "Maggie, did your mother know the Pennington's? I remember my grandmother talking about how grand Mrs. Pennington was."

"No, not my mother. My grandmother was Mrs. Pennington's housekeeper for a while. I remember her talking about the plans for the town. This town is a failed Utopia."

"How so?" asked Lori.

"Mr. Pennington was a wealthy businessman from New York City who wanted to change his focus from making money to making a family. He wanted an environment for children that was safe and friendly. He arrived in Minnesota and traveled about looking for such a place. He did not find one, so he decided the best thing he could do was create one."

Maggie continued to tell the story of how Mr. Pennington settled on this track of land because of the fertility of the rich, black soil where things grew easily if they could hack the bitter cold winters, and because a number of farmers already inhabited the area and were looking for better ways to get their crops to market besides horse and buggy. He was able to accomplish that for them by using his business contacts to get the railroad to come through and stop in the center of the brand new town where he immediately built a general store and hired someone to manage it for him.

Maggie bragged about the town she loved so much. "He built that magnificent home right at the corner of Main and Cedar Avenue, just over there." She pointed in the direction where part of the roof could be seen from the bleachers. Everyone knew the house well. It was nearly empty and dilapidated now. City council meetings were held there. The mayor's office and city clerk spent many afternoons alone there day after day. No one bothered to question what work was accomplished.

She went on. "That officially became known as Pennington's Corner in 1878. It didn't take too long for other people to move in to set up a blacksmith, a carpenter shop, a bar, a post office, a couple of churches, and other establishments. New homes popped up in the blink of an eye.

"All that was left for Mr. Pennington to do was to find a wife. However, men arrived before the women, and the women were taking longer than Mr. Pennington was willing to wait. He did not allow any prostitutes in town because of his Christian-based, family-oriented vision for the community. He did what any good Christian, red-blooded, American man would do: he sent for a bride from back east."

"She was a mail-order bride?" asked Lori.

Maggie eagerly responded. "Yep. Can you imagine how she must have felt? His former business associates were more than happy to interview ladies of quality for him. They chose the best and sent her on her way by train. She arrived in time for the tenth anniversary of the founding of the town on September 1st, 1888.

"Mr. Pennington was pleased with the choosing of his bride. The wedding ceremony was held within minutes of her arrival in the middle of the anniversary festivities.

"Sadly for Mrs. Pennington, time was not on Mr. Pennington's side. It had taken years too long, or, at least, that was the reason Mr. Pennington believed to be the cause of his change in luck. Mr. Pennington was not able to plant sufficient seed into his young bride for a child to arrive. He died childless. No family except his wife, who never remarried and never had children. Nonetheless, he died a very well-respected man of the town."

"No family left," said Mrs. Peterson. "That's sad. Wonder where they are buried?"

Maggie answered, "Probably somewhere in the municipal cemetery. Who knows? With no family around to care enough to manage the gravestones, graves get lost."

Maggie Johnson was more correct than she realized. The citizens did their best to keep the original intentions for the community alive as long as they could; but, with no descendants to care for them, their gravestones were left to overgrowth and decay. The couple's designs for Pennington's Corner were lost in the weeds. In 1982, almost a hundred years later after the founding of the town, no one knew where they were buried.

The ladies in the stands continued to watch Mrs. Benson slowly make her way to the softball field on the opposite side between game plays.

Mrs. Carol Benson, 73 years old, widowed at the young age of

32 in a freak farming accident, was a praying powerhouse in the community. She was a descendant of a long line of devout Catholics who instilled in her a vision of the Virgin Mary that teetered on the edge of fantastic. Mrs. Benson didn't just pray her rosary every day like a good Catholic. She prayed three times a day. She didn't humbly pray for the souls of others like a good Catholic. Oh, no. She prayed for the souls of the town to be changed so they all would become Catholic. She wanted to be given credit for saving souls, and to be given the coveted place in heaven next to the Virgin Mary as her equal. Except every good Catholic knows there is no such place in heaven.

There was a religious arrogance in her attitude. It was the way she waved around her rosary about town, in and out of prayer, and pointed it at other people in a way that said, "I know you are bad, and I am going to force you to be good!" She always talked about the Virgin Mary as if they were close confidantes who gossiped daily about other people.

That was how the rumors spread that at one time she had been a mistress to Mr. Pennington. No one could believe any single human being could be so devout to prayer unless their soul was tainted by sin. Intense prayers come from intense guilt from sins of highly immoral behavior. What sin could be juicier gossip than a Catholic whore and a man so moral that he attempted to build the perfect utopian community? Gossip did not require proof. However, gossip without proof often died out over time. Not this time.

Under her breath, Mrs. Peterson ended the conversation with, "Nah. Where there's smoke, there's fire. I bet she was his mistress at some point."

With bases empty and two outs, Jake struck out the next batter. That saved him from being banned from all softball games for all of eternity.

"Jake," said Coach Meir. No other words came. All he could do was shake his head at the kid in disappointment. The other team should not have been able to score so many points that half inning.

Daisy arrived at the scoreboard. She wondered how these things worked. They seemed like giant puzzles from the other side of the field. Turned out they weren't like giant puzzles at all when close up. They were rather boring. Daisy turned her attention to another moth. Or was it the same moth? Ketchup filled the palm of her hand as another bite of hotdog entered her mouth.

Sean, in his excitement that his church's team was next at bat, almost knocked Daisy down. There had never been an exciting finish to any of these games since he was old enough to pay attention.

Bottom of the seventh inning, Marty hobbled out to pitch for the Catholics. The Lutherans felt the pressure. Marty's exhaustion was beginning to show, and the Lutherans intended to take advantage.

"Fr. Andrew," said a player on the Catholic side still in the dugout with him, "Marty is too tired to pitch. He's been pitching the whole game, and he just hit that homerun. You've got to take him out."

"No. No. He's got this. This game is just as important to him as it is to me. Right? It is. Right?"

"I don't know what you're waiting for. A sign? Something huge? A bolt of lightning? I'm telling you, he's too tired."

Fr. Andrew ignored the player and cheered Marty on. "You've got this!"

Marty did not have this. First batter hit a line drive double. Second batter followed suit driving the first batter all the way home. Seven to six.

"Told you," said the other player to Fr. Andrew, but he would not relent. He still kept Marty on the mound believing God would intervene for the team. He struck out the next two batters making Fr. Andrew feel confident in his decision.

Bottom of the seventh, the last inning, a runner on second base, score of seven to six, and Jake Keening was up to bat facing Marty again, this time in opposite positions. The favor was settled with Marty's home run in the fifth inning. Jake didn't owe him anything anymore. The young man sized up the older. Marty's arm was definitely tired. He played hard all game. The young man had not. He had energy, strength, and youth on his side.

Daisy put the very last bite of hotdog in her mouth and followed the moth even closer to the scoreboard.

Marty pitched, Jake hit, and the ball was in play heading straight out to center field. By some miracle, a fly ball that should have been an easy catch was not. It was dropped. If the spectators hadn't seen it, they wouldn't have believed it.

Larry attempted to capture the moment on the radio. "The center fielder dribbled the ball like a toddler playing t-ball. The runner on second got all the way home. We've got a tie game, folks, at seven runs each!". Jake got all the way to third base, arriving at the same time as the ball.

"Safe!" said the second base ump.

"Out!" yelled the home plate ump.

Sean jumped for joy and, as he reached to put up the run on the scoreboard, he bumped Daisy again who was intently studying the moth. She reached out her ketchup laden hand to catch herself on the lower part of the scoreboard. "Oh! Sorry, Daisy. I didn't see you there."

Daisy shrugged and went about her business with the moth. The teen turned his attention back to the game. No harm done. The moth flew away, and Daisy walked on following it, licking the ketchup off her hand in the process.

There was a commotion at third base. There seemed to be some dispute between whether or not the ball made it there in time to tag Jake out at third base making it the third out and the end of the game, or if he was safely on third base and the game had to continue. Sean moved in closer to the game away from the scoreboard to listen in.

At that moment, Mrs. Benson reached the scoreboard. She poked around it to follow the worn path that wove through the tall grass intending to follow it the long way around the field along the fence line to the bleachers near home plate. But, as soon as she got around the scoreboard, she stepped on a rock which gave a little twist to her ankle causing her to nearly fall over. Her hand made contact with the scoreboard to prevent her fall and potential injury – directly on the spot where Daisy had also made contact with the scoreboard to prevent her fall and potential injury with her ketchup drenched hand.

Mrs. Benson withdrew her hand from the scoreboard. She noticed an odd sensation in the palm of her hand. She lifted her hand to examine it. Blood. Mrs. Benson saw what she believed to be blood on her hand. Her eyes grew large. Did she put her hand on an exposed nail or something? She gently moved her fingers. She felt no injury. She looked to the scoreboard where her hand had touched it. There it was. Blood in some sort of circular type of shape. She bent down a bit lower to get a better look. Yep. She decided it must be blood alright. How did a spot of blood get on the lower part of the scoreboard?

Something about it caught her eye. She looked closer. She adjusted her angle and tilted her head a bit. Something about the circular swirls of blood seemed oddly familiar. She tilted her head a bit further...

Mrs. Benson's eyes almost fell out of her head. The blood rushed out of her face. Her mouth gaped open wide enough for Daisy's little yellow moth to make a home in it.

And then it happened. The scream. The scream of pure terror pulsated all over the park. The argument at third base was halted. The spectators froze in their positions. Even Michael heard it from half a mile away with his friends stealing a bra from a girl's bedroom they broke into who was two grades ahead of them in school. Mrs. Benson screamed loud, screamed hard, and screamed unceasingly until Sean approached her.

"Mrs. Benson! What is it? What's wrong? Are you okay? Are you hurt?"

Players, umps, Fr. Andrew, Pastor James, and spectators from across the field came running to find out if Mrs. Benson was dying from some strange stroke symptom.

Fr. Andrew was the next person to reach her. He was surprisingly fit for a priest. "Mrs. Benson! What is it? What's wrong?"

Mrs. Benson simply stammered. Words would not form. Once the scream stopped, no vocal sound offered to take its place. She was struck silent.

"Mrs. Benson, please! You've got to tell us what's wrong. We can't help you until we know."

Fr. Andrew could see Mrs. Benson's gaze slowly change from focusing on something deep in her mind to focusing on him. "She's coming back," he said to the crowd closest to him.

She blinked. Twice.

"Any moment now," he continued. "Come on, Mrs. Benson. Spit it out."

"Blood."

"Excuse me? Did you say blood?"

She nodded. "Blood."

"Where?"

"On my hand." She was definitely coming back to life now. "Jesus's blood."

"Did you say, 'Jesus's blood?'"

Pastor James out of breath pushed his way through the crowd to reach her at that moment. "What's going on? Is she alright?"

"I'm not sure," responded Fr. Andrew to his softball and religious nemesis. "What she is saying is not making sense."

"What's not making sense? What is she saying?"

"She is saying, 'Blood. Jesus's blood.' On her hand.'"

"What? That sounds crazy."

"Mrs. Benson," Fr. Andrew bent down and attempted to pry deeper. "May I see Jesus's blood on your hand?"

Mrs. Benson slowly lifted her hand to show the two men her palm. The red liquid bright in the center of her hand.

"That's not your blood?" continued Pastor James.

"No," was her simple reply.

"How do you know it isn't your blood?"

"I'm not hurt."

"Well, maybe you are," Fr. Andrew took back control of the conversation again. "Does someone have a towel or something?"

"No!" she hissed pulling her hand away. "Don't wipe off His blood from my hand."

"Mrs. Benson, we have to get to the bottom of this. We have to make sure you are not hurt. How could you have gotten the blood on your hand like that unless you were injured?"

"I got it from the scoreboard."

"The what?"

"The scoreboard. There." She pointed to the spot on the lower part of the scoreboard where she caught herself from falling. "It's the face of Jesus. In his own blood."

The two men bent down to see more clearly the small swirl of red. At first, neither could see what she was referring to.

"I don't get it," said Pastor James. "The face of Jesus?"

"Look harder," said Mrs. Benson. "Tilt your head to the right. You will see it. The face of Jesus staring right back at you."

The two men tilted their heads. Their eyes grew bigger at the same time from the revelation that if a person tilted their head just enough to the right, the face of Jesus was quite easy to see in the swirls.

They stood up simultaneously and stared at each other. Then they looked at Mrs. Benson.

"See?" She shouted. "You see it too! It is the face of Jesus! It is!" She turned to the crowd and announced, "God has given us a gift! God has used my hand to bring us a miracle! He gave us the gift of the face of Jesus himself as a sign to us! He did it using my hand and the blood of Jesus! It is a miracle!"

"Oh, God," exclaimed Fr. Andrew to Pastor James. "We're in trouble now."

3

If You Tilt Your Head...

Reactions to Mrs. Benson's proclamation that the face of Jesus was visible in the swirl of blood on the scoreboard varied. Some people scoffed and turned away. Some ran as if Satan himself was hot on their tails. Some stayed back observing the scene. Some dropped to their knees and immediately began to pray. Some reached out to touch the blood on her hand, but she pulled it away from all of them. Some reached out to touch the hem of her skirt, hoping holy magic would rub off on them. Some tried to search for the face in the red stain on the scoreboard. As the face of Jesus came into view for individuals, some fainted, others backed off in terror.

Jake openly rejected the idea that Jesus did this. "You all are crazy. You know that? This is stupid." He bent down to investigate it himself. He searched and searched for the face in the blotch but saw nothing. "It's just blood." The idea of it being blood made him nauseous and dizzy. He backed off from the crowd and sat in the grass in the middle of center field with his arms around his knees and his head bent down. He started saying a prayer from childhood uncontrollably. Before he finished it, he shook it off and got up to return to the crowd to ridicule them more. "We should get back to the game. I was safe! Who's next at bat?"

Larry arrived on the scene carrying a microphone attached by a cord to heavy equipment slung over his shoulder by a strap. "Seems, we have breaking news, folks, here at the scoreboard, excitement has built upon excitement. God himself has come to Pennington's Corner! Details to follow shortly." He shut off the microphone for a moment. "What is going on here?" he asked no one and everyone simultaneously.

"It seems," said Pete, "that Mrs. Benson has encountered Jesus Christ on the scoreboard."

"Huh?"

Pete explained, "She claims the face of Jesus appeared on the scoreboard drawn in his own blood that somehow came from her own hand even though she's not injured."

"What? That's crazy!" Larry pushed his way through the crowd to see for himself. He looked at Mrs. Benson, her hand outstretched towards the dumbstruck men of God. He turned his attention to the red blotch on the scoreboard. He tilted his head to the left, then to the right. He took one step back, and there it was. At first, he smiled. Then he turned pale and backed away like something had given him a little jolt of electricity. He cleared his throat and turned his microphone back on.

"Breaking news, folks. Breaking news. God himself has come to Pennington's Corner. It seems Carol Benson, yes, Mrs. Benson, has been touched by God. Word is Mrs. Benson touched the scoreboard and blood came forth in the shape of the face of Jesus. Yes, folks, I have seen it for myself. There is the face of Jesus Christ himself in blood on the scoreboard here at the softball field in the middle of the city park. Details to follow." He shut off the microphone, shaking.

He knew he should start interviews. But he couldn't. He stood there breathing heavily.

Pete watched the reaction of Larry, his friend. He could tell whatever Larry saw was affecting him deeply. He thought *it couldn't be that profound*. He started to step closer to the scoreboard to see for himself. He took two steps closer. He took two steps back. He tilted his head left. He tilted his head right. He saw nothing but a blood stain.

Maggie came up behind him out of breath with Lori on her heels. "What's going on here? Why is everybody praying?"

Her husband responded, "Apparently, there is a likeness of the face of Jesus in blood on the scoreboard. It appeared when Mrs. Benson touched it. She's got blood on her hand. Jesus's blood, I guess."

"What? Well, that's crazy!"

"I know."

She scoffed. "Let me see." She stepped forward to investigate herself, shoving her husband aside. She bent way down to look. She tipped her head to the right. It was clear as day to her. "Oh my God!" she exclaimed. "It's beautiful!"

Lori looked at the red. The eyes looked deep into her soul. She cried out. She felt a squeeze of her stomach and a deep sense of shame. She fell back into the grass pale as a ghost.

Maggie dropped to her knees and wept.

Shocked at her behavior, Pete attempted to get Maggie to control herself. "Maggie. Get up. What are you doing? Why are you crying? Come on. Let's go home. Maggie. Get up." She refused to budge.

"Pete," asked Marty. "What's up with…" he pointed at Maggie and Lori.

"I don't know. Help me get her up," Pete answered indicating Maggie. He tried again to force her up. Marty didn't interfere. He walked over to Fr. Andrew. Jake followed.

"Hey, Fr. Andrew. What's going on?"

"I wish I knew." Fr. Andrew didn't take his eyes off Mrs. Benson. He asked questions to himself: *Did she do this on purpose? Could this be real? Everyone knew she wanted to turn all the citizens of Pennington's Corner Catholic. Heck, so did he. But would she go this far?* "Mrs. Benson?" he asked out loud. "Can you explain to me again how this happened?"

She was beginning to find her voice again.

"I stepped on a pebble which twisted my ankle a bit. By the grace of God, I wasn't hurt. I reached out to the scoreboard to catch myself so I wouldn't fall..." She paused. Her gaze intensified, her bottom lip quivered as the next words came to her. "I touched it and blood flowed out from the palm of my hand even though it was not pierced. And the face of Jesus appeared before me!"

Murmurs from the growing crowd fueled the fervor as word spread how this miracle happened. "She said blood poured forth." "She said God saved her from injury." "Did she say Jesus stood before her? Yes, she did."

"This is so stupid!" yelled Jake for all to hear. "You don't actually believe this is real, do you?"

The men of God looked at each other in fear. Pastor James motioned for Fr. Andrew aside to speak more privately.

"You know her," Pastor James stated plainly. "I really don't. What do you make of this?"

"I honestly don't know. This is all so unbelievable. And yet, I am a man of God. I am supposed to believe in such things."

"I am too! I don't believe it either. Now what? What are we supposed to do?"

"I don't know."

They both turned to look at the crowd. Everyone was looking at them for direction. They looked at each other hoping one of them had an answer. The shared look of bewilderment helped neither. Anxiety was growing by the minute.

Officer Helen Schafer arrived. "What is going on here?" "Do I have a bunch of sore losers to deal with?"

Marty pointed to the red on the scoreboard and the red on Mrs. Benson's hand.

"What is it?" she asked.

"Blood," answered Marty.

"Blood? How did it get there?"

"From Mrs. Benson, except she says it isn't her blood. She says it's Jesus's blood."

"Jesus? As in the big guy up in the sky?"

"That's the one."

"Well, that can't be..."

"Nonetheless, there it is."

"Mrs. Benson, may I have a look at your ha-"

"No!" she pulled her hand away. "No one may touch!"

"Okay," responded the officer. "I guess I will leave that alone then. Well, you all can't stand around here like this. It's like a mob happening. What are you all doing?"

"We don't know," responded Maggie, coming out of her state of prayer. "We don't know what we are supposed to do. We don't know what God is trying to tell us."

"I know," replied Mrs. Benson. "He is trying to tell us all to repent for our sins! Just like Jonah in the city of Nineveh. God sent Jonah to tell the people they must repent or they would perish! Jonah did not think the people would listen, but they did. They did repent, and the city was saved. We must save our city. You must all repent for your sins!"

"Repent for what?" someone yelled out from the back of the crowd.

She looked intently at Jake Keening and Lori Greenfield. "You must repent for your sins of the flesh. They will be your undoing." She looked at Pete and Larry. "You must renounce your actions that caused pain to others." She looked Marty directly in his eyes. "You must account for your sin of pride." She looked at the crowd in general and continued, "You must repent for your violence, your lasciviousness, your adultery, for your raucous behavior. You must repent for your transgressions against the Lord God!"

Silence took over the crowd.

Lori attempted to stand. She dry-heaved, expelling nothing. She turned and fled the scene with Daisy helplessly watching her go. The little girl shrugged her shoulders and started her own trek home.

Craig stayed on the other side of the softball field. He watched Lori run. She started in his direction. When she looked up and saw him, he reached out his hand. She let out a faint squeal of pain and darted further away. "Lori!"

The weight of the atmosphere became suffocating. Even Officer Schafer could feel it.

"Okay," she attempted. "How about we all go home and contemplate what Mrs. Benson has just expressed?"

"Home?" asked Maggie. "Go home? No. We must go to church and pray and ask God for guidance and forgiveness."

Everyone froze. They looked at each other. No one moved for a few seconds. After Mrs. Benson's long list of sins, there was fear that if one person moved, God might strike them all down at once with bolts of lightning. People eyed each other suspiciously. The worst offender exposed by running for a steeple could be the first taken out. When no lightning came, the crowd went from immovable statues to frantic chaos in the blink of an eye. There were even some screams of panic.

The two men of God looked at each other in horror as they both realized simultaneously that their houses of worship were about to be overrun with panicked souls. Pastor James ran west to St. Paul's, Fr. Andrew ran east to St. John's. Whatever this challenge was God had thrown at them, it was on.

Fr. Andrew was fast. He was a runner. A former minor league

baseball player, he still kept himself fit. He took off at a solid run and passed by everyone heading to the church.

Fr. Andrew was always head of the pack, any pack he was a part of, his entire life. He was popular as a kid, dated a lot in high school, played in the minors where he fell in love, and was headed to the major leagues as a pitcher until he tore a muscle in his rotator cuff. It never healed properly. He started drinking and sleeping with women at every opportunity. He felt a failure in all aspects.

Until one night he had an encounter. He stupidly decided he was capable of driving home drunk, and broken hearted, even though he could barely stand. He drove right off the road and into a tree.

A man opened his car door to make sure he was okay. It was a miracle he was able to get out and walk. The car was totaled. Andrew barely had a scratch.

The stranger did not call the authorities, but someone did. The man who helped him out oddly disappeared. No one else had seen him. Andrew was given a citation for drinking and driving and had to appear before court.

While waiting for his turn to enter the courtroom and face the judge, a man came and sat next to him. That same man.

"How are you? I've been concerned about you," he said to Andrew.

Andrew was surprised to see him at all, much less in a courthouse. "It's you! You!"

"Yes, it's me."

"What are you doing here?"

"I'm here to help out a friend. How are you?"

"I'm, I'm good. I mean, I have this," he indicated at the courthouse, "but I'm good. I didn't get to thank you that night for helping me out of the car. I was so drunk. I'm so sorry about that."

"You were pretty drunk. I am happy to see you are okay. Are you still drinking?"

"No, sir! I quit after that night. I hope I can convince the judge of that. Maybe he will take pity on me."

"I'm sure you'll do fine." He continued on a different topic. "You know, I followed your baseball career as far back as high school. I'm sorry that didn't work out for you."

"Yeah. I guess that's why I started drinking so much. I really thought baseball was going to be my life. Now, I don't have much of a life at all."

"Nonsense. You have a life. You have an opportunity right now to change course to have an even better life. Can you see yourself doing anything else besides baseball?"

"Well, I have sometimes felt that a higher power was calling me to do something else. Something that would help people for a lifetime. You know? Some way I could be important to people, maybe help them be happy with their lives."

"Like a therapist?"

"I don't know. Maybe something like that. I know I want to help people."

"That sounds like a calling. You should follow that. Now, if you'll excuse me, I have to get back to work. Thanks for sharing your story with me."

"Thanks for taking an interest."

The man disappeared again, and Andrew realized for the second time he didn't ask him his name.

When it was Andrew's turn to go into the courtroom, he couldn't believe his eyes at who was the man sitting behind the desk holding the gavel. He did take pity on Andrew, and gave him an opportunity to reexamine his life, which eventually led him to the seminary.

Now, he was in St. John's Catholic Church in Pennington's Corner, two decades later, no regrets, racing ahead of his flock so he could do what he always wanted to do – help people for a lifetime. The opportunity to help others examine their lives under the microscope of a miraculous act from heaven itself was not to be missed and not to be taken for granted. Lives were about to be changed dramatically, and he was all excited he was going to be a part of it.

Fr. Andrew was able to run ahead of everyone, including his star player, Marty, which gave Fr. Andrew pause to think about his need to maybe recruit some new softball talent like he knew Coach Meir did for the Lutheran team with Jake as he was graduating from high school. The moment Jake was handed his diploma, he qualified to play.

Fr. Andrew shook those thoughts away. This was not the time to contemplate players. He had souls to save.

He leapt into the sacristy and jumped into his robes. He ran into the sanctuary but slowed his steps way down as he rounded the corner in front of the altar. He wanted the people to see he was calm and in control. The pews were filled. There was a line out the door. He knew what to do. After all, this was a Catholic church. He entered the confessional where two people, one on each side, were prepared to lay bare their souls.

Pastor James was not a fit man. He was heavier set and older. He did not eat particularly well. He did not care for exercise. The only exercise he entertained was exercise of the soul with prayer and Bible study.

By the time Pastor James arrived at St. Paul's Lutheran Church, the building was filled to the brim with people all looking to him for help. He wheezed trying to catch his breath before he could say a word. What could he say anyway? He didn't have confessionals to tackle these people one at a time in a systematic method. Fr. Andrew was lucky he had that. A group prayer or service was not going to adequately meet the needs of the people. No. Pastor James needed to think how to do this quickly, compassionately, biblically, and individually.

"Give me one minute," he said to the crowd, so out of breath only a few could hear him. He went to change into robes hoping the proper attire would help him get into the spirit of the moment and to contemplate what he would say.

Many, many years ago, when James decided as a twelve year old that he was called to be a preacher, sermons came easily to him. He prayed over every meal for his family under the guidance of his grandmother, prayed over every special occasion, and started leading the Sunday evening family Bible studies by the time he was fifteen because he seemed to have a God-given ability of discernment to understand what God was trying to tell them at that time in their circumstances.

As the years went on and he had a family of his own, a wife and teenage daughter, Angela, sermons became automatic. He pumped them out like a manufacturing machine, creating an identical product over and over again. They became routine. It was hard for him to think God had become routine to him. He loved Jesus over everyone and everything.

His relationship with Angela became more strained due to generational differences, a baby boomer with all the answers versus a Generation Xer who questioned all those answers. Routine became an anchor. And yet, his love for the Word of God remained true in his heart.

Pastor James embraced his favorite King James Bible and stepped into the sanctuary to face the crowd. In his mind, he prayed, *Jesus, show me the way. Give me the words. Use me as you used Jonah in Nineveh. Help me help them, Lord.* He shook as he stood before them, his mind blank. The words he was counting on did not arrive. All was silent as the congregation waited for his words of wisdom to free them of their fears. Rivers of sweat poured out of Pastor James's armpits. He needed something. Anything. There was nothing. His mind was blank.

4

What's the Right Thing to Say?

Pastor James stood before his flock not knowing what to say or do. A high level of anxiety permeated the whole church. *How can I calm the spiritual crises of others when one is growing inside me too?* he asked himself.

After standing there nearly five minutes not knowing what to say or do, he remembered he had his Bible in his hand. He took the book and opened it. God would guide them all with whatever words came forth. He would open it randomly.

"Behold, thou art fair, my love: behold, thou art fair; thou hast doves' eyes within thy locks: thy hair is as a flock of…"

He quickly realized Song of Solomon was not the way to go here. He cleared his throat. "Excuse me. Let me try this again."

He opened the book further along, and this time read silently to himself before starting again with the confused crowd.

"Ah, yes," he said before reading. "Ephesians 6 seems the right way to go."

He cleared his voice again. "Finally, my brethren, be strong in the Lord, and in the power of his might. Put on the whole armour of God, that ye may be able to stand against the wiles of the devil."

"Are you saying what happened at the softball field was an act of the devil?" came a question from the back.

"Could be," came another voice. "Came from a Catholic."

"No, no," replied Pastor James. "That is not what I am saying. We don't yet know where this came from. Although, I am not saying we should be questioning the wisdom of God either. I'm just saying we should put on the armour of God, meaning we should get deeper into the word, so we can discern effectively what is happening in our little town."

"We should run those Catholics out of town. That's what we should do."

Everyone started talking. Some in agreement, some in opposition.

"Yeah!"

"No! Those are our friends and fellow Christians."

"They aren't Christians. The Catholic Church is a cult."

"We grew up with those people. Those are good people."

Pastor James stood before his flock wondering where he went wrong. He trusted God to give him the answers, and, instead, more chaos reigned. He put up his hands trying to get the cooperation of the crowd.

"Quiet!" someone yelled from the front. "Pastor James is trying to tell us something."

"This type of rhetoric isn't going to get us anywhere. The Catholics, though somewhat misguided, are not our enemy. They are our friends in Christ. We must be mindful of that. In the meantime, we must contemplate our own actions in light of these circumstances. I need a volunteer. Jenny!" He indicated to Angela's friend sitting there alone in the front row with her backpack. "Do you have paper and pen in your bag you could use?" Jenny nodded in agreement. "Good. Jenny will take a list of names of people who would like to speak with me privately. We'll discuss what is giving them reason to have so much introspection in their lives after what has happened."

"Sounds like a Catholic confessional, Pastor!" Some laughter came from the back.

"I agree," responded Pastor James. "Maybe it is good I use a similar tactic to get a handle on things. Jenny, if you would please? I will be in my office. Send in the first one as soon as you are ready, and then make the list."

"Yes, sir." Sixteen year old Jenny was immediately overwhelmed with people scrambling to be first.

Pastor James closed the door to his office to have a minute to himself. "Jesus," he prayed aloud. "I don't know what your plan is here, but I would appreciate it if you would share it with me so I can handle it right. This is too much, Jesus. Too much." He looked out the window wiping sweat from his brow before continuing his prayer. "I don't know what I can do to bring order again. Now we are going to hate on the Catholics? Wasn't there enough animosity? Am I supposed to come in with some flaming sword of truth and make everybody like each other again?"

He stopped and waited for an answer. No thundering response came.

A knock at the door broke the silence. "Come in." He expected to see a parishioner. Instead, it was his wife, Laura. Her blonde, Norwegian features appeared unusually haggard. Pastor James assumed it was due to the chaos unfolding in the community.

"James, what is going on? I heard it on the radio, but I just can't believe it. Blood? The face of Jesus in blood on the scoreboard?"

"So it seems."

"What does this mean?"

"I don't know, dear. I do not know."

"Well, honey, there is practically a mob out there. They are all demanding to see you. You put little Jenny to the task of organizing all those people for you?"

"I didn't know what else to do. Could you go help her, please?"

"Yes, I can do that. Is there anything else you need?"

"Nope. I think only God can help me now."

"Okay, sweetheart. I'll go help Jenny. Just try to relax in the meantime."

"Relax. Right."

Back at the Catholic Church, Fr. Andrew had already absolved the sins of two dozen people through the confessionals. He had a church filled with more sinners and more arriving. There was a common theme of adultery in confession after confession. He knew there was inappropriate sex happening in this town, but he had no idea it was so prevalent. He needed a break.

"Mrs. Peterson, I know I'm not supposed to know it's you in there, but you know I know it's you. Can I ask a favor?"

"Certainly, Father."

"Could you please tell the others to give me a few minutes break? I need to use the bathroom and get a drink of water."

"Of course. I can do that for you."

"Thank you. I absolve you of your sins in the name of The Father, The Son, and The Holy Spirit. Say five Hail Marys on your way out. Go in peace and sin no more."

"Thank you, Father."

Fr. Andrew breathed a sigh of relief. He should have had a scoreboard in the confessional with him. He was getting people to heaven left and right. Adultery, gambling, lying, abuse, alcoholism, drug use, lust, two women and a man who confessed they were in love with Fr. Andrew specifically. And there was a potential murder confession, but that one was questionable.

Some were not Catholic. Some were not even Christian. One confessed to being Atheist. He didn't anticipate that. But, hey! More for the Kingdom of God as far as he was concerned.

He wondered how Pastor James was handling this. Was he meeting with people one on one? That's what he figured he would do if he was in his shoes.

"Here, Fr. Andrew. I made you a sandwich. I thought you might be hungry after meeting with all those people." Fr. Andrew looked up to see, of all people, Lori Greenfield.

"Um, thank you, Lori."

"You're welcome." She handed him the sandwich and stood there waiting for him to eat it.

He awkwardly examined the sandwich before taking a bite. Lori was not known for having respect for the church, and certainly not for the priest. In fact, he was pretty certain he was the only man under seventy whom Lori had not tried to seduce at one time or another. She avoided him like the plague.

Ham and turkey on whole wheat with all the fixings including a nice slathering of mayonnaise and mustard together. It was just how he liked it. How did she know?

"I asked Mrs. Carver how you like your sandwiches," she responded to his unasked question. "I brought you a bag of your favorite chips and a can of root beer. She told me that's what I should get you."

"Should get me? For what reason would you feel the need to get me anything?"

Her features dropped from his reply. He tried to walk them back, but he was genuinely suspicious as to her motives for bringing him food.

"What I mean is," he continued, "if you need to talk, you don't need to bribe me with food. I will talk with you."

"You will? But I never come to church anymore. I haven't been since I was confirmed back in high school."

Fr. Andrew didn't even know she was Catholic. "Sure. How about we sit down in the cafeteria and you talk while I eat? You were right to assume I would be hungry. I am famished!"

She smiled the first genuine smile he ever witnessed on her face. He never realized before that she was truly beautiful when her smile was real.

They sat opposite each other at a circular table. He took his first bite. To his delight, it was as good as it looked. The creamy mayonnaise oozed out. The lettuce was crispy and fresh. The garden-fresh tomatoes were sliced thin. Mrs. Carver gave her specifics. She would not have given Lori Greenfield of all people this level of access to him unless she believed it was necessary.

"This is an amazing sandwich! I thank you from the bottom of my heart. Now, tell me what is bothering you."

Lori's smile faded away. Darkness overtook her lovely features, and tears poured forth. Her shoulders shook with anguish as she sobbed. Fr. Andrew put the sandwich down, unable to take another bite until he could find a way to help this poor creature.

"I've been such a bad person, Father," she sobbed. "I have done terrible things."

"Let's take this one thing at a time, okay?"

She nodded and continued. "I have been with almost every man in town. Oh! Except you, Father. Not that you aren't attractive! I mean, I would if...but you are a man of God, so I didn't think..."

"I understand."

"The men, they come to me when they feel lonely or sad or just want some. I use them to get things I need." She thought deeply for a moment. He didn't interrupt. "Does that make me a prostitute?"

He decided gentle honesty was the best course. "Possibly. How do you feel about that?"

She burst into tears.

Their conversation, outside of a confessional, continued on for another forty minutes and ended with, "Go forth and sin no more."

Back at St. Paul's Lutheran Church, Pastor James looked at the list. It was difficult to read Jenny's scribble, but he made do. His wife brought in cup after cup of coffee for every individual or couple that entered the office, and kept his cup full too. Eventually, she brought him Twinkies. He needed comfort food.

He looked over his desk at the couple before him, Pete and Maggie, with Charlie, their ketchup loving puppy, at Maggie's feet.

"I just don't know," said Maggie. "I feel like he doesn't love me anymore. Something always seems terribly wrong. I can't put my finger on it. Pastor, you need to get him to admit he is sinning and get him to change his ways."

Pastor James looked at Pete to see what he had to say.

"She's crazy!" exclaimed Pete. "I'm not sinning. I mean, we all sin. I get that. But I'm not doing anything. Of course, I love my wife. Why wouldn't I?"

Pastor James gave Pete a stern look because he, like everyone else in town, knew full well Pete was regularly having sex with the one and only infamous Lori Greenfield. If Jesus was trying to tell this town anything, it was definitely along the lines of, "Hey! Stop sinning, straighten up, and start flying right!" But Pastor James did not think it was a good idea to say that to Pete in front of Maggie. It would be better if it came from Pete himself. But Pete stuck to his claim of innocence.

"Maggie, tell me, what makes you so sure Pete is up to something he shouldn't be doing?"

"I don't know. It's this feeling I have. He doesn't touch me anymore. Hasn't for years, so that's not really a change in behavior. At the same time, he is always so happy even though he isn't getting any, if you know what I mean. He acts like a cat in the canary store with the keys to all the bird cages. And it's creepy even."

"Pete? Do you have a response to that?"

"I don't know what she is talking about."

Pastor James put his head in his hands in exasperation. This was not going well. Pete had his chance to make amends and threw it away.

While the churches were filled to the rafters with sinners, Mrs. Benson sat at her kitchen table staring at her hand. Friends, neighbors, and even some strangers were banging at her door. Some to offer support, some to touch her looking for a miracle, and some to condemn her for one reason or another. She ignored them all and sat staring at the palm of her hand. She would have to wash it off at some point. She couldn't go around the rest of her life with the dried blood of Jesus on her hand. Could she?

She went to her bedroom and dug around in the top drawer of her bureau for an old handkerchief. She found some plain ones that belonged to her husband back in the day. She continued to dig until she found the right one. A delicate one wrapped in white tissue paper with tiny, embroidered flowers and lace edges. It wasn't so white anymore. A little yellowing was here and there. She unfolded it carefully and used it to remove the red from her palm in one violent swipe. Her hand was almost clean, the red now stained the delicate piece of fabric.

She sat down on the bed and stared at the red stain. *God, will you speak to me now?* she thought. *Virgin Mary, will you come and take me home to heaven with you? Take me to my Paul?*

Mrs. Carol Benson's mind traveled back to spring, 1927, when cloche hats, flappers, and long beaded necklaces were all the rage. She was sixteen and known as Caroline Brown. She and her friends were skipping school with parental permission to spend the day shopping at Dayton's department store in downtown Minneapolis. After all, what did these girls need to learn at school?

Caroline walked into the store wearing her school clothes and walked out in her first ever flapper outfit. She instantly felt grown up. It was amazing what a new dress could do to a young woman's self-esteem. Part of the new outfit included a small, beaded handbag with a brand new white handkerchief with lace edges.

After shopping, the girls decided afternoon tea at the luxurious Radisson hotel was appropriate. It wasn't long after they were seated at a table when they noticed another table of young gentlemen admiring them. Giggling commenced as would be expected in such a situation. Eye contact was attempted, failed, attempted, failed, attempted, and finally, succeeded.

Caroline found herself staring into the most amazing blue eyes she had ever encountered. They locked in briefly. In true structured flirtatious decorum, she quickly withdrew her gaze to look down at the napkin on her lap. A few moments passed and she dared to look again. There they were. The blue eyes were still locked on her.

Caroline's friends giggled at the exchange taking place. Caroline was no longer in the mood to giggle. This was different from flirting with other boys. This one held the promise of a future. She could feel it.

He came over to the table with all the confidence of a bull fighter and the suave air of Valentino. He sang "Me and My Shadow" barely audible for her and her friends as he approached. When he spoke, she realized her first impression was wrong. He was as innocent as she was.

"Hi. I, I'm, I'm Paul Benson. I would like to give you this." He held out a little violet flower he had taken from the vase at his table.

Caroline smiled and accepted the gift. She tried to give voice to her appreciation, but nothing came out. She found herself staring into his eyes again, her mouth partially open.

When Paul realized the nervousness was matched, his confidence grew. "May I ask your name?"

Caroline still couldn't talk. One of her girlfriends did it for her. "Her name is Caroline. Caroline Brown."

"Hello, Caroline Brown. Would you like to take a walk in the garden with me?"

"The garden?" Those were the first words she was able to utter.

"Through that door." He indicated towards a glass door.

"I would love to."

That was the beginning of a beautiful, yet short love affair Carol had with her husband. They walked the small garden round and round countless times until her friends had to separate them so they could get home to Pennington's Corner before dark. They talked about all kinds of subjects. They agreed on next to nothing, but neither cared. They were in love. They exchanged information, and the girls left.

Paul was from west of Minnetonka where he worked on his father's farm. He was in Minneapolis meeting with bankers to learn about how the business side of farming worked. He was ready to own a farm of his own. He didn't realize until he saw Caroline that he was also ready for a wife.

That night, Caroline stayed up until four in the morning embroidering violets on her new handkerchief so she would never forget that day. She never did.

The marriage wasn't always so perfect. Paul Benson came to Pennington's Corner and bought farmland to build a house for his new wife-to-be. Caroline, a devout Catholic, pressured her fiancé to become Catholic, because her family demanded she be married in the Catholic Church. He didn't care which church he belonged to.

She gave in to his every whim in all things. She learned his housekeeping preferences, took on his views of the world, learned to cook for him, learned his preferences for her clothing, her hair style, sex positions. Whatever he wanted, she twisted herself into knots to give to him. It was not a relationship made in heaven. Nonetheless, she loved him.

They tried having children to no avail, much like the Penningtons with whom they rarely interacted as the Penningtons were Lutheran. So the rumor that Carol Benson once had an affair with Mr. Pennington was entirely false and impossible.

Tragedy struck the young couple in 1932 when Paul was killed in a farming accident. He was driving the tractor too close to the drainage ditch and tipped it over, trapping himself. By the time he was found, it was too late. The husband Carol Benson loved was gone. She felt all alone the rest of her days. She sold the farm and bought the house in town across from the park. She spent all those lonely years remembering only the good things and appreciating him for what he gave her.

Sometimes, during Mass or during prayers with the rosary, she could feel God's arms wrapped around her. She would remember Paul's arms wrapped around her. She could not differentiate between the two sensations – which was God and which was Paul. In her mind, they were the same. Longing would fill her being. She clamored for the imagined best spot in heaven next to the Virgin Mary, so that when she arrived in heaven, Paul would know where to find her.

She carefully folded up the handkerchief with the red stain and the embroidered violets and wrapped it back in the tissue paper carefully. "Thank you, Paul," she said out loud as she closed the drawer.

5

Marty, Born Again

Marty felt the pull to run to the church along with most of the other Catholics in town. He ran as hard as he could like a rope was pulling him from his stomach. When Fr. Andrew passed him by, that pull stopped. He slowed to a halt and stood there panting. Sweat dripped from everywhere. He was hot, and he was ashamed. Strange. He didn't know why he felt ashamed. "Why am I doing this?" he asked out loud to no one. He decided to go to the bar instead. He walked back to the park to get his car. Before he drove away, he saw Craig packing up the beer from the game. He remembered it was Sunday which meant the bar wasn't open. He drove home instead to take a shower.

Marty lived in a tiny, older home built in the 1950s near the center of town. He was a man of average to short stature, yet he barely cleared the doorways in his house. He stepped around the exhaust manifold sitting on a newspaper on the floor of his living room from his 1958 Chevy stored in his garage that he had been restoring since he was in the 10th grade of high school. He walked into the tiny kitchen in the back of the house, grabbed one of his own homemade strawberry scones he left cooling on the stovetop that morning, and walked out the back door to his fenced in fruit and vegetable garden to check the status of his raspberry patch. He reached over, plucked a berry, and popped it in his mouth. *Not quite ripe enough*, he thought. He headed back into the house as he finished eating his scone and jumped into the shower.

The shower felt good. It washed away all those bad feelings. Marty wrapped himself in a towel and sat down to watch something on television like a baseball game or something to relax and get his mind off the day's events before getting dressed and going out to find something to do. The Twins were playing. He tried concentrating on the interplay between centerfielder, Kirby Puckett, and first baseman, Kent Hrbek, but it did no good. That pull in the pit of his stomach would not settle. He could not sit there another minute. He got up, got dressed, and headed out the door.

Marty cruised up and down Main Street like a bored teenager looking for someone to hang out with. He noticed a lot of cars at the bar. Marty smiled with relief and pulled into the parking lot. The place was packed. Marty walked up to the bar where Craig was busy handing out bottles of beer and asked, "Craig, what gives? Open on Sunday?"

"You're not gonna believe this, but Officer Schafer asked me to. But only to sell beer. No hard liquor."

"Helen? Why?"

"Helen? You're on a first name basis all of a sudden?"

"What! I've been friends with her for years."

"No, you haven't."

Marty did not respond.

Craig continued. "Well, I think she is just trying to keep people calm. Give them something to do to distract them from the chaos at the field. She's been all over town, especially at the two churches trying to keep peace."

"Everyone's lost their minds."

"Apparently. Crowds keep gathering at the park. She tries to send them all away. I guess some sort of shrine has built up."

"A shrine?"

"Yep. People are leaving stuff like flowers and candles and

crosses. Like a shrine. There have been some fights. Some have tried taking a bit of the blood off the sign as some sort of souvenir. Others are trying to protect it. It's turned into some sort of holy ground."

"Holy ground? Holy shit! Really? Here? That's crazy!" Marty could feel that pull in the pit of his stomach again. "Give me a beer, man."

"Sure thing," said Craig, giving Marty a side-eye. "You alright?"

Marty downed the beer like a man out of the desert drinking water. "Give me another."

"Okay, one more. Then you wait a while."

"Yeah, okay." He held onto the second bottle as long as he could. It didn't last long. He handed Craig cash for them. They locked eyes.

"Where are you going?" asked Craig.

"I don't know, man. I don't know." Marty stepped out into the evening air, left his car in the parking lot and walked to the softball field a few blocks away.

He approached the shrine carefully. The tug in his gut grew in strength with each step. The street lights came on creating an ethereal glow. A pile of flowers covered the ground in front of the red stain on the board. Lit candles were everywhere. Crosses. Rosaries. Even a couple of small statues of Jesus or the Virgin Mary or some other saint. Some people were on their knees praying. Others standing. Helen was sending two older gentlemen away who were adamant about staying to protect it. She convinced them to leave.

"Hey, Marty. Have you come to help or cause more trouble for me?"

"Hi, Helen. I just came to see what all the bizarre behavior was about. Craig mentioned a shrine."

"Yep. There's a shrine now. People are insisting on leaving

things. I am insisting on safety and order."

"Huh."

"Yep." She looked at Marty. "But, why are you here, Marty?"

He looked at Helen briefly. "I, I don't know, exactly." The words came slowly. "I just…"

"Had to come?"

"Yeah."

"I've been hearing that a lot today. You don't actually believe this is real, do you?"

"Well, how do you explain it?"

"I don't know, but…" She paused. "I can't stop asking the question no one seems able to answer. Why in the world would Jesus come and leave his face in blood in this godforsaken little town?"

Marty could not believe the words coming out of his mouth. It was as if a complete stranger took control of his being while at the same time he never felt more aware. "Well, why don't we flip your question around. Why wouldn't Jesus come to this godforsaken town? I mean, it is godforsaken, right? Maybe He wants to forsake it now?"

"What?" She looked at Marty as if he was a complete stranger. "Why?"

"Again, why not? Aren't we people? Real people? With feelings, and lives that are difficult? Why wouldn't God, Jesus himself, come here for us?" *Who am I?* he asked himself.

"Because it's Pennington's Corner, Marty! It's not Las Vegas. Or Chicago. Or Minneapolis. Bigger places with bigger problems. We don't have drugs on every street corner, gangs, prostitutes, all that trouble. Some, but not rampant. Why would God want to come and tell us that we need to repent or else? How does that make any sense?"

"It doesn't. I don't know if God ever completely makes sense to

58

us."

"Well, I think it's all some sort of practical joke."

"You think Mrs. Benson would do something like this on purpose?"

"No. I think somebody else did, and she got caught up in it. I'm going to find out who."

"That's some joke for someone to pull."

"Yep. And whoever is pulling it is making a mockery of the whole town too."

Larry came running up to them carrying a great big clumsy VHS tape recording camera. "Hey. Helen. Could I interview you?"

"What for?"

"I ran and got a camera." He lifted the heavy thing up onto his shoulder. It was bigger than his head. "I want to make a tape of everything happening and send it in to the news stations in Minneapolis."

"Do you even know how to work that thing?" asked Helen.

"Not really, no. I'll figure it out as I go. Marty will help me."

"No, I won't," quipped Marty.

"Come on, Helen. I need to interview an authority figure to give credence to the story. Let me just ask you a couple of questions. I'll be real quick about it." He started fiddling with the camera.

"No, Larry! I don't want to be interviewed. Go away."

"I have to get some sort of story, Helen, before the big news stations find out and take over."

As if his words conjured them up, three vans pulled up labeled ABC, CBS, and NBC – the three major local networks from Minneapolis. Van doors simultaneously flew open as people and cameras and microphones flew out. Bright lights lit up the evening twilight back to high noon. Three reporters descended upon the bleeding Jesus believers and created brief recordings of hasty interviews. They rudely interrupted private moments with God. Just as fast as they arrived, the melee of people and equipment jumped back into their vehicles and departed leaving the faith-filled people to ponder *what the hell just happened.*

Still clutching his giant camera to the side of his face, Larry started to chase after the news vans. After a few steps, he turned to Helen and Marty. "Damn!" He turned away looking in the direction of the highway as the vans disappeared. "Damn!" He kicked some dirt and turned to face his friends again. "I missed my opportunity!" He pointed at them both. "It's your fault! I blame you guys. Both of you." He pouted and stomped off.

They ignored Larry. "Great," said Helen to Marty. "Now, there will be even more people here tomorrow. Once word spreads all over the state that we've got Jesus here, people will flock to get a glimpse. This town can't handle a bunch of gawkers running around causing chaos. I will be dealing with trespass, vandalism, maybe more violence, theft, I don't know what else."

"It will be okay," said Marty, trying to offer reassurance.

"Are you going to help me?"

"Sure."

"I wasn't serious."

"I was."

"How are you going to help me? A civilian."

"Just give me a minute?" He motioned to the shrine, and she let him pass.

Marty approached the so-called face of Jesus with apprehension. "God. I am a Christian. I do believe you are real. My grandparents taught me all they could about you. I just wasn't interested in hearing it. I'm sorry. I should've been better. Since I wasn't, maybe I don't have the right to ask this. But, if you know where my mom or my dad are, could you tell them I forgive them for leaving me behind as a kid? I got over it.

"And, when you see my grandparents up there, could you please let them know that I am doing good? I'm sure they worry about me a lot. They always did. Can you tell Grandpa I've almost got the '58 working? And tell Grandma her raspberry bush in the garden is finally growing decent sized berries. That'll make her happy." He felt better.

As Marty wiped off his face and turned to get his marching orders from Helen, someone slumped onto the ground next to him. It was Lori Greenfield.

Marty knelt down on the ground next to her. He could feel the pain she was in. She looked up at him, her eyes pleading for help.

Marty's mind went to all the times he was with her, pounding his own hurts into her body, not understanding at the time he was transferring his damage to her. He could see it now.

"Lori, I am so, so sorry…" He wanted to apologize for every time he had taken from her and given nothing of real value in return like love. He wanted to make it alright at that moment. She couldn't hear him. Her own pains created a roar in her head drowning out all other sounds. She could see his lips move, but his words were nothing.

"Marty. I've been bad, Marty."

"Lori…" His hurt for her deepened. He didn't know that was possible.

"I have done terrible things."

"No, Lori. You haven't done terrible things."

"Yes, I have."

"I did a terrible thing to you."

"No, Marty. I, I made you. I seduced you."

"You didn't make me."

"Yes, I did. I've always had this ability to make men do what I wanted them to do so I could get things out of them."

"Lori…"

"No, Marty. No. You sound just like Fr. Andrew. He tried to tell me it wasn't all my fault. That the guys were at fault too."

"You talked to Fr. Andrew?"

"Yeah. I brought him a sandwich."

Marty almost chuckled at that. He stopped himself. It would have hurt her more.

Lori continued. "He said there were always two of us at fault, and sometimes mostly just the guy. That they were taking advantage of me. But I tried to tell him, no. I was taking advantage of them. So I could get things. Did you know Pete promised me a car today?"

"No, I did not know that."

"Yeah. I guess I won't get my car now, will I?"

"I don't know. I've seen your car. You do need one, don't you?"

"Yes."

"Well, maybe I can help you get a better car without having to compromise yourself."

Lori looked at him. "You would do that for me? No one has ever helped without getting something in return."

"Lori, I always thought of myself as your friend. It never occurred to me until today that I was using you. That means I have not been your friend. I want to be your friend, Lori. A real friend. Someone who helps without expecting something in return."

Lori sniffled. "I would like that. I don't think I've ever had a real friend before."

She seemed so child-like. It made Marty want to reach out and hold her, but something prevented him. Maybe he was afraid he would give her the wrong impression?

Instead, he helped her to her feet. "Lori, why don't you go home and get some sleep. We'll talk more tomorrow about this after we have both calmed down, okay?"

"Okay." Then Lori turned and saw Officer Helen. "Helen, I don't know where Michael is."

"What about Daisy?" Helen asked.

"She's home. She's fine. I made her a sandwich too when I made one for Fr. Andrew."

"When's the last time you saw Michael?"

"Not since the game this morning."

"I'll look for him. You go ahead and go home and try to rest. I will keep you posted."

"Okay. Thank you."

They watched Lori hobble off home still crying.

"Well," said Helen. "That's a first."

"What is?"

"First time Lori has ever asked me about Michael. I've tried so many times to get her to show an interest in those kids."

Marty turned to Helen to ask, "You still think Jesus wouldn't bother with the people of this town?"

"Maybe I'm wrong about Him."

"Maybe we all are."

"Marty?"

"Yeah?"

"How about you go find Michael while I keep watch here? You did a great job with Lori. Maybe you can get through to her son, too. I know I haven't been able to."

"Where do you suggest I look? Train trestle?"

"No. Too dark. He doesn't go there in the dark. Start with the grain elevators. Or maybe the water tower."

"On it."

6

The Gospel According to Marty

Marty briskly walked to the other side of town in search of Michael where the elevator grain bins stood alongside the railroad tracks on the north end of Main Street. He remembered climbing in these bins himself about the same age when they were empty. Right now, some were partially filled as the first harvests of the season had begun. It would be especially dangerous for Michael to go climbing into one of those now. *Michael wasn't a dumb kid. He would know not to climb in. Right?* thought Marty hoping that was true.

He walked over to the water tower and looked up into the darkness. A figure was definitely up there. "Michael? Is that you?"

The figure shuffled but did not respond.

"I'm coming up."

He climbed up the ladder carefully in the dark. He hadn't done something like this in decades. He quietly muttered a prayer that he wouldn't fall. Marty had done more praying in this one evening than he had in years, since his grandmother passed away. It felt good. Climbing up the water tower did not.

The world looked so beautiful from up there. Lights from homes in the town and farms in the distance twinkled. He could even see the lights from other towns nearby. With the giant letters spelling out the name of the town behind him like sentinels standing guard, Marty slid his legs through the railing and sat next to Michael trying to get comfortable. He searched his mind for words to open up the conversation. Michael reached out first.

"Isn't today the 4th of July?" asked Michael.

"Yep."

"Then where are the fireworks?"

"Ah. Yes. The fireworks. I believe they were postponed because of everything that happened today. Maybe we will have them later this week."

"Bummer."

"Yeah. Bummer. You like fireworks?"

"I have some."

"You have some?"

"Yep."

"Where?"

"In my pocket. I wanted to set them off today. I didn't get to."

"Well, I think you should hold onto them until we do have the fireworks display."

"Okay."

"I assume they are just the little pocket sized, you know..."

"Yeah. Nothing big. Probably not big enough to dissect a frog."

Marty chuckled. "Dissect a frog. Well, thank you for that visual." They both chuckled together.

"Did you ever do dumb stuff like that when you were a kid?"

"Oh, boy! Do I have to admit to stuff like that?"

"Yeah." Michael prodded him along.

"I do? Well, shit. I don't know if I can remember that far back. I'm an old man, now, you know."

"Yeah."

Marty didn't feel old at the age of 38. But to a twelve year old boy,

38 would feel ancient.

They sat in silence a while looking out over the town. They could almost look directly down Main Street all the way to the highway running east to west on the south side. Just off the highway, the lights from the park adjacent to the softball field beckoned in the distance. They watched headlights from cars pull in and out of the parking lots by the softball field as people arrived to see the shrine and at Craig's bar. Lights from the television sets of nearby houses told them who was at home awake and who was not.

The sliver of moon wasn't enough to block out all of the stars. "Do you see those stars over there?" asked Marty. "Kind of look like a crooked square with a diagonal line through it?"

"No. Oh, wait. Yeah. I see it,"

"That's Orion, the hunter. He's the coolest set of stars up there."

"A hunter, huh?"

"Yep. A hunter. Do you like to hunt?"

"I don't know. I've never been."

"You've never been? I can't believe you have never been hunting. You and me, we have got to go hunting. What would you like to hunt?"

"Deer."

"Deer hunting?"

"Yeah."

"Okay, then. This fall. I will take you deer hunting."

"Okay."

"I used to go deer hunting with my grandfather. I haven't been in years. This will be fun!" It was time for Marty to change the subject. He didn't know how. Thoughts started wildly entering Marty's head. *These are conversations a man should have with his son.* That was when the most important thought crossed his mind. *Michael is twelve.* He began calculating. *Twelve, thirteen years ago... Could Michael be...* He shook his head to get the thought out. *It couldn't be. Lori would have told me, right? If she knew... What if she didn't know? Does Michael know? Bet he doesn't...*

Panic started to sink into Marty. Could Michael be his son? He had been sexually active with Lori along with so many other men for years, even back then when Lori was seventeen. He could conceivably be Michael's father. But so could a number of other men.

He got back to the subject at hand. "Michael, have you seen your mother today?"

"Not since this morning."

"I saw her just a little while ago. She's pretty upset."

"Why?"

"Um. That's complicated. But she is also pretty worried about you and would like you to go home. Would you like me to walk you home?"

"Why? She doesn't normally care when I come home."

"That's kind of why she is upset. Because she feels she hasn't cared enough before. Now, she does."

Michael scoffed. Marty was losing him. He could feel it. "Why now? What happened that now she cares?" They were both quiet. Michael was trying to make sense of this new information, and Marty was trying to find the words to explain without explaining.

"Wait... Is my sister okay?" asked Michael. Real concern filled his voice. He did love his sister.

"Oh, yeah. She's fine. She's at home."

"Ok, good." Marty could hear the suspicion in Michael's voice. He needed another approach.

"Something happened today at the softball field. It got a lot of people upset, including your mother."

"Did that Pete guy, did he hurt my mom again? Cause I told him I was gonna kill him if he…"

"No, no, no. Nothing like that. This was something that affected a lot of people emotionally. Your mom got affected emotionally. I did too."

"What happened to you?"

"Things. Like things I've done in my life that I shouldn't have done."

"Like what things?"

"Like not appreciating the people that were in my life who cared about me."

"And my mom is feeling that?"

"Yeah. Something like that."

Michael got very introspective. "I don't understand. Why now? Why today? She's never cared before."

"I think she's sorry about that."

"Well, she should be. I mean, I know a lot of my friends think it's cool I can just go do whatever I want, and nobody cares, so I can be out all night hanging out like this. And, yeah, it is cool." Michael swallowed hard. "Except it's not. I don't have a dad to take me to Twins games. Or get taken deer hunting. My mom doesn't bake me chocolate chip cookies. I see my friends have parents to do stuff with. I just have my mom, and she doesn't like me very much."

"She does. She loves you. She just didn't know it until today." Marty started to reach out and give him a hug, but Michael pulled back. Instead, Marty said, "And I can take you to a Twins game. I'm a huge Twins fan."

"Who isn't?" Michael asked.

"Who's your favorite Twin? I'm a Hrbek fan."

"Puckett all the way, man."

"And if your mom isn't good at making chocolate chip cookies, guess what? I make fantastic chocolate chip cookies. I have a secret that makes my cookies the best. I'll teach it to you."

"Baking is for girls."

"I used to think that too. But, nope. Baking is baking no matter who does it. You like to eat, don't you?"

"There's never anything good to eat at my house."

"I can teach you how to cook and bake."

"How did you learn?"

"My grandma."

"You didn't have a dad either?"

Marty paused before responding. "For a while. Not for long. I never had a mom. She left right after I was born."

"I don't think my mom knows who my dad is."

"And that bothers you."

"Yeah."

"Have you ever asked her?"

"No. I've heard people talk about me."

"Voices travel."

Michael squirmed. "Do you know why I like to sit up here?"

"Why?"

Michael got a sly smile on his face. "To get away from adults like you."

"Like me? Why would you want to get away from me?"

"I don't know. Adults don't let me do what I want. But you seem alright."

"I'm alright. I remember what it was like to be your age."

"Like what types of things?"

"I don't think I should tell you. You'll get ideas, and your mother won't like that much."

"I've probably already thought it, or worse."

Marty hesitated but smiled.

"Tell me! You gotta tell me," prodded Michael.

"Okay. Okay. There was this one time. I was fourteen." He looked around the town towards the school. "Do you see the parking lot near the bus shed at the back of the school?"

"Yeah."

"That's where I..." Marty stopped himself. "No. I better not tell you that one."

"Oh! Come on!"

"Nope. Let me think. Oh! I know!" He pointed in the other direction. "Over there at the gas station, I once..."

"Once what?"

"I better not tell you that one either."

"Man! You are no fun."

"Okay. Okay. I will tell you a story." Marty went deep into his recall abilities. "When I was eleven, I stole something."

"What did you steal?"

"A girly magazine."

Michael's eyes got big. "With naked pictures?"

"Yep."

"Did you get caught?"

"Not by the store owner. Initially, I got away with it. I got caught the next day by my grandma."

"What did she do to you?"

"Nothing."

"Nothing?"

"Nothing. Instead of punishing me or anything like that, she made Grandpa come and talk to me about the birds and the bees."

"The birds and the bees?"

"Do you know what that means?"

"Yes. I know what that means."

"Grandpa came in my room, asked to see the magazine, and when I handed it over expecting to get spanked, he proceeded to fold up the magazine and tell me about, you know, that."

"Were you embarrassed?"

"I was mortified."

"Then what happened?"

"When he was done, he handed the magazine back to me. Later that day, I found I couldn't handle looking at it any more. I couldn't get thoughts out of my head that those women were mothers to other kids like me. I took the magazine back and confessed to the owner. He gave me a job sweeping floors for a few months."

"Is that all?"

"It was enough. To this day, I can't stand looking at those magazines."

"That's not right, man."

Marty laughed.

"I didn't tell you the real reason I like sitting up here."

"Why?"

Michael almost whispered it. "I kind of feel like maybe this is what God feels like. Looking down on everybody."

Marty looked around with a new perspecitive.

"Marty, do you think God can read our minds?"

"I've never given God as much thought before in my life until today. But, yeah. I think he can."

"What does he think of us? People aren't that nice to each other. And the nice ones, sometimes even they do things they shouldn't do. I thought God wanted people to be nice to each other."

"He does, Michael. He does. Come on. Let's get you home so your mom can feel happier tonight, okay? We'll be nice to her."

"Okay."

After returning Michael to a grateful Lori, Marty returned to the park to give officer Helen a full report.

"Well done, sir! I haven't made progress like that with Lori or Michael ever. I've tried so many times." A tinge of jealousy in her voice made him scoff.

"Oh, please. I don't think it was about me or you. I think it was timing. He wanted to be heard by someone, anyone."

"Nah. I think you have a natural ability with kids. I don't. I am all about law and order."

"You are. That's true." Marty got to deep thinking again. "Why is that?"

"Oh, wow. What a question. Since when did you get a license to practice psychiatry?"

"It's a good night for going deep."

"I guess." She paused a moment to contemplate the question. "I don't know why."

"You like rules?"

"Maybe… I suppose I do. I mean we have rules. As a society. Like 'don't walk on the grass.' Someone will have to walk on the grass, not because they have to, but because there is a sign telling them not to. What's up with that?"

Marty started to chuckle thinking he had done the same thing in the past. "Some people feel they are being controlled. They don't like it. They have to do something to break that hold."

"But they have to be controlled. That's why we have rules and laws. Or else we have," she motioned to the shrine still being built up before them, "chaos."

"How is this chaos?" Marty indicated a woman getting out of her car in her nightgown, face wet with tears, slowly approaching the scoreboard as if under a spell. She mumbled something to the blood stain, and quietly left. "This. This right here in front of us. How is this chaos? I see something else."

"What?"

"Worship. Love. Change. Devotion."

Helen looked back at the shrine trying to see what Marty was seeing. "Nah. I don't see it."

"What do you see?"

"Stupidity. Naivete. Following the herd mentality. Belief in fairy tales. People who can't think for themselves."

"Are you atheist?"

"I wouldn't say I'm an atheist. There could be a god of some kind out there. A higher being. I just don't think he, or she, would do something like this. I don't think a god like the ones talked about in churches would allow so much bad to happen in the world if he or she really loved mankind. There is too much bad in the world to make me believe."

"What about the good?"

"What good?"

"The good."

"Like…"

"Like babies being born."

"That's just Mother Nature."

"Okay. What about relationships."

"Same."

"No. Not the same. Look at people who have been friends all their lives."

"Not everyone gets to have that."

"True. But hear me out. What about forgiveness? What about falling in love?"

"Falling in love is also Mother Nature. People have to fall in love to keep the world populated. It's evolution."

"I disagree."

"Based on what?"

"My grandparents. They only had so many years to have children. They didn't just fall in love for those years to have a child, my dad. No. They loved each other over a lifetime. That's got to be beyond Mother Nature."

"I don't know. That's not what I see in the world. My parents, my grandparents, they stayed together out of societal obligation."

"That's pessimistic."

"Maybe. Still true."

Marty took her hand and looked into her eyes. "I need to find a way to change your mind about love."

"Love? Were we talking about love?" asked Helen.

"I was." Marty leaned over to give Helen a kiss on the lips. She accepted it and blushed.

They stood a while staring at each other until a car honked, knocking Helen back to reality. "You should head home and get some sleep, Marty."

"What about you? You can't sit out here all night. You have to get some sleep too."

"Yeah, I know."

"Why don't you go rest a while, and I'll keep watch?"

"Can't do that."

"Why not?"

"Cause I'm the cop. You're not. I'm the one with the authority to keep order. Anybody hell bent on causing problems would walk all over you."

"What? You don't think I could handle this?"

"I know you couldn't."

"But you do need to rest."

"I do."

"What about your car? Where is it?"

"It's just over…"

"Oh, I see it. How about you go take a nap in your car? Roll your window down a bit. You'll be able to hear if something comes up."

"That sounds like a good idea. I could use a rest."

"I'll walk you over there."

"I can walk myself to my own car."

"I know you can. Doesn't mean you have to. Does it?"

"I suppose not." They started walking along. "You know, Marty, I'm beginning to get the impression that you are flirting with me."

"That is the impression you should be getting." There was something about today that had Marty doing all kinds of bold things he wouldn't normally do. Holding hands, they slowed their steps to prolong the flirting. The car was not far away. "Do you have a guy in your life?" asked Marty.

"Nope. But I do know you have been…" she searched for an appropriate word, "active."

"I can't deny that."

They reached her car. She spun around and leaned against the driver's side door to face him. "Is there anything I should know if we intend on pursuing this thing between us?"

"This conversation has suddenly turned quite direct."

"I need to be direct. I need to know what I am dealing with. I have to be that way with the public, which means I have to be that way in my personal life too."

"Okay. I can accommodate that."

"You need to know, in my official capacity, I have seen you sneak off with Lori Greenfield."

"Yes. Yes, I have. I cannot deny that. I can't defend it either."

"I don't feel right being in a relationship with someone who has taken advantage of her like that."

"I agree. I can't be in a relationship with a guy like that either."

They both chuckled. "I'm serious, though. That is a hurting woman who is hurting her own children because her pain runs deep."

"I agree. I see what you are saying. I didn't see it that way until today, but I do now. After talking to Michael, I, I am done with things like that. I am done causing more pain to Lori. She deserves better. Her kids deserve better. It even occurred to me today that I might be the father of one or both of them."

"You think so?"

"I don't know. I would think, if she suspected me, that she would have said something. You know? She would have come looking for support, help, something. She never did."

"Maybe you aren't. She has been with a lot of men. I mean a lot."

"Still, I need to take responsibility for the hurt I have caused those kids even if I didn't mean to."

"You are becoming more attractive to me by the minute."

"Oh, really?"

"Yes, really." She reached up her arms to wrap around his neck. He placed his hands at her hips. Strange to them both, it felt like they had done this a thousand times before.

He opened the car door for her. She got in, and he closed the door. She rolled down the window to look at him. She was grinning from ear to ear. He bent down and kissed her again.

"Goodnight. I'll be right over there watching over everything for you."

"Goodnight," she replied. "And thank you."

"For what?"

"For opening up to me. It was wonderful."

"I suppose we could thank Jesus for that."

"Ha, ha. Very funny."

7

Blessed are the Poor in Spirit

Pastor James rubbed his eyes until he was nearly blind. 4 a.m. He couldn't believe he'd been talking to people all night. There were still people who wanted to speak with him, but he wanted to go home to eat, pray, and sleep.

He needed sleep. He leaned his head back in his chair and closed his eyes. For one blessed moment, his eyes rolled in REM. It didn't last long. There was a light rap on his door. He opened one eye and invited whoever it was to enter.

"I'm sorry to interrupt you, sweetheart." It was Laura. "You must be exhausted. I wanted to check on you. Now that everyone has left, I thought you might like help getting to bed to get some shut eye for at least a few hours. Or maybe you might like some breakfast before lying down. I could make you some pancakes."

Pastor James grimaced at her. "I think I can get myself to bed."

"So, no breakfast then?"

"No breakfast, thank you."

"Anything else I can do for you?"

"No," he said as he started to leave his office. "I need to lie down and get a few hours of sleep. What time will people start arriving again?"

"You told them 10 a.m."

"I should have said noon."

"Would you like me to call the…"

"No. Just leave things as they are. Let me get some sleep."

She followed him to their home next door to the church. Even though he said he didn't need any help getting into bed, he silently allowed her to do exactly that. She removed his shoes, led him down the hall to their bedroom, removed his clothes, put his pajamas on him, and tucked him into bed like a little child. He was sound asleep before his head hit the pillow.

He dreamt about his wife. It was a beautiful day. The sun was shining. He was watching her walk along a dirt road. She watched the birds flying between the trees back and forth and smiled. She was beautiful. He tried reaching out to her to touch her hand. Some unseen force held him back. He tried to call out to her. He yelled out her name. She gave no response. His heart began to pound in his chest. He tried calling out with no voice. She was standing on the precipice of a deep canyon. She wobbled back and forth about to fall into the darkness below. She called out his name. He reached out but he was not able to catch her. She was gone.

He awoke with a start. The sun was shining. The clock said 9 a.m. Five hours wasn't bad for a night of sleep. A hot cup of coffee and a homemade cinnamon roll was on the table next to him. That wasn't normal. He looked over at her side of the bed. It appeared as if she had not been in it at all.

"Laura?" There was no reply at first. He called out again, louder. Still no reply. He shrugged his shoulders and had his breakfast in bed. The coffee was way too fresh for her to have been gone long. He got up to shower and dress.

He searched the house for his wife. She was not home. The television was still on to a Monday morning news and talk show. Laundry was piled up near the washing machine. One load was half in. Dishes were piled up in the kitchen. This was not like her at all. Normally, the house was spotless. Order reigned in his house. Not today. So, where was she?

He called out to his 16 year old daughter. "Angela!" In the church, it was his habit to speak in soft tones. At home, his voice boomed through all the rooms at once.

"What!" Her tone matched his. He turned in the direction of her response and headed down the hallway towards the bedrooms. He opened her bedroom door. She was on her bed listening to music and reading a Stephen King novel.

"You know I don't approve of you reading those," he said.

"Yeah, I know."

He switched back to his original subject. "Where is your mother?"

"I don't know. I saw her a little while ago in the kitchen."

"Okay." He shut the door to her room. *She is probably at the church preparing for parishioners*, he thought to himself.

There was no time to dawdle. People were coming to the church for more guidance. Pastor James had never felt so needed before. It gave him a feeling of importance, like he was a part of something much bigger than himself, and he had a very important role to play in it. He stepped outside to walk over to his office at the church. Right there at the bottom of the front steps of his home was Fr. Andrew standing in the shade of the house against the late morning sun.

"Ah! Pastor James! Just the man I wanted to see."

"Hello, Fr. Andrew." Pastor James felt sorry for Fr. Andrew. Unable to take a wife, Pastor James knew what Fr. Andrew was missing. A lifetime partner to help one minister to a large flock of people was a blessing not to be taken for granted. Fr. Andrew had to do it all on his own. That had to be exhausting and lonely. "What can I do for you?"

"I wanted to know how you are doing?"

"I'm fine. Why?" Pastor James hurried along the sidewalk towards the church next door.

"Well, I'm sure your night was as difficult as mine." Fr. Andrew tried to keep up with his hurried pace.

"Probably."

"I just wanted to know how it went."

"How it went?" he repeated. He stopped and turned to look at Fr. Andrew. His brows furrowed together.

"Yes. I got through most of my congregation through the confessional. You don't have that."

"No, I don't."

"How did you get through your congregation?"

"I'm not through them all yet."

"You must be through most of them."

"Nope. I am expecting many of them back today. In fact, I am pretty sure there is a line at my office door now." They both looked over at the church.They both shielded their eyes against the hot white glare of the sun bouncing off the stark white sidewalk that connected the parish house to the church. The office door was on the opposite side of the dark brick building, People were haphazardly forming a line that wrapped around the front entrance of the church towards the house. "Yep. There is a line." Pastor James was pushing his hint to leave hard.

"I have people today too, but only a few. I hope." Fr. Andrew attempted to get back on the topic he wanted to discuss. "So,what happened with your congregants last night?"

"Nothing happened. As you pointed out, I don't have a confessional. I sit and talk with each person or each couple individually for as long as it takes."

"Then, this might take you the better part of the week?"

"Maybe."

"Alright. Well, guess I'd better leave you to it, then. How about coffee later so we can compare notes?"

On the one hand, Pastor James wanted to tell Fr. Andrew to bug off. On the other hand, getting a different perspective from another man of God might be helpful. "Okay. Downtown café, say 2 p.m.?"

"See you then!" Fr. Andrew trotted off with a smile on his face that disappeared once his back was turned while Pastor James headed into St. Paul's Lutheran Church almost whistling.

On the other side of town, Lori was doing her best to give her children a healthy breakfast. Michael and Daisy weren't quite sure what to make of the situation. They never all three sat at the 1950s kitchen table together before.

"Pancakes? Would you two like pancakes?"

"I want pancakes," piped up Daisy.

"Can I just have a bowl of cereal and go find my friends?"

Lori was disappointed at Michael's response. "I thought we could spend the day together."

"Doing what?" asked Michael. As much as he wanted a mom who gave him attention, he wasn't at all comfortable with this new version. She looked terrible. Her eyes were bloodshot with dark circles. Her hair was an even bigger mess than normal. She kept sniffling. He knew she'd been crying and mumbling all night. He could hear her.

Lori spun around the kitchen looking at what little she had to work with. She gave a sigh and her smile turned downwards. She tipped her head to one side, took a deep breath, and said, "If Caroline Ingalls on *Little House on the Prairie* could do this and make it look so easy, then so can I. She cooked and cleaned and talked nicely to her kids. I can do that too. I have modern appliances." Except she didn't have modern appliances. They were old. They needed replacing. She held up the box of pancake mix and bottle of syrup and declared, "I have these! I can do this!"

Twenty minutes later, she served up charred pancakes drowned in syrup. Daisy liked them well enough. Michael pushed his away and was allowed to go find his friends.

On his way, he passed by the growing shrine and stopped to have a look. He knew the sudden change in his mother had something to do with it. Anger grew inside of him. He irritated some in the praying crowd by deliberately knocking over a few of the flowers. He rode away before anyone could stop him.

One of those intently praying was Mrs. Benson.

Shortly before Michael arrived, Mrs. Benson prettied herself up with her best attire in black. She put on her most comfortable black shoes, grabbed her favorite rosary, and marched across the street to the softball like a soldier going to war. People parted for her like the Red Sea parted for Moses and she marched herself directly in front of the ketchup stain on the scoreboard.

Mrs. Benson ignored the pain in her knees as she got down on them and held the rosary by the cross to begin her prayerful meditation out loud. She blessed herself with the Sign of the Cross with an air of violence and recited the Apostles' Creed at the top of her lungs. By the time she reached the second Hail Mary, she realized her voice was not going to carry on at that volume for the entire duration, so she quieted down.

Other women joined in with her. Some loud and exuberant, others in quiet whispers, all Catholics intent on taking over that area in front of the scoreboard. They followed their religiously fearless leader, Mrs. Benson, with gusto.

Maggie was there as well with her own Lutheran entourage. She didn't bother trying to claim the prime location in front of the ketchup stain. She felt no need for an insurrection. Instead, she led a prayer group on the other side of the shrine. They were focused on the Sermon on the Mount.

Michael ran through the Lutheran circle before he took off. Maggie set the example of focusing on prayer and not on the infidel in their midst.

A total stranger from a nearby town was trying to get people to allow him to lay hands on them. He believed he could miraculously heal them. Not many people were taking him up on his offer. Eventually, he quieted down.

People from communities all over the southern half of the state were swarming the park and the whole town. The same three vans from the night before were back again with fresh reporters.

Larry was there too in the press box above the concession stand at the softball field watching everything unfold. He was there the entire night. His gloomy mind went from one dark place to another. *I should be the reporter on this story,* he thought.

He sat there a while longer into the lunch hour watching people come and go, crying out in ecstasy as they felt the Lord touch their souls, or crying out in shame as they faced their demons. He watched some strange exorcism attempt that ended in abject failure and giggles. He watched people intent on causing unrest get chased away by Officer Schafer and Marty.

Someone caught his eye. It was Lori holding hands with Daisy. Lori had come to the shrine. *Lori. I need to talk to Lori. She'll make me feel happy again.* He hopped out of the tower like a man of 28 instead of the man of 58 he was and ran right over to her.

"Hi, Lori!"

She looked surprised to see him talking to her. She was feeling all alone in her shame. "Hi, Larry. How are you?" She tried to be nice without getting into too much conversation with him. She didn't feel comfortable with him around her daughter with everyone acting erratic.

"I'm fine. Say, uh, how about going to get a bite to eat with me?"

"No, thank you, Larry. I am spending the day with my daughter."

"Oh, yeah. Hi, Daisy. How are you?"

"Fine."

"That's good. How about I give you money to go get yourself a candy bar down at the grocery store?"

Lori intervened as a mother should. She swung Daisy around to her other side and put herself between them. "I don't think that would be appropriate, Larry. I told you, I am spending the day with my daughter."

"I just need a few minutes alone with you."

"I said no, Larry."

"I could make it worth your while."

Lori was beginning to feel fear in the pit of her stomach. She often thought of Larry as eccentric, but never thought of him as dangerous before. "Larry, I appreciate all you have done for me over the years. I have never felt afraid of you before. In fact, you have always helped me whenever I needed help. But, I promised Fr. Andrew I would reconsider my actions towards men. I need you to quietly go away, please." She had one hand holding Daisy behind her back, and her other hand she held out in front of her to block him as she took two steps away from him.

"But, Lori, I need you."

"You are going to have to find someone else to ease your loneliness, Larry. I am out of the lonely hearts business."

"You mean prostitution," he retorted.

"You can call it whatever you like, but I am done."

"I could spread the word around town that you are a whore, a prostitute, that you exchange sex for money."

Lori went white. He could. He could ruin her reputation even more than it already was. Lori could lose clientele at Maggie's shop. She could be fired if Maggie ever found out Pete was her best client. *Oh, God,* she prayed inside herself. *Help me. Tell me what to do.*

No word from God came to her. She was on her own. She bent down to speak to Daisy.

"Daisy, honey. How about you go over to the playground so Mommy can have a few minutes alone with this gentleman, hmm? I won't be long, and then we can go play at the swimming pool together. Would that be okay?"

Daisy did not like this. "No, Mommy. I want to go to the pool now."

"We will, honey. Can you just give me a few minutes with him?"

"Okay." Daisy did not go to the playground. She refused to budge an inch. She watched as Larry took her mommy by the arm and hastily took her back to the media booth.

They entered the concession stand and Larry got the window covered by a wooden board that was made to slide into place making it much darker inside. The air was stifling. Sunlight seeping through the crevices gave just enough light. Larry began unbuckling his pants. He fumbled from excitement. He felt young and energetic. He felt wanted.

He stopped when he heard sobbing. He had never heard Lori cry before. He had always heard her giggling like a schoolgirl. The eyes searched for her face in the confined space. She was pressed up against a corner table as far away from him as she could get, her face turned as far to the side as possible, her eyes pressed shut, and water pouring out of her eyes and her nose. Larry had never seen her like that. His heart moved.

"Lori," he whispered.

Nothing about her changed. She was still in that position bracing for some sort of violent impact.

"Lori," he whispered again. "I could never hurt you."

She opened one eye slightly. His pants were done up again. He stood pressed up against the door, as far away from her as he could be. His hand was outstretched in an attempt to make peace.

"I don't want to hurt you," he repeated.

She relaxed just a bit, not sure if she could trust him.

"I have hurt you, haven't I? Often."

She said nothing. She slowly stood up. Her arms down at her sides, she turned the palms of her hands toward him as if she was offering him peace and comfort. She took a step towards Larry. He cried out.

Craig came to see what all the hullabaloo was about at the park. He did not anticipate the scoreboard stain creating so much drama.He walked over to the shrine but couldn't see it through the growing size of the crowd. Towards the back of the mob he spotted Daisy standing there as if she was frozen. He walked over.

"Hi, Daisy!"

"Hi, Craig," she responded without looking at him.

"Something wrong, Daisy?"

"I think so."

"You think so? Can you tell me what you think might be wrong?"

She didn't answer.

He bent down to her level. "Daisy, can you tell me, please, what is wrong?"

Without moving her head she answered, "You know Larry, the radio guy?"

"Yes."

"He took my mom over to the little building way over there. Where they keep the hotdogs. She looked like she didn't want to go with him."

Craig stood up and spun around. "You mean the concession stand?"

"Yeah."

"Stay here!" Craig sprinted as fast as he could through the opening in the fence and ran across the softball field. When he got there, he stopped to listen for sounds. He heard crying. "Lori!" He yanked open the door to it so hard he almost pulled it off its hinges.

The scene before him was baffling at first. Lori stooped over Larry partially holding him. Larry was almost in a fetal position on the filthy wooden floor crying like a baby.

"Shhh...." scolded Lori. "Larry's having a moment of clarity with God."

Mouth wide open from shock, Craig slowly backed out and started closing the door to give them privacy. He opened the door again to have another look. He could not believe what he was witnessing. He closed the door again, backed up, and let his mind spin. *Is Lori ministering to Larry? Is that what is happening? Is Lori capable of doing something like that?*

He glanced over at the scoreboard on the other side of the field surrounded by worshipers and thought about the so-called face of Jesus on it. He asked out loud, "Is this why you're here?" Then he looked over at Daisy still standing way over by the shrine exactly where he told her to wait. She waved. He waved back.

He reopened the door and whispered a question to Lori trying to be lighthearted as if this was an everyday occurrence. "While you are busy doing this, may I please take Daisy back to the bar and give her some lunch? Like a burger or something?"

She whispered back, "That would be great, thanks! I'll be there soon."

"Take your time."

He closed the door again and listened for a moment as the sobbing continued. He could hear Lori offer words of comfort in return.

Completely dumbfounded, he went back to collect Daisy. "Okay, Daisy. I found your mom. She is fine. Nothing to worry about with her. But she might be gone for a while."

"What's she doing?"

"Well, turns out Larry, the radio guy, isn't feeling too good, and your mom is being nice and taking care of him so maybe he can feel better. In the meantime, she would like for me to get you some lunch. How about coming with me to the bar and getting a burger and fries and a milkshake?"

"Yes, please!" Daisy happily placed her hand in his and smiled. "Thank you, Craig, for making sure my mom was okay."

It wasn't too long before Lori showed up and found Daisy and Craig sitting together at a table laughing. She smiled as she thought, *Too bad he isn't Daisy's father.*

8

Blessed are the Peacemakers

Pastor James was exhausted when he arrived at the café about twenty minutes late. The smell of coffee and the murmur of gossiping voices soothed his soul until he heard the voice of Fr. Andrew fielding questions from people from across the cafe every time he turned around in his stool at the counter. Pastor James grimaced before taking the stool next to the would-be pontiff. A steaming cup was immediately placed in front of him without him asking.

Fr. Andrew loved talking to all the people about God and Jesus and things heavenly. He greeted his Lutheran counterpart with a question. "I wonder if this was how Jesus felt when he finally had to escape his followers in a boat in the Sea of Galilee. Being surrounded by people constantly pestering you with questions gets tiring." He changed topics before a sarcastic retort could be tossed his way. "Pastor James! Good to see you! You have saved me from this crowd."

"Glad I could be of service." Pastor James offered up the sarcastic reply anyway.

Fr. Andrew ignored it. "How was your morning?"

"Exhausting."

"Really? Mine was productive."

"Productive? I don't know if you realize this, but we don't create anything, you and I. We shepherd people. We help point souls in the right direction. We don't create them."

"Of course. You know what I mean." Fr. Andrew changed the subject quickly. "So – have you seen your wife today?"

He could see James's face make a sudden change. "Now that you mention it, not since late last night. But I know she was at home because there was a steaming hot cup of coffee and a cinnamon roll next to me when I woke up. I know Angela didn't make breakfast." He looked suspiciously at Fr. Andrew. "Why are you asking me? What's going on?"

"I'm asking because I know where she is."

"Where?"

Fr. Andrew looked around trying to keep them both quiet. "She's in my rectory."

"She's where?" Pastor James was not quiet. He caught everyone's attention. Fr. Andrew attempted to shush him. Pastor James attempted to calm himself down and lower his voice. "What is she doing in your rectory?" Even in his quiet tones, the anger was unmistakable.

"She needed someone she could trust to talk to."

"Someone she can trust? She's got me!"

"Shhh… She didn't feel like she could talk to you."

"Why not?"

"Because it's about you."

"About me?"

"Shhhh! Yes, you."

"Was she there this morning when you came to see me?"

"Yes."

"Why didn't you tell me then?"

"I tried. You were preoccupied, for good reason. With everything going on in this community lately, it's understandable. I didn't feel it was the right moment. I thought you should get through more of your day first. But, I didn't want to wait too long either."

"Why you?"

"She needed to talk to a man of God."

In a failed attempt at whispering, Pastor James gave out an exasperated, "So she went to a Catholic priest? I, her husband, am a man of God too!"

"That didn't come out right. I meant a man of God she felt comfortable talking to."

Pastor James looked at him with murderous intent.

"That still didn't come out right. I'm sorry. Let me try again." He let out a huge sigh and thought carefully about his next words. "She didn't feel safe talking to you about you."

"I think I understand that much."

"Okay. Good."

Pastor James had a thought he didn't like for one second. "Are you and her...?"

"What? No. Nothing like that. We have not been meeting in secret. I am not doing anything with her or any other woman. Nothing inappropriate is going on. Not between her and I, anyway." Fr. Andrew rolled his eyes at himself. *I need to learn when to shut my own mouth,* he thought.

Pastor James did a double take at that last comment from Fr. Andrew. "Nothing inappropriate between the two of you. But maybe between you and another?"

"Um. No."

"You can't mean her and another?"

Fr. Andrew made no move.

Pastor James whispered, "Are you saying my wife is having an affair?"

"You know, you and she need to sit down and have a conver-"

"Oh my God!" Pastor James yelled.

"Shhhh!"

He did not quiet down. "How can she do this to me!"

"Listen. I am trying to facilitate a safe way, a safe place for the two of you to be able to talk things through. Can you handle that? A safe conversation? Where she can open up to you?"

"Safe for her? What about safe for me?"

"For you too. Come on. You must have had couples come to you with problems like this. What did you do for them?"

"It doesn't matter. This is different."

"How so? How is this different?"

"Because it's me. It's my wife. It's my marriage." He slammed his hand on the table. The coffee cups rattled, spilling coffee on the counter. The waitress started over with a washcloth. She looked at both men and receded into the ice cream display behind her without cleaning anything.

Pastor James went back to whispering. "I don't know how to handle this."

"Well, thankfully, I do.

"Oh, really?" How could a Catholic Priest who has never been married give relationship advice to a married couple?

What Pastor James did not realize was that Fr. Andrew was not celibate his entire life.

When Andrew played baseball on a minor league team in Missouri, he was in love.

Samantha was a baseball player fanatic. Not of the game. Of the players. She spent all her time at practices and games flirting with the players and looking for love. She found it easily.

Andrew fell hard. It was love at first sight for him. It took a bit longer for her. She was blonde, blue-eyed, a classic beauty. The romance heated up quickly.

She approached first. "Hi, you! That's some arm you've got there." She expertly batted her eyes and flipped her blonde waves.

He turned red. "Thanks."

"You're new."

"Yep. Scout pulled me out of college junior year. Liked the look of my throwing arm."

"I can see why. How about you take me out for a burger after practice today?"

"Sure!"

Andrew fell into a hot romance hard and fast. They went everywhere together. He played better when she was around. Most of the off season was spent in bed.

Spring training was looking very good for Andrew professionally. Scouts from the major league teams were showing up and making inquiries.

She was giddy. "An offer will come your way soon. I am sure of it!"

"I hope so." He didn't want to get his hopes up and be disappointed. He was right to be cautious. Scouts came and went with no offer. He continued on with the regular season. That's when he started to feel her pull away.

"Babe?" he asked in June of his second season on the team. The romantic setting at her favorite restaurant was perfect for the moment.

"Yes?"

Sweat dripped from his body like it did on the pitching mound at the bottom of the ninth inning. He pulled the little box from his pocket and pushed it across the table. His voice cracked when he asked, "Will you marry me?"

The smile on her face was much smaller than he anticipated as she opened the box and put on the ring. "Yes. I will marry you." She put the ring on her finger and continued to eat her dinner.

"Is that it?"

"What?"

"Is that all you have to say?"

"I said yes." She looked at him, eyes wide with surprise at his question.

Three weeks later, during the 4th of July game, it happened. Samantha was missing from her usual seat in the stands. Andrew was distracted. His pitching was off.

The game was tied at four runs each. A runner on third and another on second was not a good recipe for a stressed pitcher on the mound with two outs in the eighth inning. Batter was up and ready.

Andrew nodded when the catcher signaled for the fastball. This batter's less than stellar average at bat called for it. Out of anger Samantha wasn't there, Andrew put more power behind the throw than necessary. Something felt like a pop in his shoulder. He grabbed at it and made his way off the mound.

His pitching coach approached him. "What happened?"

"I don't know. It hurts. I heard a pop."

"You heard a pop?"

"Yeah."

Andrew was pulled from the game and was out for the rest of the season.

Months later, Samantha was beside him when he got the news. His career was over before it began. It should not have happened. The injury should not have been that severe. But it was true.

"Sorry, kid," said the team doctor. "That torn ligament in your shoulder is not going to heal properly. I hope you have a backup plan for a career."

He didn't.

She didn't talk to him about it. She didn't give him the opportunity to fight for their relationship. She simply went off with another player. No discussion. No "thanks for the fun" conversation. No goodbye. She simply had a walk-off base hit in the bottom of the ninth inning leaving Andrew alone in the dugout to lick his wounds. He lost the game of relationships. He never got over it.

Months later, he had his drunk driving trip to the courthouse. He turned to God and realized the seminary was where he belonged. Still, the pain of that betrayal stayed with him his entire life. Forgiveness and healing took a long time. Fr. Andrew never told anyone from Pennington Corner about her.

"She even kept the ring," said Fr. Andrew out loud.

"What?" asked Pastor James.

Fr. Andrew's mind was elsewhere. He returned to the problem at hand. "Sorry. I was just… Never mind. It doesn't matter. Except to say that I do understand how it feels to be betrayed and abandoned."

Pastor James now had to face the same demon Fr. Andrew had. Except this was Pastor James's wife, a woman with whom he was in a life-long committed relationship. *Can I forgive her?* he asked himself.

"Fr. Andrew, I should know what to do. You're right. I have had couples come to me in this exact situation before. I have guided them through it. Some made it, some didn't. Now that it's me, I don't know. My God! This hurts! I am at a total loss."

"This is what you need to do. You need to go home, make yourself a cup of tea, and rest a while. Don't see any more parishioners about the recent events. Take some time to yourself. Then, come to the rectory about six o'clock. We'll have a light supper and a nice conversation."

"A nice conversation."

"A nice conversation. That's what we'll have."

"You know, sometimes I think you Catholics live in some sort of fantasy world. Say a few prayers, and all will be well."

"I tell you what. We'll try that tonight. We'll say a few prayers and we'll see if all is well afterwards." Fr. Andrew attempted a smile. Pastor James only glared back.

Pastor James walked home with his head down to do what Fr. Andrew suggested. As he passed by his church, he saw another line had formed outside. He detoured and headed to the church office.

Fr. Andrew returned to his church to a new harvest of souls as well, mostly people who came from out of town in need of spiritual guidance after visiting the shrine. He rolled up his sleeves and muttered, "The work of the Lord is never done."

Marty and Helen were still guarding the shrine. The mob was turning into a circus. There were more and more people arriving, but fewer and fewer of them were from Pennington's Corner.

"Maybe I should call in some reinforcements?" asked Helen.

"Who would you call?"

"The county sheriff."

"I'm surprised they aren't here already."

"Don't these people have jobs?" asked Helen, indicating the crowd. "It is Monday. Why don't they go home?"

"You better call."

"Yep."

Michael was in the park at a distance and watched Officer Helen Schafer go over to her cop car. He watched Marty as Marty watched all the people. Michael had many unanswered questions about what was happening. He decided it was time to investigate again.

He dropped his bike next to some trees and walked into the crowd. He made his way as close to the shrine as he could get without being seen by Marty or Officer Schafer. He made his way to the inside of the fence from the scoreboard in the outfield expecting something to make sense to him. Nothing did. He walked over to where the television reporters were waiting around for their next live news feeds. They were all discussing Twins sports scores and the weather. He learned nothing from them.

He looked again at the mountain of stuff and the people walking through the softball field to deliver them with care. There were flowers and candles and crosses and rosaries and stuffed animals and photos and statues and so much stuff that things were falling over each other and tumbling down the pile.

Paths had formed on both sides of the fence from people walking around the mountain of stuff to get behind it to see the scoreboard. On the other side where people waited to take turns to see the face of Jesus. There were only a few feet between the scoreboard and the fence. He followed that path around and through the people.

The crowd formed a demarcation line of people about six feet away from the scoreboard to let him, and only him, in. There seemed to be a magical invisible barrier no one could cross or God would be angry. The Holy Land opened itself up for Michael to visit.

As Michael hesitated, he thought, *I'm not scared of any god.* It took only an ounce of courage for him to cross the invisible line. He waited for someone to stop him. *Am I invisible?* No one could see him. He stepped closer and closer to the scoreboard. *Will I be hit by lightning? Is that what God does? Is God going to be angry with me for being there?* Michael took another step closer, then another. Finally, Michael got all the way to the front of the scoreboard so he could easily reach out and touch it.

He looked at the scoreboard. The score was still up. *What are people all weirded out about?* He looked around the scoreboard, on the ground, around the back of it, in the tall grass surrounding it. He saw nothing to show the power of God. He even saw the red blotch, which was darker in color as it dried out. *Why are people flipping out about this?* He bent down to examine it. "It's just ketchup," he said out loud. No one heard him. He continued, "Whoever was keeping score was probably eating a hot dog at the same time. No crime committed. So, why is everyone acting so weird? Adults are stupid." He shrugged his shoulders, made his way out of the crowd, picked up his bike, and went looking for his friends.

Maggie was still at the shrine deep in prayer. She mumbled incoherent words. She felt the spirit overtake her and reveled in the intensity of the experience. Her body visibly vibrated like she was having an orgasm.

It was getting close to dinner time, and Pete was hungry. He attempted to reign in his wife. "Maggie. Maggie. Maggie!"

She continued to ignore him.

He decided to give up and go eat at the café. He got a couple of blocks away from the park when he looked down Main Street and realized the café was going to be packed with people. He turned around and marched back to the softball field. *That woman is going to feed me dinner!*

This time when he found her, she was on her knees loudly trying to speak in tongues. Her eyes were practically rolling in the back of her head. The words coming out of her mouth were gibberish. Her eyes were locked shut. He bent down and yelled in her ear, "Maggie!"

She immediately opened her eyes and glared at him. "What!"

"It's dinner time."

"So?"

"So, you need to come home and make dinner."

"No, I don't," she stated matter of fact.

"Yes, you do. I'm hungry."

"I don't care. I'm not hungry."

"You always make dinner."

"Not tonight."

"What am I supposed to eat?"

"Go to the café. Or go to the grocery store. Or go home and look in the refrigerator. There must be food in there. Have you ever opened a can of soup before? We do own a can opener, you know." Condemnation hung in the air like the flies that were beginning to circle the crowd sweating in the summer heat.

Pete furiously demanded, "Maggie! So help me! You come home now and stop this nonsense!"

"Nonsense? This isn't nonsense! This is more real to me than anything else has ever been. This is a miracle!"

Pete had had enough. He grabbed her by the arm and walked her home. She only fought him a moment and then pulled her arm away and walked quietly seething with anger. She decided maybe they should go home and have it out once and for all.

They entered the house through the kitchen door and stood there staring at each other. Charlie greeted them with all the happiness a puppy contains. When he realized they were not responding to his joy, he went into the living room to lie on his own pillow in the corner to pout.

All the words they wanted to spew at each other remained silent. Maggie turned around and started making dinner. She got out the can opener, showed it to him, and opened up a can of chicken noodle soup. As the soup splatted into the saucepan, Pete went into the living room and turned on the TV. If anyone had asked him what he watched that evening, he could not have given an accurate response. He was too upset to pay any attention.

A few minutes later, they sat at the dining room table with their food in front of them. Neither could eat. They stared at the steaming bowls of noodles and chicken and carrots and celery and little bits of parsley – a mixture that seemed as discombobulated as their marriage.

Finally, as the untouched soup turned as cold as Maggie's heart, she looked at him and spoke. "Pete, I know you have been sleeping around for years."

He remained silent, staring into the chicken void.

"I think I've known the whole time. I just didn't want to admit it was true."

"How did you find out?"

"I don't know. I put it all together today. At the scoreboard. It just came to me."

Silence.

"I think we should get a divorce," Maggie whispered.

His eyes lifted. He met her gaze for a moment. He looked past her at the framed picture behind her. "You know what? I hate that painting. The one behind you."

Maggie turned slowly and looked at it. She slowly turned back to face him. Her brows tipped up. "Why?"

It was a scenic picture, a print, of a not famous painting by a not famous artist, something purchased years ago to decorate a wall because it matched the dining room décor. *Why does this painting mean something to me now?* he asked himself. He answered her, "I liked it when we bought it. A farm in a meadow surrounded by fields of hay and autumn-colored trees near sunset when everything is a golden haze. This entire house is decorated in the color gold. You know why I liked it? Because it screamed of financial success. But that changed. Now, it screams of boredom, of settling, of feeling like nothingness. I hate it! It makes me angry. I want to be angry, Maggie. I want you to be angry. I want you to scream at me in anger."

"We were high school sweethearts," she replied quietly. No scream came from her. "We've traveled the world together with our son when he was young. We've been all over Europe and all over North America. This is an exciting life. I'm not bored, Pete. I'm not angry about my life." The anger switched on. She screamed. "I'm angry you don't think our life together is precious enough to treasure! I'm angry you need more excitement than I can give you! I'm angry at how you can trash our lives we built like they are nothing!"

Pete wanted to rage more, but deep down he was a little afraid of her. *I always feel under your thumb. You control me. Everything I say or do has to meet with your approval.* He didn't say any of those thoughts. After all, what was left to say?

There was more to say. She felt much the same way. *He is so controlling! I can't do anything! Anything I want to do, I have to go through him. When do I get to live the life I want?* She tried to reach out. "Pete, we were happy at times, weren't we? I loved you very much in the beginning. You got so wrapped up in the dealership... I don't know. You didn't seem to have any time for me. I was busy with our son."

"I did give you the salon."

"And I love the salon!"

The salon made her think of Lori Greenfield. Now she felt angry.

"Was Lori Greenfield one of your women?" she asked.

He opened his mouth to say something. No sound came. He closed his mouth again and continued to stare.

"How did I not know?" she continued.

"Should I pack a bag?" asked Pete. His voice was small and child-like. Nothing like the big bully who dragged his wife home from the park earlier.

"No. No point. You can stay in the other bedroom until we get things sorted out." She got up from the table to start clearing away the dishes.

Pete sat there a while longer, his head in his hands, listening to the clang of the dishes. It never occurred to him she might want a divorce. It never occurred to him she would ever figure it out. He always thought of her as too naive. He felt dumb. Maybe he could stop this.

He got up and walked into the kitchen. He intended to walk up behind her while she was at the sink, wrap his arms around her, kiss her on the back of the neck, and make her see that none of this mattered and they could go on as usual.

He approached her from behind cautiously, with all the stealth of a rhinoceros stalking a blade of grass. She read his mind. She spun around and glared at him with the daggers of a legion of first century Roman soldiers. He didn't stand a chance.

He took two steps back. "Is there anything I can do to make this better?"

She glared at him in silence. The daggers were annihilating him.

Pete suddenly looked like a very old man. His shoulders slumped. His already frowned face drooped. His heart grew cold to match her own.

He started to turn and walk out of the kitchen when a gust of hot wind blew through him. He physically turned red with anger.

"This is all your fault, you know!" Unable to take responsibility for his own actions, he went on the attack. "If you weren't such a cold fish in bed, I never would have gone looking for another woman! Besides, I never loved you. I felt sorry for you. I knew if I didn't marry you, nobody would. And, I needed your dad's money to start up the dealership. So, thanks for that, anyways!" He stormed out of the kitchen, grabbed his things from the bedroom, and hastily moved into the spare room.

His nuclear bomb hit its mark. She turned back towards the sink filled with dishes, stared into it blindly, and wept for hours.

9

A Soul in Search of Itself

Larry spent hours by himself in the closed-up concession stand after Lori was done cradling him like an infant. The door was ajar enough for air to circulate, but Larry still couldn't breathe. Sweat poured off his body leaving puddles on the floor. He remained in that position dwelling on the angel that swaddled him in friendship and love until the late afternoon sun made the heat unbearable in the enclosed space.

Larry pushed his body up with a grunt and pushed open the door using more strength than should have been needed. He walked past his car and headed a mile out of town to his tiny house next to the radio tower.

Larry's house was not much more than a converted one room shed with an added bathroom. It had just enough room for his broadcasting equipment, a sofa and chair, a television on a small stand, and a tiny kitchenette with a small stove, some shelves, a small sink, and a dorm room sized refrigerator with only a few cans of beer in it. Only two windows gave any light besides two lampstands from the 1960s. One window faced south. The other faced west and let in a little flashing red light at night from the looming tower above his roof, the beacon that always called him home from a night of drinking and meeting up with Lori.

Larry got himself a beer and sat on the sofa to drink it. He stared at the television in front of him. He didn't turn it on. He finished half the beer, set it down on the coffee table in front of him, and walked out the door.

He walked back towards town along the main east to west high-way. Cars and semis drove past causing blasts of air that nearly propelled him into the ditch numerous times. He continued walking unheeded.

He turned left onto Main Street and walked right past the bar, the shrine with all the people, and the cafe as it was closing for the day.

"Hey, Larry," called out the cafe owner as she locked the door. He didn't respond.

He stopped in the center of town in front of the large American Foursquare that was originally the home of Mr. and Mrs. Pennington.

Larry remembered back in the day when this was his home. Larry's parents purchased the home when he was a child from the profits of their grocery store that was in the building where the cafe now stood. Larry was seven years old in 1929 when his parents purchased the home and they moved in.

"Larry!" called his father. "Get in there and finish emptying your boxes! Get those toys of yours put away."

"Yes, Dad." Larry hurried up the stairs. It was hard for him to not roam around in the new house. It was much larger than the previous bungalow they lived in where slept in the parlor right by the front door. That used to scare him. But in the big Foursquare, he had a bedroom all to himself with room for toys and all kinds of creepy corners and hidden cupboards. There was some sort of monster carved into the woodwork around the fireplace. His mom said it was just a carving of vines and flowers. But Larry saw a dragon in the intricate details with large eyes and razor sharp teeth to protect them from invaders.

It was nice being closer to the grocery store. Two blocks away was much easier than walking more than half a mile with short legs. Larry was at the store almost every day after school and all day during the summer helping empty boxes and stack shelves.

He bagged groceries as soon as he was old enough to handle the delicate eggs.

As his short legs became long legs, his voice took on a deep soothing tone, and his mother became a widow, Larry became the man of the house and the store. He was so preoccupied, he never got his high school diploma. He was the sole breadwinner of his family.

"Larry," said his mother in the fall of 1939. "You should go out with your friends."

"Yes, Mother."

"No, really. You should go out and get ice cream with a pretty girl and listen to the band play on Friday evenings in the park."

Larry stopped sorting out the bad apples from the good and looked at his mother. "I would, Mom, if I had any friends."

"Oh. Okay." She walked back to the checkout counter. "I still think you should go," she mumbled.

The bell on the front door gave a little jingle as the beautiful Maeve Wilson walked in the door. Larry stopped to gawk, an apple in each hand. With her pretty blonde hair and upturned smile, she was the loveliest thing in the entire school. Larry was just as in love with her as every other teenage boy in the county. Head cheerleader, she was on the arm of the football captain where she was socially expected to be. She let go of her companion's arm and walked up to Larry.

"Larry, can you give me the best apple you've got?" she asked, eyes wide open. She batted her eyelashes just the perfect way her mother told her.

Larry paused a moment before realizing she was talking to him. He looked down at the two apples. He examined them both, put them both down, and dug deeper in the box of apples he was unloading. He pulled out the most perfect one he could find. "Here," was all he said as he blushed.

"Thank you." He held out the apple and she took it. The sleeve of her sweater pulled up a little showing a bruise on her forearm. She quickly covered it up with her other arm with an embarrassed smile. She took a bite and turned to leave with her companion who purchased some candy without paying for the apple. She turned back at the door. "You have a nice voice." Larry stared after her.

Larry spent all his free time walking around town Friday nights in the park as the band played watching for Maeve. She was always on the arm of the football team captain. If she ate ice cream, Larry ate ice cream. If she sat on a bench, he sat nearby. Usually, she ignored him. Every now and then, she would give him a sly smile, and he would smile back.

Larry often noticed bruises on her arms, and one evening at the park he thought he saw some around her neck. The band was playing as he got himself a bag of popcorn and searched for Maeve. He saw her sitting on a bench near the bandstand next to the football captain. He was half turned talking to other guys from the team. Larry didn't see him. He only saw the purple around her neck. Her sadness and his anger attracted each other like the gravitational forces of the earth and the moon. Larry approached rapidly. Maeve stared in silence. As Larry was about to approach, the football team captain turned. Maeve flinched at his movement causing the gravitational pull to cease. She looked at Larry again and carefully shook her head no. Larry stopped in his tracks. The football team all started to move away from the bench. The team captain put his arm around Maeve, and she went with him without a word. Larry knew he had missed his only opportunity.

Larry went to the senior class graduation ceremony and watched her get her diploma. Within months, Maeve was married to the football captain, and they were living in Minneapolis. Months after that, in November of 1941, he overheard gossip being shared between two older ladies of the community in the middle of the vegetables.

"Did you hear about Maeve Wilson?"

"You mean the girl who married the football player? No. What about her?"

"She's dead."

"What?"

"That's right. She's dead."

"How?"

"No one knows. At least, no one's talking. I think we all know."

"Oh! Her poor parents! What are they going to do?"

"I hear her husband has agreed to move them to Minneapolis to be near her grave."

"Really? Is he doing that out of a guilty conscience?"

"Shhh… Probably, but you won't hear me say that."

"Me neither."

Larry froze. *Maeve dead?* He quietly finished stocking the cans in the box in front of him and took the box out to the back of the store to crush and throw in the trash heap. In a blind rage, he started kicking and throwing the trash cans and the trash that came flying out of them. He grabbed a pallet off a neatly stacked pile and started ripping it apart. The torn wood sent splinters into his hands. When he was done venting, he looked down at his bloody appendages, clenched his fists to stop the bleeding, and snarled.

"Next time I see him, I will kill him!" Those were the only words he said about it. He never had the opportunity.

Less than a month after Maeve's death, two days after Pearl Harbor in 1941, Larry joined the army. He sold the store, sold the big house he loved as a kid, and bought his mom a tiny house on the north end of town that was torn down to build an apartment complex years after her death in 1945. Larry got word of her passing in a letter from the town priest at the time.

Larry didn't see much military action. During basic training, he was pulled aside by his commanding officer.

"I hear you have the perfect voice for radio," said the officer.

"Radio?" asked Larry.

"Hm. Sounds like it. Say something else."

"Like what?"

"Talk about the weather."

"Well, it's sunny out. A little hot. Humid. Could use some ice cream." Ice cream made him think of Maeve.

"Alright. That's all I need to hear. You will report to Sergeant Dennehey at 05:00 where you will be transferred. You are going on the radio."

Larry spent WWII at a base in the South Pacific playing music and reading the news to the troops. He saw no action, but he read enough about the tragedies happening on the islands around him to hurt.

Larry returned to a town filled with strangers, even amongst the people he attended school as a kid. It was time for the annual 4th of July baseball game. The band was setting up in the stands.

A young, widowed Mrs. Benson was sitting in a corner of the stands closest to the concessions table, the booth had not been built yet. She was holding a rosary close to her heart and holding back her tears from missing her deceased husband so much. Larry didn't know her well, but he remembered her from the store when her husband was still alive trying to navigate the particulars of buying vegetables and cooking them the right way to please a meat and potatoes man.

He got himself popcorn from the concession table and sat to watch the game. The stands were filled with ladies in their Sunday hats and gentlemen too old to play. The typically peaceful game started off with a battle of fists between two players, one from each team.

"What's that about?" asked Larry of the ladies in front of him.

"Pickerson from St. John's and Veley from St. Paul's are having a dispute over who tore down the tree line that blocked the wind from eroding Pickerson's field. Thing is, everyone knows neither of them did it, But Pickerson insists Veley did it out of spite because Pickerson made eyes at his wife."

"Yes," said the other woman. "It was Norton's sons who did it. They just wanted the wood to build a fort. What a waste. They'll never get around to building it."

"Don't you know it," replied the first lady again. "Those boys, always doing something stupid, wreaking havoc, and starting things they'll never finish. Oh well. At least we have yet another reason for this game. Think these games will ever stop?"

The second lady finished the topic. "Do you mean will we ever run out of disputes in this town? Doubtful. Always someone sleeping with someone else's wife around here."

Larry munched on his popcorn, watched the game, and eavesdropped on the ladies gossiping. He recognized some names and not others. He learned one interesting piece of information that made him happy.

The first lady asked, "Did you hear what happened to that guy that married that real pretty girl, you know, the prom queen back in um, what year was that, 40? 39? Her name was Mary or May or something like that."

"No," said the second lady.

"You mean Maeve?" interrupted Larry.

They both turned to look at him. He expected them to be annoyed he was eavesdropping, but they were not. "That's it!" said the first woman. "That's her name. Anyway, I heard her husband got killed in France during the war."

"Really?" said the second woman.

Larry smiled.

As Larry watched the game, he realized he was hearing a play-by-play of the action coming from the other side of the bleachers. He climbed down to follow the voice and investigate.

There was a table set up with large equipment, a large microphone, and cables running everywhere. There was a little man sitting behind the table trying to keep up with the game and run the equipment at the same time. He fumbled around and missed two plays in a row. Larry decided to ask.

"Can I help you with that? I have radio experience."

The gentleman behind the table at first looked offended that someone was offering to take over. "What experience? Make it brief. I am on the air."

"Military radio. Music and news."

The man's demeanor changed to relief. "Switch with me." Within moments, Larry was in the driver's seat of the only local radio station in town. Over time, he purchased it with the money he still had from the sale of the store and the Pennington house, and became the only local radio station in the county. However, even though he was better than the guy who originally owned and ran it, he was never good at it.

Larry continued to stare at his childhood home. It was nearly 6:00pm. Dinner time. He wasn't hungry. The sun was lowering itself but was still above the horizon. He turned and continued walking.

Pastor James looked at the clock on the wall as it struck 6:00pm. Dinner time. He was not hungry, but Angela would be. He sent everyone home from the church and headed to his house next door. As he rounded the corner of the tall brick structure, he observed how his shadow from the evening sun disappeared into the shadow of the church steeple on the sidewalk. He turned up the smaller sidewalk path to his front door and disappeared into the house.

He could smell the pizza Angela was making. "I hope you don't mind frozen pizza, Dad," she said as he walked into the kitchen. "I really don't know how to make anything else. I haven't seen Mom all day and I want to go out later tonight, so I didn't want to wait for dinner. Is that okay?"

"That's fine." He walked to the stove and took over the cooking duties. He opened the oven, pulled out the pizza that was not quite ready yet, and started slicing it up. He put some slices on two plates, handed one to Angela, and indicated to her to go into the dining room. She complied, confused because the pizza was obviously not done. They sat at the table, neither touching their food.

"Dad? Where's Mom?"

Pastor James stared at his plate.

"Dad?"

"Hm? Oh! She is out with a friend. I will be bringing her home later."

"Okay." Angela changed the subject. "Can I go to Jenny's house after dinner? Her mom wants to take us to see the movie E.T. Can I go?"

"Yeah, sure."

"Can I have some money?"

"Um, yeah." He pulled some money from his wallet. He could not comprehend what he was giving her from the shock of the day. He gave her all the cash in his wallet.

She counted out $60. $20 would have sufficed. "Wow! Thanks, Dad!" She gave him a big hug. He barely noticed. She looked at the slices of pizza sitting on his plate and then looked intently at his face. "Are you alright?"

"Yes." He looked at the pizza. "I don't know why I made myself a plate. I'm having dinner with Fr. Andrew later."

"Oh, ok." She looked at him oddly, then smiled knowing she was free from parental eyes all evening. She said a quick goodbye and left.

Pastor James sat at the dining room table staring into his pizza until the clock on his mantle in his living room that matched the one in his church office struck 7:00pm. He got up, put on his shoes, and walked out the door.

As he walked, his thoughts roamed all over Mrs. Benson's declaration about the blood stain face of Jesus on the scoreboard, the reactions of the people not only from Pennington's Corner but from all over the surrounding area, the confessions he was hearing, and Jesus himself. He thought about Jesus coming to town. *Why, Jesus? Why are you here? Is this real? Did you come just for me? Did you come so I could forgive my wife for doing the unforgivable? If I can't forgive my own wife, how can I pastor others on forgiveness?*

He reached St. John's Catholic Church, walked around to the rectory, and stood frozen in the warm evening staring at the door three steps up from him. A hard lump formed in his throat. He tried to swallow it down so it wouldn't burst out of him in the form of a wail. His mind traveled back to a cold evening on January 16, 1963, in Madison, Wisconsin. It was his 24th birthday.

The weather was not kind that day. The high temperature when the sun was out did not reach ten degrees Fahrenheit, and the winds were brutal. The recently ordained minister was on his way to a party being given in his honor by one of the congregates of his first ever parish. He was nervous. He stood on the doorstep not wanting to enter. Was Mrs. Winkleman going to attempt to set him up with her niece again? That Laura seemed like a nice girl, but he had no interest in marrying anyone at the time. He wanted to get settled in first. Besides, he had very little experience with women, and she was pretty. Nevertheless, he thought he could do better. He thought someone prettier, less shy, and with more of a talent for organization would be better suited for the life of a minister's wife. The one time he met her at the Winkleman's Christmas party a few weeks previous, she seemed incapable of organizing her purse much less a bible study group. Plus, she could not hold down a conversation without turning red and looking away.

He rang the doorbell. Mr. Winkleman opened the door and gave him a pleasant welcome. "Oh, by the way, I'm sure you have already guessed, but my wife does have her niece, Laura, seated next to you for dinner. Just thought I would give you fair warning. I know my wife's tendencies to play matchmaker can get annoying, but it keeps her out of my hair. So, good luck to you." He gave the young minister a hard pat on the back.

Pastor James just smiled as nicely as he could as he groaned on the inside. He handed Mr. Winkleman his coat and went into the living room where the other guests were warming themselves by the fireplace.

As he entered the room, he braced himself for what he thought would be a barrage of unwanted attention from this Laura girl. Instead, he was warmly greeted by some of the other parishioners, a total of six others in the living room. No Laura. He found himself looking around for her.

He was brought a warm cup of coffee from Mrs. Winkleman who gave him a funny look when he accepted it. Pastor James felt uncomfortable. *Have I offended Mrs. Winkleman?*

He and the other guests talked at length about the cold weather, his last sermon, did he miss his parents back in Missouri, and more. Finally, it was time for dinner. They were all called into the dining room to take their seats. Pretty little place cards with the names of each guest directed the individuals. As Pastor James sat down he noticed Laura was not seated on either side of him as expected. He caught himself scowling. *Why is this bothering me? I'm not attracted to her anyway. She's not my type.*

After all the guests were seated, Pastor James noticed the open spot that must have been reserved for Laura was as far away from him as it could be. He looked over at Mr. Winkleman at the head of the table who also seemed to notice the situation.

He returned pastor James's confused look with a shrug of his shoulders.

Soon, Mrs. Winkleman and Laura came out of the kitchen with a flourish of dishes. They all looked delicious!

"Now, Renae," piped up Mrs. Schmidt to Mrs. Winkleman, "I know you didn't cook all this. You try your best and all, but you are not nearly this good a cook."

"Of course not," returned Mrs. Winkleman. "My niece did all this. Except for the salad. I can take credit for the salad. She just got a college degree in home economics. We are so proud of her!"

Pastor James could not believe what he was seeing. A beautiful rack of lamb, well-seasoned mashed potatoes, two kinds of vegetables, a sauce that smelled divine, homemade buns, Mrs. Winkleman's green jello salad, and a beautiful birthday cake at the center of it all. He was amazed at the spread! *The young woman who couldn't organize her purse made all this?* he thought to himself.

He looked over to her to give some sort of nonverbal thank you. She refused to look at him. She kept her head down and covered her face with her dark blonde hair.

"Wow!" he said. "I feel so honored with such a spread! Thank you!"

She gave a simple nod of her head and a whispered, "You're welcome," as she sat down in her chair.

Pastor James looked at Mrs. Winkleman with as big a smile as he could muster, but she refused to make eye contact.

I'm in trouble, he thought.

The food was delicious. It was the best lamb he had ever eaten. The potatoes were creamy and flavorful. The buns were freshly baked. He marveled over every bite so much so that it was painfully obvious to everyone that he was trying to get the young chef's attention. Dinner was turning into a spectator sport.

She wasn't having it. She ate very little of her own food and took part in very little of the table conversation.

It was time to clear out the main course dishes to make room for the dessert plates. Laura still refused to make eye contact even as she took his plate. He moved his head under her face so she had no choice but to look at him. Her eyes lifted just far enough for them to make eye contact.

Whoa! She's beautiful! Her eyes were radiant gems of green set against flawless pale white skin. Her bobbed blonde hair framed her features perfectly. His breath caught in his throat. He knew he was destined to marry her at that moment. She simply looked away and headed into the kitchen with the stack of dishes.

Pastor James got up, looked at everybody around the table, and said, "I can't believe I'm doing this."

"Go get her, son," said Mr. Winkleman.

Pastor James motioned for Mrs. Winkleman to remain in the dining room with a wave of his hand. He entered enemy territory quietly. He was hoping for the element of surprise.

Behind him, everyone at the table strained to eavesdrop.

"What are they saying?" asked Mrs. Schmidt.

"Nothing yet," responded Mr. Winkleman. He was closest to the kitchen door.

In the kitchen, Laura had her back to the door. She was busy scraping off the plates and creating a stack next to the sink. "I know you want to get to the cake, Aunt Renae, but why don't you go ahead and start that without me? I don't know if I want to watch the birthday boy blow out his candles."

"She can't. The birthday boy isn't in there."

Laura spun around nearly dropping a plate. "I didn't know...I didn't hear you come in."

"I followed you."

"I see that. Do you always do that?"

"Do what?"

"Sneak up on girls in kitchens?"

He chuckled. "No. This is my first time."

They stared at each other for a moment. Holding a fork in her hand and waving it around, she asked, "Is there something I can do for you?"

"Yes. You can tell me why you are angry with me."

"I'm angry with you?" She pointed the fork at her own chest.

"Sure seems that way."

"Why would I be angry with you?" She pointed the fork at him.

"I don't know. That's why I'm asking."

"I'm not angry with you." She was back to being unable to look him in the eyes.

"You can't look at me. That tells me you are angry with me."

She lifted her eyes. They were so beautiful. "Okay. I'm looking at you."

"Good. Now, please, put the fork down and tell me why you are angry with me."

She looked at the potential weapon in her hand and gently tossed it into the sink filled with suds. She turned back to face the enemy. "Because..."

"Yes..."

"Because when we met at the Christmas party, you were rude to me."

"I was?"

"Yes."

"How?"

"You wouldn't look at me. I was trying to be nice. I knew you were uncomfortable here, brand new to the community, your first parish, and my aunt trying to push us together. I was trying to help you, but you wouldn't look at me, or talk to me, or acknowledge me at all. You were rude."

He was rude. He could see it in his own memory. He hadn't intended to be, but he was. "I'm sorry. Thinking back, I agree with you. I was rude. It was not my intention. I'm very sorry."

Laura took a step back at the unexpected apology. "Thank you." She didn't know what to say after that.

"Can we start over?"

Laura shrugged her shoulders. "I don't know. I guess that would be the Christian thing to do."

He walked over to her, his hand outstretched, and said, "His. I'm Pastor James. I am the new minister over here at Word of God Lutheran Church. It's very nice to meet you."

"Hi, Pastor James. My name is Laura. It's very nice to meet you too. I'm sorry my Aunt Renae keeps trying to set us up. You should probably be aware it isn't even appropriate given I am a Catholic."

Pastor James's smile dropped from his face. No matter. He was in love. He was going to convert her and marry her. He did.

Here he stood, 19 years later, in front of the rectory of St. John's Catholic Church in Pennington's Corner, Minnesota wondering if he even wanted to win the heart of his wife back again.

10

Though I Walk Through the Valley

Pastor James stood there contemplating whether or not to ring the doorbell when the door to the rectory flew open. Fr. Andrew peered out at the pained soul at the bottom of the stairs looking up at him.

"Are you coming in? Dinner's getting cold."

"I don't know," said Pastor James.

"Don't you think you should?"

Pastor James searched for an excuse. "It is a rather lovely evening out here. Maybe I'll keep walking"

"Good idea. I'll go with you." Fr. Andrew stepped outside and got in sidestep with Pastor James. They walked a while in silence following the setting sun.

Larry turned back south on Main Street and walked to the cafe he had passed by earlier now closed for the evening. He stopped to peer in the windows. He remembered how it looked when it was a grocery store. It was still a grocery store eleven years ago when he first met Lori there.

The first time he noticed her was at a high school basketball game. She was already into using sex in exchange for homework assignments and grades by then. He was announcing the game on the radio. He happened to glance in her direction, saw her bell-bottom jeans, blue eyeshadow, long blonde hair, and was hooked. He was 48, and she was 16.

Larry went right to work courting her. He sent flowers and love letters. She ignored them. He pursued her for months until his world caved.

Larry was announcing the local high school boys late season basketball game when Lori walked in front of the media table between plays. She was carrying a hotdog in one hand and a soda pop in the other. What caught Larry's eye wasn't the typical curve of her frame he normally gawked at. It was the perfectly round, significant bulge beneath her breasts. Larry's radio went silent as Larry searched for his voice beneath his rage. At first, all he could get out was, "Who did it?"

"What?" asked the scorekeeper teen sitting next to him.

"Huh?"

"Who did what? You asked, 'Who did it?' In most movies, the butler did it."

Larry looked at the kid. "Oh, just...shut up!" Larry put his attention back on the game.

Soon after her high school graduation and after giving birth, Larry discovered her staring into the grocery store window holding her crying baby boy and looking distraught.

At first, he walked by. He couldn't help himself. He turned back and asked, "You look upset. Is there something I can help you with?"

"Um, no. I just..." She didn't want to tell. She didn't want to admit there was a problem. *How else will I feed my baby?* she thought to herself.

He gently put his hand on her shoulder and pulled her to the side to make her feel safe enough to tell him her secrets. "It's okay. You can tell me. Let me help you."

"Well, I don't have enough money for formula."

"Formula?"

"You know. To feed the baby?" They say it's healthier than coming from the mother. I don't know, but I can't feed him anyway. They don't seem to be working right." She looked at her breasts. He could hardly control himself. "But he's starving. He's got to have some food, and I am out of money."

"What about the father?"

"He can't help. He doesn't have any money. He's gone off to college anyhow."

"Does he know?"

Lori shook her head.

"What about your parents? Can't they help you?" Larry already knew her home situation.

"I don't have a father. My mother doesn't have any money either. Besides, she's pretty angry at me for getting pregnant in the first place. Not like I did it on purpose. She's going to kick me out pretty soon, I think."

"I can help you."

"Really? Oh, thank you! How?"

"I can get some formula and some food. And, I can help you find a place to stay."

"I would be ever so grateful! I will pay you back somehow."

"Yes. Yes, you will."

Larry gave her the supplies she needed for the time being and went to work securing her an apartment on the west side of town not far from his radio tower. Even though he could afford to buy her all new furniture, he gave her money to scour garage sales for secondhand items.

Once settled, she called Larry to thank him for his generosity.

"Would you like to come over for dinner on Sunday?" she asked. "I would like to thank you for being so kind." Lori was naive and scared but not stupid. She knew what Larry wanted in return.

What other choice did she have?

Larry came with a bottle of wine while Lori served hamburgers from the local bar. The wine gone and the burgers half eaten on paper plates, they moved to the sofa. Lori turned on the television and feigned interest in a news program hoping Larry would get the hint. She started to sit in a chair, but Larry took hold of her hand and guided her to the sofa next to him. Without a word, Larry began fondling her breast and kissing her neck.

Lori attempted to distract him with guilt. "Larry."

"Hm?"

"Have you ever been in love before?"

He didn't answer for the longest time. Without stopping his advances, he thought of Maeve. Her blue eyes and golden curls bounced out of his mind for what he hoped would be the last time. He unbuttoned Lori's top and removed it. He fumbled with the clasps on the back of her bra. She made no move to help him. He felt like a soldier storming into battle. He pushed her over her own knees ignoring her groan to unhook it, pushed her back, and then abruptly repositioned her on her back.

Lori did her best to endure the sofa springs digging into her back and Larry's weight on top of her. His kisses felt like he was sucking the life out of her. She started to push him off but made herself give in. Her baby in the next room sleeping needed formula and shelter. She let Larry have his way.

Larry read her lack of participation as permission. His first time having sex was with a prostitute while he was in the military. That prostitute was also uninterested in his advances but allowed him to do what he wanted because he was a paying customer. Larry was not understanding that Lori was basically doing the same.

He bruised her as he forcibly removed her jeans and underpants. He fumbled with his own pants and pushed them down around his ankles. He inserted himself and finished quickly.

"That was amazing!" he groaned as Lori thought to herself, *Thank God that's over.*

Baby Michael began to cry for a bottle in the next room. She slowly removed herself from underneath him, dressed, and went to care for the baby. Larry put his clothes back on and indicated for her and the baby to sit next to him to watch television like they were a family.

That was the beginning of Lori using sex for more than grades and attention. This ritual became a regular Sunday evening event until Michael was two, old enough to leave the bedroom on his own.

"Larry," Lori ventured on their last Sunday evening playing house, "I appreciate all you have provided for me here, but I would like to go to school."

He was not happy. He asked, "For what?"

"I want to be a hairdresser."

"You want to give women perms?"

"Yes. I think I can be good at that."

"What for?"

"So I can make some money. Provide for Michael myself."

"Okay. I'll pay for you to go to school."

"Larry, that's not what I am-"

"No, no, no. Let me do this for you." He reached over to kiss her and stop her from arguing.

Larry did pay for her to go to school in exchange for more pretend family time in her apartment.

When Maggie saw how skilled she was with the latest trends, she hired her. It didn't take long for Maggie's husband, Pete, to get in on the Lori action. Word started to spread throughout the men of the town that Larry and Pete both had special arrangements with Lori. They wanted in too.

Larry arrived at her apartment late one night unexpectedly. "Did you sleep with Pete Johnson?" The volume in his voice awakened the neighbors in the apartment and little Michael.

"Yes," she responded calmly.

"Why? How could you?"

"I needed a new sofa."

"What?"

"I needed a new sofa." She moved aside to open the door further so Larry could see it. "I couldn't stand the old one anymore. The springs were broken and hurt. Pete said he would buy me a new sofa."

Larry looked at Lori as if he didn't know her at all. "How could you?" He started to walk away but turned to her. "You need to move."

"What?"

"You need to move. I used up my money. I can't afford to pay the rent anymore. You need to move."

"How much time do I have?"

"Two months."

Within two months, Pete secured a mortgage for Lori in a little two-story house not far from the park and softball field.

Larry stopped seeing Lori for a few months, but he couldn't stay away. Sunday evenings remained his until the face of Jesus appeared on the scoreboard.

Larry found himself in the dark standing in front of the scoreboard staring at the face of Jesus in red. He didn't know how he got there. His mind flipped back and forth between Maeve who looked like an angel and Lori who was the angel he ruined. He wanted to weep for all the damage he had done. No tears came. Lori emptied them out of him in the concession stand when she cradled him like a baby.

Larry did something he hadn't done ever in his life. He prayed. "God, how could she do it? How could she forgive me for all the wrong I did to her? I hurt her. I ruined her life. I hurt her children. I forced her to stay in this god-awful town and let people abuse her, starting with me. I was going to rape her today! How could she forgive me like she did?"

He replayed the earlier exchange in the concession stand that afternoon.

"I'm so sorry, Lori! I'm so sorry I did this to you!"

"It's okay, Larry," whispered Lori. "I played a role too."

"No! It was me. I did this. I hurt you."

"I forgive you, Larry. Isn't that what God does? Forgives? I can do that too. I can forgive you."

She sounded like the innocent girl she used to be. It hurt him all the more. He was in hell. She pulled him out of it. She cradled his broken being with her pity and held him like a mother holds a helpless child.

As Larry continued to stare into the face of Jesus, he wanted to die.

He started thinking about ways to end his life. He looked around for ideas. He saw a light flashing in the dark from the top of the water town on the opposite side of town.

Out near Larry's radio tower, Fr. Andrew was able to steer them back into town off the loud gravel that inhibited conversation and onto newer, black pavement. It didn't matter. He had difficulty finding the words to say anyhow. The two men walked past St. Paul's Lutheran Church and past homes with families gathered together in peace and safety, where parents tucked their children into bed with a storybook, and husbands and wives kissed each other goodnight. They stopped at the school where they sat on the swing set behind the elementary school classrooms.

Fr. Andrew forced himself to take the plunge. "Are you ready to face her yet?"

"How is she?" asked Pastor James, wondering if he really wanted to know.

Fr. Andrew gave careful thought before answering. Off and on all day he attempted conversation with Laura. Mostly she cried and drank tea. When she attempted words, she cried more. Eventually, he put her on the couch in his office and closed the door to give her the space she seemed to need. The only broken up words he could get out of her were, "Bless me, Father, for I have sinned. It has been eighteen years since my last confession the day before I married my husband, and I have been cheating on him for the last two years." She recited that four times throughout the day when she came out for more tea.

He attempted to give her the opportunity to complete her confession, but she kept breaking down and returning to the confines of his office. He didn't know she used to be Catholic until now.

He was ready to answer Pastor James's question. "Broken."

"Good."

"That's not talking like the man of God you are."

"Right now, Fr. Andrew, I am not a man of God. I am a broken husband."

"I see that. You can't leave God out of it, though. You need Him to get you through this."

"I know."

They got up and started walking again. Fr. Andrew let him lead the way. Before long, they found themselves in front of the shrine. It was 11:00pm. The crowds were mostly dispersed for the night. There were only a couple of people praying including a tearful Larry who was walking away from them towards the north along Main Street. They paid him no attention, and he did not see them at all. Only a nearby county sheriff remained alert to the happenings.

Pastor James motioned to the shrine. "Did this kill my marriage?"

Fr. Andrew wasn't sure how to answer that question. "Um. No."

"No?"

"No."

"So, whatever is going on started before all this?"

"I would say this is what is leading to the end of what's been going on."

"That sounds cryptic."

"I'm sorry. I don't want it to sound that way."

"She is for sure having an affair. I didn't imagine you saying that before. You did say that at the cafe."

"She should be the one to tell you what's been happening. Not me."

"Jesus!"

"Let's not go down that road."

"Why not? Isn't He supposed to be the one in control?" He motioned to the red stain as he paced back and forth like a pro-wrestler looking for the best way to start the fight.

"Okay," continued Fr. Andrew. "Maybe we need to calm down before we go back to the rectory."

"Calm down? I don't know if I will ever be calm again!" Pastor James did something no one had ever seen him do before. He became violent. He punched the scoreboard. "This miracle of God is ruining my life!" The county sheriff took a couple of steps closer to them. Fr. Andrew motioned to him that it was okay. "It's ruining my church! The congregation is filled with people more lost than ever! It's ruining my marriage! My wife is sitting at the Catholic Church of all places contemplating leaving me for another man while I don't know if I even want her back! This isn't a miracle! It's a curse!" He punched the scoreboard again. He didn't yell out in pain, but Fr. Andrew was certain he was injured.

"Okay," he said as calmly as possible. "I think we need to go to the rectory and get this," he indicated Pastor James's hand, "taken care of, and then we need to decide whether or not we should even have this conversation tonight. Maybe we should wait until morning."

"No! We are having this out now! Right here and now with God!"

As the sheriff again approached, Fr. Andrew gave a quick glance up to the clear sky wondering if a bolt of lightning was about to reign down on them.

"No, no, no. Don't look to Him." Pastor James pointed up to the sky as he continued to spew his anger. "I'm the one talking. I'm the one in charge. He can't do this to me! I won't let Him! He is not going to ruin my life. Some other man is not going to come in and take over my family. No one can fill these shoes. No one. God is not going to get away with this!"

Again indicating to the sheriff to not intervene, Fr. Andrew said, "James, you know God does not want this for you. You know how God feels about marriage. You two have a wonderful life together. This does not have to be the end of it."

"Oh, no. This is the end of it. The marriage is over. She can't do this to me! I won't let her humiliate me! I won't let Him either!" He pointed to where the face of Jesus was on the scoreboard. Then he broke down and cried.

Fr. Andrew allowed him to sob for about half an hour before directing him towards the rectory.

The moon was full above Larry as he walked towards the water tower. He didn't notice. He passed by the closed shops including the cafe that used to be the grocery store and past the big house he grew up in. He arrived at the grain bins near the water tower and looked up. Maybe there was a place for him to hang himself on top of the grain bins? Or, maybe he could get inside and suffocate himself by falling in and getting buried? Maybe he could jump off the top? He had no idea suicide could be so complicated given how easy people died in the war. *I should have died in the war.*

He spotted the water tower and decided his original solution was the best. He would hang himself from up there. He walked over to the ladder barely within reach thanks to a smaller ladder added from someone's garage.

He started the climb as tears fell from his face. He wasn't afraid of the height. He was afraid of meeting God on the other side and having to explain himself. He reached the top assuming he was alone and started removing his belt.

"Hey, Larry," came a voice to the right of him a few feet away. "I thought that was you."

Startled, he nearly fell off the water tower. "Hey," he looked to see who he was addressing, "Marty. How are you?" He tried to sound nonchalant, as if they were out for a nice, leisurely stroll on top of the water tower as they would any other day of the week close to midnight. He wiped his face on his sleeve. He looked closer at Marty. "Is there someone sitting there with you?"

"Yep."

"Hello," came the voice of twelve year old Michael. "You should sit over here by us. It's a nice view of the town and the moon."

Larry looked up at the moon. It seemed bright and cheerful in complete contrast to the darkness in his heart.

"Yeah," said Marty. "Come join us over here. There's plenty of room."

Larry replaced his belt. Michael did not notice the belt, but Marty did. Larry sat down next to Marty, and the three of them sat in silence for a while staring at the happy moon.

Michael finally broke the silence continuing his conversation with Marty before Larry joined them. "I don't know. Maybe someday I could be on the moon. Maybe I could be one of those astronauts who does stuff like that."

"You could do that," replied Marty.

Larry stayed quiet and listened.

"I mean, I never thought about stuff like that before," continued Michael. "What do I want to be when I grow up? I never thought about growing up. I suppose I should. I'm getting there, right?"

"Right," came the simple response from Marty.

"I will need to take care of my mom and my sister, so I will need a good job."

"Possibly," said Marty.

"Did you go to college, Marty?"

"I went to a trade school to be a mechanic. I'm glad I went. I do pretty good for myself."

Michael leaned his head out to see Larry better. "You own the radio station. Did you go to school to learn how to do that?"

"No. the army taught me. When I came back, I bought the station. I should have gone to school for it though," Larry answered. He tried taking cues from Marty on how to talk to this kid. This kid, the same kid whose mother he could have destroyed. *I owe this kid for all the damage I did to his mom. If it hadn't been for me…*

"You bought it? Where'd you get the money?" Michael was amazed anyone could simply have money to buy a radio station. "It must have cost a lot."

"I did. I bought it." *And your crib when you were a baby.* "See the cafe? That used to be a grocery store. My parents used to own it. When my dad died, it became mine. I didn't want it, so I sold it and bought the radio station. Problem was, I didn't know how to properly run it. In the army, I was given information to read on the air. Here, I have to know what to say. I should have gone to school to learn. I'm terrible at reporting the news, and I am terrible at putting on music people want to hear. The only thing I do well is read the obituaries." Larry chuckled. Marty and Michael did not.

"If you do such a bad job, why do you keep it?" asked Michael.

"I don't know. I've never asked myself that question before. Maybe I should stop."

Marty interjected. "Or, maybe a better idea instead of giving up is to find a way to run it better. Maybe hire someone who did go to school to learn broadcasting and needs to get their foot in the door into the industry. What better place than a small radio station?"

Larry's face lit up. "Where would I find someone?"

"The school in Mankato. Or maybe the next biggest radio station which is also in Mankato. Someone might be looking for a new job."

"Or," offered Michael, "maybe you could hire someone closer to you who wants a job like me."

Both grown men chuckled.

Fr. Andrew and Pastor James arrived at the rectory. Pastor James hesitated. Fr. Andrew put his hand on his friend's shoulder and led him in like a scared executioner on his first assignment.

11

A Lutheran Confessional

Shortly after midnight, an already emotionally drained Pastor James allowed himself to be led into the rectory by Fr. Andrew. The rectory was a small apartment connected to the back of the church. It had only the basics in its construction: a living room, a kitchen, a small dining room, a bedroom, a bathroom, and an office. Laura was nowhere in sight. The dining table was filled with cold food and dishes from a partially eaten dinner including one used half-filled plate, one clean unused plate, and one untouched filled plate, and a couple of serving platters with food on them. Dinner was ruined thanks to one particular guest who refused to enter a few hours earlier.

Fr. Andrew sat his injured friend into a chair in the living room and went to find an ice pack and bandages for his hand. He examined the injury when he returned with the items. It was black and blue. He tied the ice pack directly on with the bandage.

"There. That should help. You might need x-rays tomorrow."

Pastor James did not respond.

Fr. Andrew then went to the office and lightly rapped on the door. "Laura, he is here now. It is time."

It took a moment for Laura to come out of the office. She came through the door and stood looking at her husband. She tried fumbling with her hair a moment in an attempt to look more pleasant. It didn't matter. He kept his head down and refused to look at her.

Fr. Andrew led her to a chair opposite her husband and grabbed from the dining room a third chair for himself and formed the shape of a triangle. Pastor James looked at the physical arrangement.

"Pizza," said Pastor James.

"What?" asked Laura.

"Pizza. I gave Angela pizza for dinner."

"Oh. Okay," she replied.

Fr. Andrew cleared his throat to begin with some sort of prayer, but nothing came to mind.

Pastor James looked up at his wife. She looked terrible. Her skin was pale. Her bloodshot eyes were sinking in darkness. Seeing her that way flared his anger. His eyes flaming red and his cheeks burning with heat made him look like he was possessed by a demon.

"Who is it?" he demanded. "Who are you in love with?"

"Go ahead," she whispered. "Punish me. I deserve it."

"Tell me who it is!"

Fr. Andrew attempted to intervene. "This line of questioning won't help anyone. Maybe we should start with a pray..."

Pastor James demanded again. "Tell me who it is! Do I know him?"

"No," came another whisper.

"A stranger?"

"Yes."

Fr. Andrew attempted a prayer. "Dear Heavenly Father..."

Pastor James, "Are you in love with him?"

Laura, "No."

Fr. Andrew, "...we come to you Lord to ask you to intervene..."

Pastor James, "How long have you been together?"

Laura, "Two years."

Fr. Andrew, "…in this troubling time…"

Pastor James, "Who is he?"

Laura, "I'd rather not say."

Fr. Andrew, "…in this holy marriage…"

Pastor James, "Why the hell not?"

Laura, "It doesn't matter who it is."

Fr. Andrew, "Let's try this again. Lord, we ask you to join us…"

Pastor James, "Was the sex good? Is he better than me?"

Laura, "No."

Fr. Andrew, "…in this moment of high emotion…"

Pastor James, "No?"

Laura, "No."

Fr. Andrew, "…and broken hearts…"

Pastor James turned to Fr. Andrew. "Is this always how you conduct these sorts of interventions?"

"No," he replied. "This is a special case. I'm not sure how to navigate this for a Lutheran Pastor and his wife who are also friends of mine. This is new territory for me."

"Well," stated Pastor James. "You're not doing too good here."

"I noticed. Let's go for attempt number three. This time, how about we let me get this started properly." He looked up to heaven. "Lord, thank you for being here. Amen." Then he directed his attention to his friends. "James. Let's state things simply. Your wife has broken your marriage vows."

"No kidding."

"She came to me because she wanted to find a way to confess to you and try to save the marriage. As someone raised in the

Catholic Church, even though she is now Lutheran, this is where instinct brought her to do this. She has come to confess to God and you and receive forgiveness. Can you accept her confession to you for the wrong she has done?"

Pastor James was all about anger until that last question. "Can I accept her confession? I…" He paused to think. "I don't know."

"How about we try?" Fr. Andrew turned to Laura. "Laura, you came to me with a story. Why don't you start by explaining your story to your husband?"

Laura, in too much shame to meet her husband's eyes with her own, continued to look down at her hands as she attempted to confess her indiscretions. "It started two years ago at the annual softball game. You were in the dugout with the team. I was sitting in the bleachers with the other ladies. 4th of July was a Friday that year. Craig was preparing for extra beer sales because it was the beginning of the weekend, so he had ordered an extra shipment. Well, the shipment arrived."

"It's a beer delivery guy?" Pastor James's anger intensified, shutting Laura down.

Fr. Andrew tried to get things restarted. "Let's try and help Laura recount what happened."

"Help her? What about helping me?"

"I'm hoping I can help you both. Laura, can you continue?" asked Fr. Andrew.

She nodded her head. "He came out of the truck and started unloading the barrels and the cases. I was expecting to see him flirt with Lori Greenfield. All the men flirt with Lori Greenfield. I've even seen you look at her periodically, especially during those games."

"I do not flirt with Lori Greenfield!"

Fr. Andrew attempted a gentle correction in the narrative. "Let's not get into finger pointing…"

"Finger pointing! This is all her fault!" yelled Pastor James.

"Let's get back to the story. Laura…"

She took a deep breath. "He didn't flirt with Lori. He started to notice me."

"I'll kill him."

"Shhh…" said the priest.

"I didn't know what to do. I looked over at you, but you were all about ministering to the men on the team. I looked around to the other ladies. No one seemed to take any notice. It was almost as if he was some ghost that only I could see." She stopped.

"He's a ghost," interrupted Pastor James. "You're telling me he isn't even real."

"Go on," prodded Fr. Andrew.

"I don't really know what happened after that. It's kind of a blur. We ended up behind the concession stand…"

"I'm going to burn down that concession stand."

"No, you aren't," said Fr. Andrew. "Continue, Laura."

"We exchanged names and phone numbers."

"Is that all?" asked the injured spouse.

"He immediately started calling me that evening. You answered the phone."

"I did?"

"Yes."

"What did he say to me?"

"He simply asked for me. You didn't question. You just handed me the phone."

"There is no way I did that."

"I swear to God, you did."

"Don't swear to God! That is a lie, and you know it. There is no way I would allow some strange man to call my wife."

"You assumed it was some parishioner calling about the choir. He told you he wanted to join."

"I don't remember this."

"It doesn't matter," intervened Fr. Andrew. "He called, you answered, you had no suspicions, you trusted your wife, so you handed her the phone expecting her to properly handle whoever it was."

Both gentlemen looked to Laura expecting her to take it from there. She felt a bit cornered but pushed on. "He asked if I was going to the fireworks later that evening. I said yes. He said he would be there. I said that had nothing to do with me. You and I went to the fireworks display. He was there. He sat where he could look at me instead of the fireworks the whole time."

"He was after you."

"Yes."

"Why would he be after you? You must have done something to lead him on."

"I suppose I did."

"Hang on, Pastor James," interjected Fr. Andrew again. "We still don't know the whole story of what happened. I'm not sure she should tell all the details. But we do know Laura is not in the habit of leading men on. Laura, is this the only affair you have ever had?"

"Yes."

"Were you looking to have an affair?" continued Fr. Andrew.

"No."

"Okay. I didn't think so. You are definitely guilty of the infidelity, but we don't fully understand yet how it started."

Pastor James chimed in. "We do know. She should have never met him behind the concession stand and given him her, our, phone number."

"Laura, do you have a response to that?"

"I needed the attention."

"What?" Pastor James could not believe what he was hearing. "Are you saying this is my fault because I wasn't paying enough attention to you?"

"Maybe..."

"Oh, no! I reject that outright! I paid attention to you all the time."

Fr. Andrew gently interjected yet again trying to keep things on track. "Let's not point fingers. Right now, let's focus on getting the truth out. Laura, remember, you are the one who had the affair. You may have been feeling neglected, but ultimately, you made the decision. James, you do bear half the responsibility of the condition of the marriage going into this. There. That is enough finger pointing for now. Let's get back to the confession. Continue..."

Laura choked back tears. She thought she had cried enough for the day. Apparently, she had more tears inside herself. "I tried ignoring him. He kept calling. He figured out you were gone almost every day from 10 a.m. to 4 p.m. He would call almost every day. After a few times, I stopped answering the phone. You got mad at me because then I missed some important calls from parishioners. So, I had to answer the phone. We got to talking and became friends."

"What could the two of you possibly be talking about? What could you have in common?" asked Pastor James. "You are the wife of a pastor, he is a beer delivery man."

"Well, he also felt neglected at home by his wife."

"He's also married? So, you weren't just breaking up our marriage, you were destroying another?"

"I guess... I didn't think of it in that way."

"Do they have children too? What about our daughter? Do you have any idea how this will affect Angela?"

"They have three children, younger than ours, and yes, I do understand this will devastate her. All of them."

"Devastate. Yes, devastate. Think on that word. Let the weight of that word hang on you." The anger in Pastor James's voice only seemed to intensify.

"Okay, Pastor James," Fr. Andrew emphasized the word pastor to try and remind his friend he is a man of God. He turned back to Laura. "Then what happened?"

"The phone calls went on for weeks. He made deliveries to Craig's bar every Thursday afternoon so Craig would be ready for the weekend. We decided to meet for lunch on one of those delivery days."

"You met with him at the café on Main?" Pastor James could not believe the audacity.

"No. We met in Rochester." She paused, bracing herself for the impact.

"You drove all the way to Rochester? Do you know how far away that is?"

"About two hours one way."

"Why?"

"So no one we knew would see us."

"Where is he from?"

"Minneapolis."

"So once a week, you drove a long distance to have an affair? How did I not know?"

She didn't respond to that question.

"How much time did you actually spend together in bed? Who paid for the hotel rooms? I assume you had your flings in hotel rooms." Pastor James was digging for details Laura didn't want to give.

"I don't know if I should answer those questions."

Fr. Andrew suggested she try without too much detail.

"We would be together for about an hour. I would have dinner cooking in a crock pot while I was gone. You never noticed."

"Every week? This happened every week?"

"No. Not every week. It was along his route. If I wasn't there, he would just go on with his route. We met at the same hotel each time. They always had rooms available."

"A rent by the hour sort of place?" Pastor James's eyes got big.

"I guess…" She stumbled on her words.

Pastor James looked physically ill. He wanted to vomit. He ran into the bathroom and braced himself for it. He dry heaved some. Nothing expelled itself. He rinsed his face off with water and returned to his chair.

He looked over at his wife. Up until a few hours ago, he loved her with all his heart. He would have done anything for her. In one day he no longer knew how he felt about her.

"Okay," said Fr. Andrew in an attempt to lighten the mood a bit. "It's getting really late. How about we stop here, we all go home. Laura, you sleep in your bed, James, you sleep on your couch, and we pick this up again in the morning?"

They both ignored him.

"What is the state of this relationship now?" pushed Pastor James, starting another round of dialogue between the two of them.

"I told you, he broke it off."

"Why?"

"He found another woman he liked better to fill the Thursday slot."

"Thursday slot? You were a slot?"

"I guess."

"When did this happen?"

"A month ago."

"So, he dumped you."

Laura cried a bit more. "I've been saying that. Yes."

"You are hurt by that."

"Yes."

"How do you think I feel?"

"Devastated."

"There's that word again."

They stared at each other in silence letting the weight of that word hang on them more.

Fr. Andrew was tired and wanted to end the conversation for the night, but he felt this might be a good time to ask about future intentions. "So, Laura, what is it you want to get out of this conversation?"

She squeaked before answering. "I am asking James to forgive me." Fresh tears poured out of her eyes.

"Pastor James?"

"I can't think about that right now," Pastor James responded.

"Let me attempt to bring some clarity to this," continued Fr. Andrew. "Your wife has confessed and is asking for forgiveness." He directed his next question at Laura. "Are you hoping to stay in the marriage or leave it?"

Through a shaking voice wet with flooding tears, "I want the marriage. I have done a terrible, terrible thing. I want to make things right between us. If he will have me."

"Pastor James? You have obligations here."

"What about her obligations?"

"She has obligations as well. We will get to those over time. I want to focus on yours right now. You are a husband, father, and you have a congregation who look to you to be the epitome of God's grace and mercy. Where are you on forgiving her and working on the marriage?"

"This is unforgivable." Pastor James's brokenness was palpable through his voice.

"Is it?" Asked Fr. Andrew. "Is it unforgiveable? Or is this a human, moral failing that people do recover from? Marriages are often rebuilt. You've been through this with other couples. I know you have. You yourself have personally helped couples recover from this. What makes your situation, her infidelity, unforgivable? Look at her and tell me how after all these years of marriage, this can be over in one day?"

Pastor James looked at his wife. She looked like a different person, a complete stranger. "You are not my wife," he spewed. "My wife would never have done such a thing. You don't even look like Laura. Laura had a glow about her, a vitality. You have none of that. You are devoid of life. And now, you have a major moral failing. I could never love a woman like you. It can be over. It is over."

Laura slowly rose up from her chair. With an extremely hunched over demeanor full of contrition, she approached her husband slowly. When she got in front of him, she got down on her knees before him and allowed her tears to pour out onto his feet. And then she kissed his feet as had been done to Jesus in the bible. She repeated over and over again, "I am so sorry. I am so sorry. Please forgive me. I am so sorry."

Pastor James recognized the biblical scene being played out before him. He pushed her back. "Don't give me biblical dramatics." She sat on the floor in the middle of their chairs, a place of judgment. "Answer me this because I am sure that damn shrine has a role to play in all these theatrics. Why are you telling me now?

Why today? Why in the middle of all this chaos in our church, in our town, are you confessing this now?"

"You're right," she said, partially raising her eyes to meet his. For the first time during this exchange, some sort of certainty was in her face. "I heard Larry report on what was happening at the park, some sort of miracle from God on the scoreboard. That first night, well, early morning actually, after you fell asleep exhausted from meeting with all those other people, I went to the park to see for myself. I put you into bed, took a flashlight, and left. There were quite a few people there. People were down on their knees praying. Others were bringing things. A pile had started up, what everyone is now calling a shrine to Jesus. The intense prayers – I could actually feel them in the air. It was as if I could reach up and grab someone's prayer right out of the air and look at it.

"Then it occurred to me," She continued," that I had lost the ability to pray since the affair started two years ago. I was too ashamed of myself to pray to God. I couldn't look to God any-more. I couldn't look at you anymore. The shame was over-whelming.

"Larry had said that the blood stain was in the shape of the face of Jesus. I thought, 'I can look at Jesus. I can look him straight in the eye and confess to him what I had done. I can pray to him directly.' I went over to the scoreboard and searched for a while with my flashlight. It was dark, so it took me a bit to find it. But I found it. There He was. It was Jesus. I could see Him clear as day.

"I tried to confess to Him everything." She continued her dia-tribe against herself. "It was hard getting the words out. It was hard admitting to all the wrong I had done, the betrayals to you, the man I swore to love till death parts us. I had failed to keep my vows.

"After I finally got it all out to Jesus, I started begging for forgive-ness. I asked Jesus himself to cleanse me of my sins. Then I asked Him for the strength to confess to you and beg you for forgiveness. I owe it to you to be honest, and take whatever punishment you decide I deserve."

Still on the floor, she stretched out her hands to him. "James, do whatever you must do to punish me for my transgressions. I can take it. I will take it. I will do whatever needs to be done to make this right for you. Please! Forgive me. Take me back. I am a sinner. I have sinned against you and against God. I want to make this right. I will do whatever you demand of me. Please, James! I love you!"

Those last three words were too much for Pastor James. He got up without a word and walked out the door.

12

Bearing False Witness

The door slammed behind Pastor James leaving his wife a pile of ashes on the floor of the rectory and Fr. Andrew helpless to do anything about it. He was shocked at the level of rejection by his Christian friend.

Fr. Andrew composed himself and helped Laura up off the floor. "You need some rest. Let me walk you home."

"What about James? He'll be there. He won't let me in."

"He won't be there. I don't know where he'll be, but he won't be there. Let's get you home."

He was right. He delivered Laura to her daughter who looked at her mother and the priest completely confused. After neither offered up any explanations, Angela quietly helped her mother into bed, and Fr. Andrew went off in search of his friend. It was nearly sunrise when he gave up the search and went back to the rectory to get some sleep.

Pastor James had been home briefly before Laura and Fr. Andrew arrived to get the car. He drove to Rochester. He entered from the north side of the city and started driving around looking for whatever hotel may have been the place. He was expecting God to lead him there and give Pastor James the satisfaction of being able to confront this man, this stealer of wives, destroyer of families, and have it out with him. It wasn't until he arrived at a rundown old hotel that he realized his expectations were ridiculous. He drove most of the way back and got himself a room at another motel to try and rest. His failed attempt at sleep lasted until well past sunrise. He got back in his car and finished the drive to Pennington's Corner. He parked the car in front of the church and entered the sanctuary.

It was time to have it out with God.

"Can I talk to you here? Or do I have to go talk to you face to face at the park?" His hot anger at God for the entire scoreboard situation rushed out of him like hurricane force winds on the Florida coast. "Can you meet me here? Can we have this out?

"What are you trying to tell me? That I'm a failure? That I have failed in all areas of my life? As a minister? As a husband? As a father? Is there anything I have succeeded in? Huh? Tell me. Tell me! I need to know! I need help here. I need guidance. Why are you talking to all those people through a blood-stained scoreboard instead of through me? I have been trying my best to serve you for years, to be your hands and feet to your people. I have been available to you. And you had to use that – spot? Why, God, have you rejected me? Why?"

He sat down on the first pew looking for a sign Jesus was in his midst. There was nothing. No sounds, no miraculous creature to come forward and speak, no human with a message from God, no Mrs. Benson with blood on her hands, no voice from the rafters. Nothing. Pastor James felt empty.

He continued, more subdued. "Are you even there, God? Is this all a big joke to you? Has my life been a waste because you are nothing more than a myth we have been believing in for all this time? Is that what this is? If that is true, then someone needs to take my life cause I don't believe I can recover from something like this. I dedicated my life to – no one? Nothing? Something that isn't real?

He began to weep. "How could she do this to me? Of all people to hurt me, why her? I loved her. I depended on her. I trusted her. How could she hurt me like this? How could you hurt me like this? How could you allow me to fall in love with a woman who could do such a terrible thing to me? How?"

He fell into silent sobs for the rest of the morning. He did not hear people come in searching for his guidance, see his despair, and quietly leave. Word spread that Pastor James was in the midst of a crisis of faith. Was there anyone able to help him? Phones rang throughout town. A few people from both congregations dropped to their knees and prayed. Others, many others, jumped on the gossip bandwagon.

Word got to Maggie. She was in the garden with Charlie trying to occupy herself against the pain she was in from her own marriage falling apart when a neighbor approached and told her the news.

"He is in a crisis of faith?" asked a shocked Maggie.

"Yes," said the gossiping neighbor lady.

"But nobody knows why?"

"No. Everybody needs to get down on their knees and pray for the man, but more needs to be done. Has anyone spoken to his wife? Does anyone know what happened?"

Maggie jammed her trowel into the dirt in frustration at all the issues happening throughout the populace and left it sticking up. "All I know is that their daughter, Angela, has been hanging out at her friend Jenny's house since early this morning. No one has seen Laura at all. She did not attend this morning's bible study meeting."

The neighbor inhaled sharply at a thought. "Do you suppose he's been having, you know, that, with Lori Greenfield too?"

Maggie now had the idea that this was very possibly a marital issue similar to her own. But, being in the middle of a marriage crisis herself, she was not about to say anything about it. She didn't want her marital crisis being gossiped about; therefore, she didn't think she should encourage others to gossip about

Pastor James and Laura's issues either. She thought carefully and replied, "Normally, I would suggest we round up the troops and start making a bunch of hot dishes to fill their freezer. But not this time."

"What?"

"This time, we will do nothing."

"Do nothing?"

"Yep. That's what I said. I feel deep in my heart that this is a private matter best left to the two of them alone. We should leave it alone. We should leave them alone. And while we are at it, we should stop gossiping about them. That hurts them and us."

The neighbor lady walked away confused and thinking, *That isn't like Maggie at all. She loves juicy gossip.*

Maggie, however, did not intend to leave it alone. She intended to have a visit with her favorite pastor's wife.

Maggie brushed the dirt off her hands and headed into the house to clean up and whip together a quick rhubarb dessert. Armed with comfort food, a prayer, and, maybe for the first time in her life, an understanding heart, she headed into battle.

No one answered the doorbell for a long time, but Maggie felt the need to keep ringing it. She knew someone was in there. It had to be Laura.

Finally, Laura came to the door wearing a bathrobe and looking like she was still in bed asleep. Her hair was a mess. Her eyes were dark. Her breath was terrible.

"Laura?" Laura's depressed state was so transformative that Maggie felt the need to question whom she was addressing.

"Maggie... What are you doing here? Did we have something on the calendar? Did I miss a hair appointment?"

"No, dear. I just came to check on you." She breezed by Laura not giving her an opportunity to refuse her entry. "Let's sit in the kitchen while I make some coffee."

"Coffee?"

"Yes. You look like you could use some, and I need some myself."

Maggie had been in that home many times for various church functions. She knew exactly where everything was kept like it was her own kitchen. Coffee was percolating in no time. Cups, cream, and sugar were out and ready to go. Rhubarb dessert was sliced and served on pretty little flowered plates that matched the coffee cups perfectly. She got everything on the table, but before she sat down to talk, she made one request. "Laura, honey, do you have a box of tissues on hand?"

"Yes. Why?"

"Because I know for a fact we are both going to need them. Where would they be?"

"On the bathroom countertop."

"I'll be one second." She darted into the bathroom, found the box, and darted back to sit by her friend. The two women both in dire emotional need faced each other. One knew why. The other suspected.

"Why are you here, Maggie?" asked Laura.

"Because the rumor mill is running around town talking about you."

"Oh. Well, that was fast. I suppose you want to know if it's true."

"I don't know what's true for you, but I do know what's true for me. That's what I want to talk to you about."

"I don't understand."

"You will." Maggie proceeded to tell Laura about how she found out Pete has been having multiple affairs, especially with Lori Greenfield. "I'm pretty sure the entire town knew, including you. Well, everyone but stupid me. No one thought to tell me. Figured I couldn't handle it? I guess that makes me angry, but it's also understandable. I didn't want to tell myself either. Besides, ultimately, it's Pete's fault."

Laura tried to listen as a wife of a pastor should. Her mind wasn't working very well, and she was wondering why Maggie was speaking to her once she found out she was having an affair. It occurred to her she might lose all of her friends. *What Christian wants to be friends with someone with an immoral character?* she thought as she listened to Maggie go on and on about herself.

Maggie finished her story by declaring that they have decided to divorce and are avoiding each like the plague. She blew her nose with the fourth tissue since she began her tale. Then she waited for a response from Laura. None came.

Maggie opened up a bit more. "Laura, I didn't come here to get more gossip on you. I came to tell you that you can talk to me. If Pastor James has done something terrible, or has become violent towards you or anything like that, you can tell me. If you're afraid to tell me, send me a sign and I will be your ticket out of here."

Laura was surprised. *She doesn't know it was me. She thinks it was James.* "Maggie, there is something you need to understand." She took a deep breath and braced herself for judgment before continuing down this dreary path. "James is not the one who had the affair." She paused until Maggie was looking at her intently. She wanted to be certain Maggie didn't miss this important fact. She wanted to get it over with. "I did."

Maggie was struck by lightning. In her shock, she forgot that she had already put sugar and cream in her coffee and was now doubling it up. "You?"

"Yes, Maggie. Me. I had the affair."

Maggie continued to add sugar to her cup until Laura reached out and stopped her. "How can that be? I mean, you would never..."

"I thought I would never. I was certain I would never. But I did."

"How? I mean... I'm not looking for details, but if you did, then it can happen to anybody."

"Either that, or I am not nearly as morally good a person as I thought I was."

"But you are. Or, you were." She thought for a moment. "No, you are. Oh, my goodness! I'm so confused now. I was certain it was Pastor James. It's always the men, isn't it?"

"I guess not."

They sat in silence a while staring into their cups of coffee and untouched desserts.

Laura had enough of looking at Maggie's overly sugared cup. She got up and dumped it out into the sink and poured her a fresh cup. When she returned, Maggie thanked her and asked, "What are you going to do?"

"I don't know. I think James wants a divorce. I don't. I want to try and save the marriage."

"He must feel so betrayed."

Laura's face looked crushed at that statement of fact.

"I'm sorry, honey. I only said that because that's how I feel. I don't mean to bring you down more."

"That's just it, isn't it? My staying will bring him down. Who wants a pastor to lead them spiritually when that pastor has a wife who strayed? I've damaged him far more than just my own actions. I've ruined him in the eyes of the congregation."

"That's not necessarily true."

"What do you mean? It's got to be true. He is probably at the church right now thinking that, trying to do what he is expected to do for the people of this community. He's always doing for the community first. He always puts others ahead of me. At the same time, he must be wondering how each and every one of them must be judging him so harshly. Maybe it's best I just pack up and leave. It would be best for him and everyone else."

"Leave? You can't leave. What about Angela? She needs her parents together. What about Christian forgiveness? Turn the other cheek? Love as Jesus loves? You can't leave the marriage and forget all the lessons you yourself taught to all these people."

"Some of those lessons I taught while in the midst of this affair."

"You did? How long did it last?"

"Two years."

"Two years? Oh..."

"Exactly. See? I have to leave. I have to divorce him. For his sake. For the sake of the church."

"What about for your sake? What about what you need? What about what this family needs? You might lose people from this flock, but you might gain others. You might be the right example to set how things like this should be handled." Maggie got very deep in thought for a long moment. "Like for Pete and I."

"What do you mean?"

"Maybe I am being too hard on Pete. Maybe, as a Christian, I need to seek to understand before I judge. Maybe, I need to take a hard look at forgiveness, ask myself if I am capable of forgiveness before I decide to destroy it."

"Are you saying you don't want a divorce from Pete now?"

"No. I'm saying maybe I shouldn't be so quick to decide."

Laura finally found her appetite. She picked up her fork and took a bite of the rhubarb dessert. "Mmmm...this is good. Thank you for bringing it."

Maggie took a bite as well. "You're welcome."

"And, Maggie, thanks for being my best friend in my hour of need."

"You're very welcome."

In the alley behind the house where Maggie and Laura were eating their rhubarb dessert was a group of boys looking for trouble. They never got their fireworks display on the 4th of July.

They never found a frog to experiment with their little firecrackers to see what would happen. They were itching for trouble and were having difficulty finding it. Today, they were determined. They were tired of listening to the adults talk about God and life and living by traditional morals and values. They wanted fun and excitement because that is what eleven and twelve year old boys want out of life, especially their leader, one Michael Greenfield.

They approached the tire swing next to the church's storage shed. This place, normally set aside for good Sunday church behavior, was now the backdrop for their quest for excitement. Michael still had those same little firecrackers in his pockets from a few days ago, and he had gotten his hands on more. He carefully placed them in the tire.

"Who's got the matches?"

"Me." A book of matches was ceremoniously handed over to the fearless leader.

Michael opened the book and removed one match. He closed it and prepared to strike the match. He stopped a moment and wondered if he should do this. He thought about Marty, his new best friend. What would Marty say if he knew what he was doing right now?

"Michael. Michael! What's the matter? Why haven't you lit it? Are you afraid of fire or something?" asked one of his comrades.

"Don't be stupid. Of course I'm not afraid of fire. I'm just thinking, that's all," said Michael.

"About what?"

"I'm thinking about how loud this is going to be."

He struck the match. Nothing. He tried it again. Nothing. The flimsy cardboard match was no good. He threw that one to the ground and pulled out another. That match wouldn't light either. "These are shitty matches. Whose are they?"

"I stole 'em from the car dealership," said the kid that supplied them.

"That explains it. Nothing but shitty stuff at that place." Michael hated that old man Pete. He thought he was mean to his mother.

Michael tried again with a third match. This one lit up. Deep down, Michael was disappointed this was going to work. He no longer wanted to cause trouble, but he had no choice. His friends were counting on him. Peer pressure was doing its damage.

He lit the firecrackers, and they all ran in different directions hiding behind trees, bushes and sheds to catch the action without being hit or seen.

The explosions were really loud to the imaginations of young boys! The thrill! The excitement! When it was over, they all came out laughing believing they had gotten away with some trouble where no adults were able to pin it on them. They felt like they had really accomplished something.

Except for Michael. He decided this was all really dumb and a waste of time. "Hey guys, let's go home, put on our suits, and meet up at the pool."

All the boys agreed, and the danger was over.

Maggie and Laura did hear a little bit of commotion along with a couple of other neighbors and came out to investigate. They saw the boys leave on their bikes.

"Did I see Michael Greenfield?" asked Laura.

"Yep. Probably up to no good. Looks like nothing major, thank God," responded Maggie. "That boy. He is determined to find trouble, isn't he?"

"Well, if you had the childhood he's had all this time, wouldn't you? Wouldn't you cry out for help? For someone to take notice and do something to fix things because you can't do it yourself? Look at what I did. Wasn't that a cry for help?"

"Good point," Maggie contemplated. "I never thought about things in this way before."

13

The Apostle, Officer Helen Schafer

"I should be checking in on Michael Greenfield. See what he's been up to today," said Helen as she searched for her underwear.

Marty reached out and pulled her back on top of him in his bed giving her a long-lasting kiss she would remember the entire day. "Don't you think we should eat first? I, for one, am hungry after all that exercise. I'm thinking of pancakes."

"In the middle of the day? It's well into the afternoon, you know."

"Absolutely. With strawberries from my garden drenched in butter and maple syrup."

She moaned into his chest. "You are making it impossible for me to do my job."

Marty got serious a moment thinking back on his conversation with Michael on the water tower. "Do you spend most of your time looking after Michael?"

"Yep." She climbed back off of him.

"How come?"

"He's a very troubled kid. I don't want trouble to be his lifetime pattern." She tried again to find her underwear in the entangled bed sheets and comforter. She thought she found them. "Aha! There you are! Oh. No. These are yours. Where are mine?" She handed Marty his and resumed the search for her underclothes.

"I don't think they're in the bed. I think I threw them."

"Can you remember which direction?"

"Um…" While lying there in his original position, he half-heartedly re-enacted the moment he removed them from her body trying to remember the trajectory. "Must be that way."

Helen got up and drew an imaginary line in the perceived arc of his toss and followed it to a chest of drawers with a TV on top. Behind the TV was where she found them. "Finally!" She put them on and started hunting for the rest of her uniform. "Pancakes would be delicious, but I have got to get back to work."

"Yeah, I do too. I have to help Lori find a usable car. I promised her I would start looking today."

"You're going to get her a car?"

"Yep. I can do it. I just have to put forth the effort."

"Why?"

"To help her out. Hopefully to help Michael too. You aren't the only one worried about that kid." He got up and started searching for his mechanic uniform.

"How do the two relate?"

"Lori's car is on its last leg. I know. I'm the one who usually works on it. You know, for a 'Pete's Special' discount that I promise will never happen again. Pete would pay me cash for taking care of her car. I guess during the game Sunday she used sex with Pete to get a new car out of him. He did promise, but he didn't give her one. I don't want her having to sell herself like that anymore, so I offered to find a used replacement."

"You do realize what you are saying to me, right? You are directly talking about prostitution."

"Whoa! I admit I have had sex with her a few times."

"Quite a few times. Along with half the men in this town."

"But I never paid her for it."

"What did she get out of you for it?"

"Nothing I want to admit to the town cop now that you are talking prostitution. Except I do need to admit it to my girlfriend now that we are together. What to do? Confession time: I fixed her car for her a couple of times for being with me, and quite a few times for Pete. But, I am not that kind of guy anymore. I will never do it again. Finding her a car is out of friendship only. I swear." Marty paused. "Do you really think of her as a prostitute?"

"A car for sex? Yep."

"Wouldn't that be more of a gift for a friend rather than a direct sale?"

"It could be construed that way."

"You aren't going to arrest her for that, are you?"

"No." Helen had a question. "Now that Lori has retired from that line of work, where are the men in this town going to get their action? Especially Pete, whom I could easily arrest for prostitution."

"Wouldn't he just get it from his wife?"

"Doubt it. That's not the same level of excitement for a guy who buys, or exchanges, from a prostitute on a regular basis, in public."

"You just called Lori a prostitute."

"Sorry. I know she is your friend."

"I'm not comfortable thinking about Lori that way. She is a friend trying to survive. She's had a rough life."

"Don't worry," she said as she kissed her love good-bye. "I'm not going after her."

"No. You're going after her son."

"Kinda, yeah. For his benefit. I promise. See you later?"

"Later."

Helen started her drive around town on this beautiful July

afternoon more relaxed. Not only did she have a wonderful afternoon tryst with her new boyfriend, but the crowds were significantly lessened at the park and throughout town. The novelty of Pennington's Corner's own hometown miracle was dying down except for the ultra-religious who were mostly praying and not doing much of anything else. Things were becoming peaceful again, which meant a certain Michael Greenfield would be around searching for trouble as usual.

Michael already had his trouble for the day with the insignificant firecrackers in the tire swing at Pastor James's house. Helen happily found him and his friends at the swimming pool. She first spotted their bikes along the fence line, and then she saw him fly off the diving board. With Michael preoccupied there, she felt she could concentrate on other things today. She took a deep sigh of relief.

As she drove through the park, she noticed the town council had a clean-up crew slowly working on getting rid of the shrine. They were starting with the dead flowers and staying clear of the scoreboard itself and those who were there to worship.

Main street was populated with a closer to normal amount of people on a summer afternoon with the weather warm but not stifling. All seemed well with the world. She smiled and drove on.

She headed towards the south end of town where Craig's bar was located. It seemed quiet. She realized she was hungry after all and regretted not having eaten pancakes with Marty when she had the chance. If she had known Michael was having fun at the pool, she would have taken him up on his offer. Craig had good burgers and fries. She deserved a plate.

It was cool in the bar. The air conditioning was working, a contraption that had always given Craig's uncle a hard time when he was alive and owned the place, but not Craig. He rarely had a problem with it. Craig hated the bar and everything in it. For some reason, as if the establishment itself understood, it served him well regardless. It paid his bills and kept him busy. It helped the normally shy man have and maintain friendships.

Craig used to work here for his uncle Lloyd. Contrary to Craig, Lloyd loved the place even though he could barely make ends meet. He did not have good business sense. Craig did, and Lloyd put him to work managing the place at an early age in high school.

Craig used the job to earn college money. It paid for all four years of business school. A bar was not the type of business Craig wanted to own. In fact, he didn't want to own a business at all. He wanted to work in downtown Minneapolis or downtown Chicago in the financial district. He wanted to get out of the hick small town atmosphere and live in a nice apartment where every meal came from the restaurant on the first floor of his complex. He wanted a lavish lifestyle. He never had the chance to get that.

Craig barely graduated from college when his uncle Lloyd died from a stroke. Craig inherited the bar. He considered selling it but didn't.

It may have had something to do with Lori Greenfield and the fact that he was in love with her at least since the fourth grade. Other than the occasional time together starting back in high school, Lori acted like she didn't know Craig was alive. He was just another guy. Craig was always hoping for more. His assumptions of Lori were not true. She noticed him.

After years and years of pining for her, even when he was away at college, and watching her go off with man after man time after time, he decided it was never going to happen. He gave up. Yet, he stayed in Pennington's Corner running a bar he hated just to stay in her vicinity.

Officer Helen sat at the bar. "Hey, Craig. Can I get a cheeseburger, fries, and a coke?"

"Here or to go?"

"I think I'll eat it right here."

"Okay. Coming up."

A delicious, greasy, gooey cheeseburger with buns buttered and toasted with extra crispy fries and an ice cold pop to drink was just the fuel Helen needed after her earlier exercise with Marty. Although, she still wished she had taken him up on the offer of pancakes.

"Hey, Craig," Helen inquired. "You know, all these years, I've never really gotten to know Marty until the past couple of days. How well do you know him? What's he like?"

"Oh, boy! Um. Well, that's kind of a difficult question for me to answer. He was pretty much out of high school before I got in. We didn't interact much as kids at all. I did get to know him better a few years ago, but he always seemed so private. Really nice but didn't care for anyone to get too close."

"I've noticed that too." *If anyone is getting close to him now, it's me.* "Did you know he can bake? Like really bake. Like really good in the kitchen, he should own a restaurant, kind of baking."

"I heard a rumor, but I never got the pleasure. How good is he?" Craig gave her a sly look.

"Let me tell you, Craig. As much as I am enjoying this burger, I wish I had accepted his offer of pancakes earlier today." She glanced away and turned red.

"Really? Is that so?" Craig touched his cheeks to indicate to her that she was blushing.

"Oops."

"Hey. I think it's great. You two don't make an obvious couple, but you do make a cute couple."

"Have rumors been flying around about us?"

"Not that I've heard. Maggie Johnson would be the one to ask about that."

"Or Lori."

Craig unconsciously gave a little smile at the mention of Lori's name.

Helen continued, "Craig...should I check if the rumor mill is going on about another couple in town?"

"Maybe..."

"You and..."

"Yes. You would be correct."

"What's going on, if you don't mind my asking. I promise I'm not big on gossip. Just curious."

"We had lunch here yesterday. Her, me and Daisy."

"How did it go?"

"Great!"

"My God! You look downright happy. I don't think I've ever seen you this happy."

"I have been in love with her my whole life. I tried to bury it."

"Does she know how you feel about her?"

"No. I am trying to play it cool, go slow. You know? She's got kids and all."

"Yeah...speaking of Lori's kids. Can I talk to you about one of them? Especially now that you seem to be taking a special interest in them."

"Sure."

"What do you think of Michael?"

"Michael..." Craig got very thoughtful. He took the question seriously.

Craig continued, "I think deep down he's a good kid. He does stuff, but then he always seems genuinely sorry after. Obviously, a cry for attention. Maybe Lori is better able to give him that attention now than she was before? I hope someone can get to him before it's too late."

"Marty is trying. He is planning on taking him deer hunting this fall like his grandfather used to take him when he was young."

"Sounds like the job of a father." At first, Craig chuckled at those words. The chuckle disintegrated as an idea came to him. Who is his father? Helen could see the question enter his head.

She replied to the unspoken question. "That is what Marty is wondering about himself too."

Craig began making some quick calculations. He was good with numbers. His eyes got even bigger.

Helen recognized that same panicked look. "Marty had a similar thought as well."

"How many other possibilities?"

"Well, let's see. There's obviously Pete, and Larry, and about half the male species in this town. I suppose only Lori could know."

"Shit." He thought again. "Well, no. She wasn't this..." he paused trying to find the right word to use, "active at that time of her life. So, that leaves me and Marty. And maybe half the football team. A teacher or two?"

"Are we being serious or joking?"

"I want to say joking, but this isn't funny."

"No, it isn't. It's really about a boy."

"Have people been speculating all these years, and it only just hit me? And Marty?"

"Well, now, Craig, don't take it personally. Condoms were available back then. Didn't any of you use them?"

"We were so young and inexperienced. None of us thought pregnancy was possible."

"Until Lori got pregnant, of course."

"Well, yeah..."

"And no one bothered to ask her who the father was?"

"I guess not. Not even me." Craig looked disappointed – at himself.

"Yep. Saw that same look on Marty too when we discussed the possibility."

"What do we do?"

"One of you gentlemen needs to sit down with her and ask the big question."

"Oh, God."

"God is out there." Helen pointed in the general direction of the park.

"What if it's me?"

"Excellent question. What if it's you? What if it's Marty? What if it's someone else? Then what?"

"Then what?"

"Then what? And I don't mean about your relationship with Lori, although I'm sure as a typical man, that is probably where your brain is heading. No. I mean what about that boy who needs guidance and hasn't had a whole lot of it over the years? Remember that part of this conversation?"

Craig nodded his head.

"What about him, Craig?"

"A father?"

"Yeah."

"What about Daisy?"

"Another excellent question. Is it possible for you to…"

"No. No, it's not. I was never with her during that time."

"Huh. Lucky you, you can at least pinpoint that one of them is not. Marty can't say that. And probably a number of other possibilities in this town. Nonetheless, that girl needs parental guidance too. It's great Lori is finally getting at it, but a little late. It would help tremendously if someone would step up to the plate and help her. Now that you've told me she wasn't that active back when Michael was conceived, maybe it's possible to discover who Michael's biological father is."

"I suppose so."

"Do you think Lori knows who?"

"I have no idea." Craig's mind was now very far away. Probably back to about twelve to thirteen years ago when hearts were young and minds were stupid. "I don't know if she just had casual sex back then or if she was already..."

"Hey! Craig! Wake up!" Helen wanted him back in the present. "I'm not asking about all this just to blow your whistle. I am concerned for Michael."

"Well, a lot of people are concerned for him. Is there some reason why you seem extra concerned?"

"Yes. I can't put my finger on it, but I think his antics are getting a little more dangerous. Another parental figure needs to step in. I don't think Lori can handle it herself. Maybe it doesn't matter who his real father is. Maybe he just needs more adults in his life. Ones he can look up to and respect."

Craig looked Helen in the eye. "I hear what you're saying. I will try and have a talk with Lori about it."

"Good. I think it would be best coming from you given how the two of you seem to be getting so close lately."

Craig remained in that deep thought.

Helen got concerned. "Now, don't tell me I've gone and spooked you! No. We can't have that, Craig. If you care for Lori like you say you do, then you've got to get in there and get involved. That woman comes as a set of three."

"I will. I promise."

"Okay." Helen put down cash for her dinner plus a little tip, and offered another tip. "By the way. See that guy over there in that booth with the girl in the red shirt?"

"Yeah."

"Underage undercover cop. Don't serve him. She is of age, but he is not. I don't want to have to arrest you. It wouldn't be good for Michael to see one of his potential father figures arrested for something dumb."

Craig cracked a smile. "Thanks for the multiple tips."

"No problem." Officer Helen headed back out to do her job.

Shortly after she left, Jake entered. He walked right up to Craig at the bar. "Hey, Craig. Is Marty in here? Have you seen him?"

"He seems to be a popular guy lately. Nope. He hasn't been in yet today. Why?"

Jake appeared anxious. "I'll go ahead and tell you. Maybe you'll let me have some anyway. I wanted to ask Marty to buy me some alcohol. I gotta have a drink."

"You do know he is dating Officer Schafer, right? He doesn't do that kind of stuff anymore. He's trying to live within the law now."

"Could you...?"

"Absolutely not."

"Come on, man! Just a beer?"

"No."

"Why not?"

Craig looked over at the young couple in the booth. "I don't want to lose my license."

Jake used his hand to push his hair back and then slammed it on the bar.

"What's the problem, Jake? Maybe I can help you?"

"I don't know. It's that shit happening over there at the softball field. It's getting to me."

"Getting to you?"

"Yeah."

"What do you mean?"

"I don't know. I need it to go away. I feel like that face is staring at me."

"I thought you were one of the ones who couldn't see the face."

"Did you see it?"

"I haven't looked."

"You haven't looked? You gotta go look. It's something."

"So, you did see the face?"

"No, I didn't."

Craig was confused.

Jake tried to explain. "I couldn't see the face, but I could feel it's eyes. They were staring into my soul. Now, I can't close my eyes without seeing them."

"You know that doesn't make any sense, right? You couldn't see them, but you could feel them?"

"Yeah…"

"I mean, come on. You can't see it, but it can see into your soul? How does that work, Jake?"

"It can see what I've all done."

"What have you done, Jake?" Jake didn't respond. He looked remarkably guilty about something. "Jake, what did you do?"

"I haven't done it yet."

"Done what?"

Jake leaned in to whisper. "Sex."

Craig looked a bit surprised. "I thought you were the Don Juan of the high school all senior year?"

"Everybody thought that. I wanted everybody to think that."

"So, what happened?"

"I fell in love."

"With who?"

"Pastor James's daughter, Angela."

"Isn't she a little young for you?"

"Yeah."

"Okay. You haven't had sex with her."

"Nope."

"Cause she is too young?"

"Yep."

Craig chuckled. "Jake, you have no idea. You are probably the last decent guy in this entire town."

Jake looked confused.

Craig continued, "Does she even know how you feel?"

"Yeah."

"I'm missing something here, Jake."

"She has been sneaking out to meet me at night. She's been lying to her folks telling them she's been at Jenny's when she's been with me."

"And you haven't…"

"It's been really hard…that didn't come out right."

Craig laughed, but shut his laughter off as quickly as he could. He didn't want to embarrass the poor kid. "Well, I understand. I do. It's pretty remarkable that you have held off this long. So, why do you have this guilt about sex if you haven't had it?"

"Cause we keep getting closer and closer to it. I was fine until that happened." He pointed in the general direction of the scoreboard and put his head in his hands on the bar.

"Oh. I'm guessing it's getting more difficult. You don't think you can keep from sinning. Is that it?"

"Yep."

Craig watched the young couple with the underage undercover cop quietly leave the bar. He took the opportunity to take pity on Jake and handed him a half-filled mug of light beer.

"Thanks, man."

"That's all you're getting."

"How about some words of advice?"

"I don't have the right to give you any. I was far from being a virgin by the time I was your age. I can only say this. Be damned careful. She isn't just a teenager – how old is she by the way?"

"Sixteen."

"Sixteen. Geez. Can I remember sixteen?" He got back on the subject. "She is also the pastor's daughter. Don't fuck yourself over for a screw job."

"That's good advice."

"Yes, it is. Take it."

Jake downed his half a beer and left with resolve he would keep his hands to himself.

14

Charm is Deceitful, and Beauty is Vain

Wednesday, July 7th, 1982 started off with rumbles of thunder in the clouds and a little wind that blew around the offerings at the shrine. City crews scattered to pick up as much as they could because the weather forecast was predicting more windy adventures to come including the possibility of tornadoes later in the evening. Even though the clouds dissipated by noon, the growing humidity in the afternoon heat was a promise more thunder was on the way.

Business was getting back to normal. There were fewer and fewer people at the scoreboard praying. Oddly, it seemed no one was paying any more attention to the red swirl except for Mrs. Benson. She cleaned the scoreboard multiple times a day, careful not to affect the image of Jesus. To her, this was an altar and should be treated with deep reverence. She felt the need to prevent the ants from trying to climb up the scoreboard and invade the face of Jesus. A can of ant spray was her weapon of choice.

Life for Fr. Andrew was also getting back to normal. However, his continued requests for Pastor James and Laura to return to continue to work things out in their marriage were being ignored by the husband but welcomed by the wife.

Pastor James moved a few personal items to the church office after he ordered Laura to move out. She refused to go.

Larry was already making calls to hire another radio DJ from stations in Mankato.

Lori was practicing her homemaking skills on her children. Her cooking wasn't pretty, but the kids seemed happier. She also found herself busier at the salon. She couldn't fathom why. Gossip was that some of the wives of guilty husbands were looking for a showdown with the town prostitute, and others wanted to be there to watch. None of them had the courage to start the show. She was the best hairdresser around. Her talent was real. She was able to do things with perms no one else could do. Bangs were higher, curls were tighter, and mullets even for ladies were beginning to gain ground, and she knew how to do them and keep them feminine. No one wanted her to quit.

Marty and Helen were falling deeper and deeper into love. The strawberry patch was losing its berries fast.

Craig went from chasing after Lori to falling away from her after his conversation with Helen. She didn't mean to, but she spooked him. He wasn't ready to be a father type figure.

Maggie and Pete were in limbo. They woke up in separate bedrooms. They ate breakfast together at the kitchen table in silence. She went about her day; he went about his.

The atmosphere in the salon was charged. The women instinctively knew something big was going to happen, that the showdown between Maggie and Lori was on. Women who didn't have appointments came in with wide ranging excuses for being there. It was a zoo of women strutting around on eggshells waiting for the bomb to drop. There was hardly enough room for the four hairdressers to work.

Maggie was on fire. She was tired of the tension in her house. And she knew who was to blame. She looked over at Lori humming as she cut, colored, rolled, and curled other women's hair. She looked so happy, Maggie couldn't stand it. At the same time, Maggie, like many of the other women, had pity for her. After all, she had two children to raise on her own. Maggie knew what her salary was because she paid it. Nevertheless, the damage done to her marriage and to the entire town could not be ignored. *Should*

I fire Lori? Should I divorce Pete and leave town? She couldn't take it anymore.

In the middle of trimming bangs, her pain got so intense that Maggie let out a scream that could only be described as ferocious. Everyone jumped. The lady in the chair jumped the most. She grabbed a mirror to check to see if she still had bangs, and sighed in relief that they were fine. Then she scrambled out of the chair and out the door before Maggie could have another chance at cutting them.

Everyone else stayed frozen. This was it. The gauntlet was thrown. No one dared move. Did that inhumane sound really come from Maggie Johnson? Her cheeks were flushed, her eyes were bulging, and a vein was violently pumping in her neck. It looked like it was going to burst open and spew blood everywhere. Everyone stared in fear. Then everyone followed Maggie's terrifying gaze to its target: Lori.

Lori looked very afraid. She knew it was coming. She was hoping it could be avoided. She hoped somehow Maggie wouldn't do it.

"If you want to fire me," was all Lori could say. "I don't blame you." She turned to face Maggie, put down her scissors, and bowed her head waiting for the day of atonement to fall upon her. "Go ahead. Let me have it."

"You! You! How could you!" Women began to scatter getting out of the way of the firing line while still staying to watch the fireworks display denied them on the 4th of July. This was going to be more explosive anyway.

"Preach it to me," replied Lori, still holding her head down. "I deserve it."

"Deserve it? You deserve a beating!"

"I do."

"You deserve to be run out of this town!"

"Maybe I should go. Maybe that would be best."

"Stop agreeing with everything I say!"

"Sorry..."

"No, you should not go. You should stay. You should be forced to stay. You know why? So every day of your life you get to see the faces of the people you've hurt!"

Lori silently looked around the room at the faces of the women. Some were nodding in agreement. Some looked at her with pity.

Maggie continued her attack. "As far as I can tell, you have been with the husband of every wife in this room."

A small sound of shock came from a mousy little voice in the corner. "Mine too?"

"Yep," came another voice.

"I didn't know for sure," replied the mousy little voice followed by a little cry.

Lori looked over at where the mousy little voice came from and silently mouthed the words, "I'm sorry."

Maggie vented on. "I hate you! I hate you! I hate you!"

Lori flinched but did not move from her spot.

"You have destroyed my marriage of over twenty years! How could you?"

Lori opened her mouth to respond but thought better of it.

"You shouldn't be allowed to get away with it!"

Now, Lori spoke. "I agree with you. I shouldn't be allowed to get away with it."

Maggie looked shocked at that response.

"I am working with Fr. Andrew..."

"Fr. Andrew?" from another voice along the wall.

"Oh! No, I've never been with Fr. Andrew. He isn't that kind of person. But I've been working with him to help me figure out how to make it up to all of you – for all the harm I have done."

"Why?" asked Maggie. "Why did you find it necessary to sleep with all the men in town?"

"Not all the men. Just the ones that could help me."

A strange quiet came over the room.

"I'm not like you, Maggie. I'm not capable of running my own business like this." Lori indicated the salon. "I wish I could, but I'm not good with numbers and money and taxes and all that. So, I got men to help me with things I didn't think I could do myself. Although, that's one of the things Fr. Andrew is helping me to understand. That I can do more than I thought I could." She smiled as she said the next sentence. "I'm even learning to cook for my kids, and they like it!" She smiled at the thought of her kids. Looking around the room again and feeling the hostility, she forced the smile to disappear. She went back to contrite.

When she paused to take a breath, someone asked a question. "What do you mean when you say you got men to do things for you? I thought they paid you for sex."

Lori was extremely candid. "Some did pay me. In cash. Others in trade. Like John did my taxes for me year after year. I was only with him during tax season. Bud took care of my leaking roof once, and painted my house another year. I'm not sure I've been with him enough yet to cover those bills."

"Oh, yes, you have!" said Bud's wife. "I'll make sure of that."

"Okay, thank you. I would appreciate that. He's a little rough."

Another woman asked, "I heard Pastor James and his wife are maybe splitting up from an affair. Were you with him too?"

"Pastor James? Oh, no. I was never with him. If he was having an affair, it wasn't with me."

"What did my husband do for you?" asked one of the other hairstylists.

"Um. He was a cash man. Oh! Except for when he fixed my phone. That was in trade. Your husband was interesting. Every time he would, you know, he would call out your name. I always thought that was kind of sweet."

"Sweet?"

Another wife asked, "What about my husband?"

"Let me think. You're married to Hank, right? One time. He fixed my lawn mower."

"And mine?"

It was as if Lori was going through a file cabinet in her head. "Raymond. Yeah. He was just out for extra fun. Things he didn't think you would be okay doing with him. Paid with cash. That's all."

Maggie spoke up again. "And my husband?"

"Well, last time we were together, on Sunday during the game, between the sheds across the street, he promised me a new car for a blow job. But he never got it for me."

Maggie looked shocked. "A new car?"

Lori tried to soothe her. "But don't worry about it! Marty is working on finding me another car anyway, so I won't have to give my body away anymore. Marty is helping me too."

"I thought Marty was one of your customers?"

"Marty wasn't a customer. He's just a friend. And sometimes we had sex? Mostly just for fun. A couple of times to fix my old car. But now, he's with Officer Schafer, so we won't be getting together like that anymore."

Lori decided to offer some comfort to the ladies. "I know it's bad, what I did. Really, really, bad. But I promise you all, none of the men fell in love with me. Or, at least, I didn't fall in love with any of them. I wasn't looking for love, they were all just looking for sex. That's all it was. Sex for them and a way of getting by for me. They married you. Nobody ever offered to marry me."

That got all the ladies thinking. Some softened up to her. Some still hated her. They all attempted to put themselves into her shoes, and none of them liked how they fit.

A strangely calm Maggie posed another question. "Lori, how did this all start?"

"Oh. Gosh. That's a long time ago. I was rather active with friends in high school." She motioned to one of the ladies in the room. "Well, you know. You were there too." That lady blushed. Lori went on, "I ended up pregnant. If you remember my mom, she wasn't exactly thrilled at becoming a grandmother. So, I needed to find a place to live and take care of my baby. Larry offered to help. Somehow, it ended up becoming an exchange of money, housing, and food for what he called favors or services."

"Didn't your mom used to do this kind of thing too to get by?" asked one of the women.

"Um, yeah," Lori teared up a little and her voice quivered. "I have been doing pretty much what she did. I didn't know another way. I thought being a hairdresser would be enough. But it wasn't. I couldn't think of a better way to do things."

A heavy, invisible weight filled the room.

Maggie got very thoughtful. "Lori, I'm going to make sure you get your car from Pete."

"You are?"

"Yes. Right before I run him out of town."

"Are you going to run me out of town too?"

"No." Maggie was not blind to the life Lori and her children had been leading. "But you aren't going to do this anymore."

"I promise."

Maggie intended to keep her word. It never occurred to her before that maybe the fault for Lori's sexual exploits belonged more to the men than to Lori, especially Larry. Obviously, Pete played a huge role in that woman's life being rough. He owed her. He owed both women.

Maggie stormed out of the salon.

"Okay," asked Lori with a hot curling iron in her hand. "Who's next?"

Maggie went storming into the car dealership. She didn't care that there were customers in the place. She wanted this done immediately.

"Pete!" The anger in her voice was evident. It reverberated throughout the building.

"Maggie! What are you doing here? Can't you see I am with a customer?"

"Yes. I see. I see a lot of things these days."

"Huh?"

Maggie turned to the customers. "Hi. Do you think you could go talk to another salesperson? Like Jim over there?" Jim was with another customer, but gave a weak wave at the invitation to have those customers join him given the obvious circumstances. "Or," Maggie continued, "You could come back another day?" They took option two and left in a hurry.

"Maggie!" Pete was steaming mad. "What the hell are you doing!"

"I am here to right a wrong you have done!"

"What are you talking about?"

"You promised Lori Greenfield a car for services rendered."

"I did no such thing."

"Oh, yes, you did. She told me. Gave me all the details." She pointed in the direction of the park. "Right over there, between the sheds behind the softball field on Sunday. You promised her a car for a blow job, which she delivered. Apparently with some considerable skill." Maggie couldn't help herself. She enjoyed watching Pete squirm for once. "Tell me. Was it good? Did you enjoy denigrating a poor, single mother almost half your age? Did that make you feel like a man? Did it once occur to you the damage you were doing to her children?"

Pete turned white and stammered. "I, I, I didn't..."

"Of course you didn't! You couldn't think of anyone but yourself!"

"No! I didn't do those things!"

"You did! And you are going to deliver her that car you promised!"

"Are you crazy? You want me to give the town whore a car?"

"A brand new car!"

"What?"

"You heard me!"

"But she's nothing but a wh..."

Maggie interrupted him. "Nothing but what you and Larry and a bunch of other men in this town made her out to be! You created the town whore! You will pay her as you promised!"

"I will do no such thing!"

"You will! Or I am divorcing you and taking you for everything you've got!" Maggie started to storm out.

Pete yelled out, "I will not! I will not! Maggie! Come back here!" He followed her out as she went shopping amongst the rows of cars.

Maggie looking over the vehicles. It had to be a vehicle that would be reliable and useful for a woman with two children. And there it was, a brand new 1982 Cutlass Ciera in a nice pretty shade of red. It was perfect! She pointed to it and said, "This one."

"Oh, no. I'm not doing this."

"Jim!"

Jim abandoned his customers at Maggie's call and came running out as a dutiful sergeant should under her command. "Yes?"

"Get this car ready for sale. Pete will pay for it out of his own pocket."

Jim looked at Pete who didn't want a scene out there for all the town to see. He nodded at Jim to go ahead and do it.

Maggie observed that Pete was falling in line. "There. That's enough for revenge. I won't divorce you now. It won't be worth it. All the expense. All the headache. And for what? No. I'll keep you. See you at home, dear! I am making your favorite. Meatloaf." Pete hated her meatloaf.

Pete watched his wife get in her car and drive away. As she drove off, he noticed storm clouds gathering west of town. A storm was coming. Pete thought it couldn't be worse than the storm that was his wife.

Jake and Angela, who told her parents she would be at Jenny's house, were in Jake's car driving past the dealership on their way to park behind the school bus garage as teenagers often did. It was quiet and devoid of prying eyes.

Angela jumped on Jake before he got the car in park and started kissing him. Normally, Jake would join in whole-heartedly. But, he was feeling uneasy about all the happenings in town.

"Angela," he attempted to gently pry her off. "Can we talk?"

"Talk?" she giggled in disbelief. "Since when do you want to talk?"

"Since now. Since the past few days."

"Since Jesus came to town?"

"Yes."

She scoffed. "Why? What is there to talk about? The old people have all gone crazy. Over what? Have you seen it?"

"I have."

She was surprised. "I didn't know it affected you too. Could you see the face?"

"Not really. You?"

"I didn't look. But, I don't understand. If you couldn't see the face, then how are you affected by it?"

"I don't know. I just know I was."

"Affected…"

"Yes."

"So, now you're a what – a goody two-shoes? A good boy all of a sudden?"

"I don't know. Maybe…" He squirmed in the driver's seat.

"You know what? If you don't want to be with me, then just take me home. I don't want to be with you either."

"Angela."

"No. I mean it. You don't want me, take me home."

"No. It's okay. I'm fine."

He reached out to kiss her with as much passion as he could muster. It took a while, but the atmosphere did start to heat up both inside and outside of the car.

15

Our Father

Lori finished up at the salon in much better spirits than the first half of the day. A number of the women from the community who used to only be nice to her when they needed their hair done were now being quite kind; although, much of that kindness seemed tainted with pity. Pity was still better than hostility.

After work, she drove home in an old jalopy Marty found for her to check on the kids. As usual, Michael was nowhere to be found, and Daisy was busy helping herself to food in the kitchen.

"Hello, baby!" she said, giving her daughter a hug. Hugs were a new activity Lori discovered she enjoyed, and Daisy reveled in them.

"Hi, Mom!"

"Daisy, have you seen Uncle Craig today?"

"Nope."

"Hm. I thought for sure he would check in on you."

"He sent someone from the bar. The waitress. The one with the ponytail."

"Oh. That's strange." She switched her focus to be more on Daisy. "How about we have dinner? What would you like? Hopefully something a little healthier than that popsicle."

Mother and Daughter made a simple meal of hamburger steaks, mashed potatoes, and green beans. The beans and potatoes Michael brought home from Marty's garden the day before when the two guys were spending time together. Lori recognized Michael was happier when he spent time with Marty. He was a good influence on her son. The beans were delicious. They'd only had them out of the can before, never straight from the garden.

After their early dinner, Lori decided to drive over to the bar and say hello to Craig. "Daisy, Mommy is going to go out for a little while. Okay? I'll be back by 9 p.m. to tuck you into bed. Okay?"

"Okay, Mom!" She was glued to the TV anyway.

As soon as Lori left, a tornado watch was declared for the area on the television. Daisy turned to see if her mother was still there to see it. She was not. Daisy thought about it for a while. She decided she should walk to the bar to warn her mom the weather was about to turn bad. She slipped on her shoes and left the house.

Lori could see the storm clouds brewing. The clouds were an ominous grey, almost an evil, sickening shade of green. She overheard someone who was leaving the bar in a hurry say to his friend, "Green often means hail or tornadoes. We'd better get back." Thunder rumbled in the distance.

Lori darted into the bar concerned the rain was about to start. She spotted Craig immediately where he normally was, behind the bar serving drinks.

"Hi, Craig!"

"Hey," he responded with a frown.

"Something the matter?"

"No. Nothing. Why would something be the matter?"

"I don't know. You don't seem yourself."

"Of course I'm myself. Who else would I be?"

"I don't know. Elmer Fudd?"

Lori chuckled. Craig did not.

Trying to find his funny bone she added, "Does that make me

Bugs Bunny? Hey! What's up, Doc?"

No response.

"Wow. You are a tough nut to crack. What gives?"

"I told you. Nothing."

"Fine. You don't want to talk? We don't have to talk. I've done enough talking today as it is. I'm going home."

"Hey! Wait! What's that supposed to mean?"

"What's what supposed to mean?"

"That you've done enough talking today."

"None of your business." Lori headed for the door determined to leave.

One of the ladies at the bar answered Craig his question for him. "Craig. She got grilled by a bunch of women at the salon today."

"What happened?"

"A bunch of ladies at the salon, wives, practically pounced on her asking a bunch of questions about who she's all had sex with, and why, and what did she get out it... You know. She got jumped."

Craig suddenly felt bad for her. He almost tried to leap over the bar to stop Lori from leaving. Too late. She was already out the door, and the bar was too high to jump over it anyway. He had to go around.

He ran out the door and caught her getting into the car. The tears in her eyes broke his heart.

"I'm sorry!" he said. "That was not nice of me. Please come back in." She hesitated. "Please? I'll be nice. I promise."

"All right. Since you promised." She locked up her old car and re-entered the bar with him.

He sat her down on the stool nearest to him as he worked so they could talk between mixing drinks. The first drink he mixed was her favorite stand-by, a rum and coke. She didn't care much for fancy drinks. Her other favorite was a simple ice-cold beer. He liked that about her. It made her seem uncomplicated.

But she was complicated. She had a traumatic history and two children she was raising on her own. He was spooked and needed to admit that to her, especially now that he was suspicious Michael might be his own son.

"So, where are the kids?"

"Daisy is at home alone, so I can't stay long. I promised to tuck her into bed later."

"And Michael?"

"Out and about as usual. I have no idea. Saw some storm clouds. I hope he finds his way into a shelter somewhere before that hits."

"Hey, Craig! How about some beer over here!"

"Coming!" He handled that customer and two others before returning to Lori. "Do you know where he goes or what he does when he's out like this?"

"He mostly rides his bike, climbs the water tower, goes looking for friends to hang out with. I don't really know, I guess. I know he's been spending time with Marty lately."

"Um, is, is…"

"Is what?"

He was trying to be careful. "Is Marty – his dad?"

Lori looked surprised at the question. She giggled a little. "No. Of course not."

"Are you sure?"

"Yes. I'm sure."

"How do you know?" *Am I getting too personal? Am I venturing into territory I don't belong? If we are going to get serious, don't I have a right to know who are the fathers of the kids?*

He was beginning to regret asking when she finished her sip and responded. "Of course I know, cause it's you. You're his father. Didn't you know that?"

Shock gripped Craig. That was his deepest fear. Even though he had played the possibility of it being true in his head a million times since Helen brought it up, the truth still hit him hard. "I, I did not know."

"Don't you remember that night?"

In all honesty, Craig wanted to ask, "Which night?" but was afraid that would be insulting. Instead, he said, "Remind me."

"Senior year Halloween dance. Don't you remember? You wore a gorilla mask. You were trying to scare all the girls. A lot of people didn't know it was you. I knew it was you."

"You were dressed as Little Red Riding Hood or something."

"Well, I was trying. I was really just wearing my mom's red coat. Someone said I looked like Little Red Riding Hood, so I went with it."

Memories were flooding back. Craig smiled. "We ended up in the upstairs wrestling room."

"In the dark."

"Just enough light."

"The mats were comfortable enough."

"I didn't have a condom."

"Neither did I."

"Was that your first time?"

"No. My first was with Marty. I don't think he knows that."

"It was my first."

She giggled. "I did know that."

They got quiet. Craig got called over by customers feeling neglected. When he returned, he asked, "If you were with Marty before, then how do you know I'm..."

"Trust me. I know. Look," she was getting annoyed with Craig, but she had had a rough day at the salon and said "if you want to get tested, I suppose we can do that."

"No, no, no. I believe you. I just can't believe I have a son. Had a son all this time and didn't know."

"I can't believe you didn't know. Over the years I figured you would have put it together. I just thought you didn't want to be involved, so I left you out of stuff. I mean, I never did tell you."

"Maybe that's true. Maybe I didn't want to be involved. But that's not right. That's not fair for you. I should have taken care of my responsibilities all these years."

"Don't you get it? That's what I didn't want. If you were going to be in Michael's life, in my life, I wanted you there because you wanted to be there, not out of some obligation. That wouldn't have been right. You weren't ready for that kind of responsibility."

"And you were?"

She looked at him hurt. At first, she was insulted at the insinuation that she failed as a mother. But she stopped herself from verbalizing it because she was failing as a mother and knew it.

"I see what you are saying," he continued, "and I appreciate it. But I had a responsibility to him. I should have been involved whether I liked it or not. I need to be now. And what about Daisy?"

"What about Daisy?"

"Am I her father too?"

"How could that be? We weren't together at all during that time."

"Craig!" yelled Coach Meir from the pool table. "Come on, man! Are you open for business or what?"

"Coming!" He went to serve up more drinks. He returned again.

"Who is her father?"

"That doesn't really matter."

"It does to me. That is another man who needs to take responsibility."

"Now you're the responsibility police?"

"No. That's not what I'm saying."

"So, what are you saying?"

"I'm saying that you handling everything on your own - those days are over. You can now get the real help you've been needing all this time."

"Craig!" came a voice from a customer across the bar.

Lori was getting angry. Anger was not an emotion often held in her body. "I've done pretty well for myself and my kids. I did everything I needed to do. How many other parents in this town can say that they have been willing to sacrifice themselves for their children? Have been willing to sell their bodies? None!"

"I'm sorry if I'm prying where I don't belong."

"You are!"

"Craig!" came the same voice. "Drinks!!"

Craig turned around again to serve up more drinks to at least three more customers. He was losing count. When he turned around, Lori was gone, and money for her drink was sitting on the bar. He never charged her before. Never. He screwed up. *I went too far. I judged her.* He could have caught up with her. He didn't try.

She sat in her car wiping away the tears. Lori did not have much of a problem with people in town judging her for what she had done. After all, the men she was with were husbands and fathers. They were men who belonged to other women. She could take the judgments of those women because she earned them.

Craig judging her was another matter. Craig treating her like a prostitute hurt so much more because she loved him. She always had and would forever. Arrows from him passed right into her heart.

For years, she thought Craig, with all his math skills, had figured out he was Michael's father, and she thought she was sparing them both the turmoil of such a relationship. She spared Craig from the responsibility of fatherhood before he was ready, and she spared Michael from the rejection felt when a parent didn't want to be around like her mother didn't want Lori around. She thought she was being kind to them both. At the same time she felt she deserved the heartache that came with it. Raising Michael alone, and Daisy too, was her self-imposed punishment for bad decisions. Somehow, deep down, she thought that was being noble. And Craig wasn't appreciating that she was putting herself through that for him. She felt overlooked, taken advantage of, treated like a second-class citizen by the one person in all the world she loved. Because she loved him, Craig was the one and only person in the world who could emotionally cut her so deep with so little effort.

Craig saw she wasn't being noble. Craig saw her for what she was – an abused woman in pain. Problem was, he recognized himself as her worst abuser.

The thunder was getting louder, lightning was beginning to shoot across the sky. Lori started her car and headed for home. She just missed seeing Daisy rounding the corner of the building. Daisy saw her mother drive away and attempted to run after her.

As she passed by the park, Lori nearly ran into Mrs. Carol Benson crossing the street carrying a large tarp, a hammer, and nails. Lori hit the breaks in time. Mrs. Benson looked intense. Her eyes were bloodshot, and her hair was unusually wild. She peered into the windshield trying to see the driver. She pounded on the hood of the car and yelled, "Come help me!" She kept walking.

Lori pulled her car over on the wrong side of the road, closer to the shrine, and followed Mrs. Benson. "What are we doing?"

"There's a storm coming soon. A big one. We have to protect Jesus!"

"I've never been much of a religious person before now, but does Jesus need our protection? Isn't He big enough to protect Himself?"

Mrs. Benson stopped in her tracks a moment. At some level those words made sense. Nonetheless, Mrs. Benson had to do what needed to be done, and this needed to be done. "Don't be sacrilegious. Come help me!" she scolded. Lori silently complied.

When they arrived, they found almost all of the offerings had been picked up by the city workers. The only few things left were new things from recent visitors to the shrine. Mrs. Benson didn't care she was stomping over them. She only cared about getting the face of Jesus safely covered.

She set down the hammer and nails and started covering up the corner of the scoreboard with the tarp. "Help me!" she repeated to Lori who stood there not knowing what to do.

Lori examined the situation. Then she picked up the hammer and nails and nailed the tarp to the scoreboard. Mrs. Benson was satisfied with the results. "That's right. Put one there. And one there."

When they were finished, the wind started to pick up, and the evening felt heavy. Something evil was enveloping the town.

"You'd better get home," ordered Mrs. Benson. "This storm is going to be bad. I can feel it in my bones. I need to get back and pray."

Lori was taken aback. She started to cry.

"What's wrong with you?" asked Mrs. Benson.

"You told me to go home before the storm hits. That's the nicest thing you have ever said to me."

"Well, you better get going. It wouldn't be good if it was the last thing I ever said to you."

Larry was all over the radio station giving updates on the tornado warning that was being posted for the entire county. He hoped everyone was listening. Some were.

No one in the bar was paying attention.

Helen was at Marty's again saying goodbye. It was her job to be out patrolling during a storm like this. Marty was not happy about it, but he promised to be a good boyfriend and stay out of trouble.

Fr. Andrew was just finishing up a late dinner, heard Larry's report, and set about praying for the safety of Pennington's Corner.

Pastor James sensed something was wrong in the air and decided to go home. He found Laura listening to the radio and grabbed a flashlight to head down to the basement for shelter.

Mrs. Benson made it to her basement, rosary in hand, fervently praying less for the town and more for the scoreboard.

Lori made it back home to discover the TV was on, lights were on all over the house. "Daisy? Michael!" Neither of her children were there.

16

Who Art In Heaven

Lori searched her home. "Daisy? Daisy, please, baby! Answer me! Michael! Where are you?"

No response. The thunder outside was growing louder and louder. The thunder inside her heart was pounding harder and harder. She reached for her phone. Only a couple of rings before he answered.

"Marty? Is Michael with you?"

"No. I haven't seen him since mid-afternoon. He was headed out to the train trestle with some friends. But that was hours ago. Why?"

"I suppose Daisy isn't with you either?"

"No. What's wrong, Lori?"

Lori started to shake. "The kids aren't here. I went to the bar to talk to Craig. I left Daisy here. I told her to stay here, that I wouldn't be gone long. But she's not here. And I haven't seen Michael since this morning. And this storm is coming in..."

"I'm calling Helen. You stay there in case they come back."

Marty immediately called the dispatcher who connected him to Helen.

"Hey, Marty. What's the emergency?"

"Lori called. She doesn't know where the kids are."

"Shit! The one day I don't keep track of him, he goes AWOL,

and of course there's a tornado warning. Okay. I'll start looking around his regular haunts. Have Lori call other people too and tell her to stay home."

"On it."

Marty called Lori back to tell her to call other people.

First on her list was Craig. He took a while to answer his phone at the bar. He was too upset with himself to care who was on the other end. "Hello?"

"Craig? Are either of my kids there?"

"Lori? No. Of course not. What's wrong?"

"They aren't here. I can't find them."

"Have you called Helen?"

"Marty did. She's out looking."

"Okay. I'll announce something here at the bar, and I'll get out and look too."

"Okay. Thank you, Craig."

Craig stood on his bar and announced, "Hey, everybody! We have a situation. Lori Greenfield's children, Michael age 12 and Daisy age 6, are both missing, and if you haven't been listening to the thunder, a major storm is about to hit. Anyone willing to help search, please do so. I am going out to look, so the bar is now closed. If you aren't going to help, please go home."

In the meantime, Helen requested the dispatcher phone Larry and get him to announce the two missing children.

Larry got right on it. "Hello, Pennington's Corner residents. We have an emergency announcement. We have two missing children and a tornado warning in place. Repeat: we have two missing children and a tornado warning in place. The children are Michael Greenfield age 12 and Daisy Greenfield age 6. Please check the area around your property immediately. This is a dangerous storm coming in. Do it quickly and thoroughly, and then get into a shelter. Again, Michael Greenfield age 12 and Daisy Greenfield age 6. Authorities have no idea if the children are together or alone. Please quickly and thoroughly search the area around your home or property. We have a tornado warning in place. Let's keep everybody safe, especially these two children. I will provide further updates as they become available."

Maggie and Pete heard the radio announcement while in their basement arguing about Lori's new car. Their argument stopped short the moment they both heard two children were missing.

"Let's go," ordered Maggie. She started up the stairs, Charlie at her heels.

"Oh, no!" said Pete. "You are staying here. I'm going to go search."

"Two sets of eyes are better than one."

"Normally, yes. But I don't need the distraction of keeping an eye on your safety while I search for those kids. You stay here!"

"Since when do you care about my safety?"

"Since now. Keep the radio on. Stay safe. I'll be back as soon as I can."

"You stay safe!"

"Since when do you care about my safety?"

"Since now."

Pete set off in search. Maggie sat in the basement and prayed.

Pastor James and Laura were at opposite ends of their basement not speaking to each other. Laura kept looking over at her husband trying to find the words to apologize for the deep hurt she caused him, trying to find a way to explain how she still loved him even though she broke his heart. Any little sound she made was met with a look of pure hatred. She was getting nowhere.

When the announcement came through their radio, they both looked at each other in panic. They thought they knew where their daughter was. They believed she was at Jenny's house. She was planning on spending the night. Even though they preferred her being with them during a storm, at least they knew she was sheltered. Except they didn't know she was in a car with Jake Koenig behind the school's bus garage. They both immediately felt for Lori.

Pastor James stood up and started heading for the staircase.

"Here. Take this flashlight. It's much better than the one you have." Laura approached him to make the exchange. Their hands barely touched. "Please be careful," she continued. She looked back up into his eyes. They were meeting hers with some softening. He shook his head to remind himself that he hated her.

"I'll start around the house, and then I'll check the church."

Mrs. Benson heard the announcement while praying her rosary. She stopped in the middle of a Hail Mary prayer in the second decade, and a thought flashed across her mind. She put down the rosary and put on her raincoat. She walked out the door and went straight towards the scoreboard. There, she found Daisy hiding behind a loose corner of the tarp she and Lori had nailed onto the scoreboard earlier. Daisy could barely hold onto it as the wind was trying to whip it around. She was trying to use it as a shelter from the storm.

"What are you doing here child?" yelled Mrs. Benson through the howling wind.

"I'm looking for my mommy!"

"She isn't here. You come with me. I live just over there. Come along."

Daisy took Mrs. Benson's hand, and they made their way across the street to her home. The wind was getting more powerful by the moment. It tried to blow them both down Main Street as they crossed. Mrs. Benson called on the Lord to give her strength to get the girl safely across. She did. She locked up the kitchen door behind them and decided there wasn't time to call anyone that she had found the girl. Instead, they headed straight for the basement as a huge tree branch crashed in her front yard.

Fr. Andrew did not hear the radio report at all, but he heard the storm approaching. He set about making sure things were locked up. The church was typically left unlocked during much of the day for anyone who needed time with God. He locked this door and that door, made sure all the windows were closed, and checked all candles were safely snuffed out. He went back to the rectory to wait out the storm.

As soon as Fr. Andrew was out of the sanctuary, Michael lit a match in the corner near the altar where he was hiding with the matchbook he used to light the firecrackers in the tire swing. He re-lit most of the candles near the altar Fr. Andrew had snuffed out moments before.

A blast of wind came through well ahead of the tornado announcing its pending arrival. After that came a brief interlude of rain and hail. And then, it came.

It started out west of town. It approached the shack at the radio station where Larry was repeatedly announcing over and over again the tornado warning and missing children simultaneously. He could hear it outside, the sound of a train barreling towards him. Larry should have ducked for cover as boards from his little shack were ripped from the walls and turned into missiles looking to impale anything and anyone. Larry refused to give up his spot in his chair. He continued to broadcast, yelling as loud as his lungs would allow. He was competing with the shrill of the tornado.

"It's here! It's here! The tornado is just west of town heading east. Take cover! Take cover now!"

As quickly as the tornado approached him, it left, leaving Larry unharmed. His home was partially destroyed around him.

Next, the tornado hit the school where Jake and Angela were half naked in the moment of a teenage sexual attempt. Jake didn't know what to do with Angela. He could only stare at her breasts as the rest of the world melted away including Angela herself.

"Jake," she started repeating as she stared out the back window of the car. "Jake. Jake!"

"Yes, Angela." He thought she was really getting into it.

"No! Jake! Look out!" A roof from some building somewhere landed on top of the car. Jake pulled Angela as far down onto the floor of the backseat with him as he could to protect them both from the crushing impact. Glass broke around them. The roof was pushed down on them. They were trapped.

The tornado bounced along drilling out ground in one area and leaving another area untouched – one house demolished, the house next door without a scratch.

Pastor James was about to step out of St. Paul's Lutheran Church to continue his search for the children. He was unable to open the side door. The wind was holding it shut. The building made a sound of a groan. He attempted the door again. It opened easily. He stepped in and pulled the door shut behind him. Now the wind was trying to keep it open. It latched. He let go of the door handle and stepped back slowly into the sanctuary. The building seemed to take a deep breath. He could see the windows bulge in and out like lungs searching for oxygen. All was quiet. He waited a moment before attempting to step outside again. The door opened, but a giant oak tree branch barred his way. He ran out another way to check on Laura. He ran out into the darkness unable to see anything. The rain pelting his face faded quickly. A flash of lightning showed him an evergreen tree planted many years before he was here as the pastor was lying in his living room.

"Laura!" He ran towards the house searching for a sign that she was still safely in the basement where he had left her. "Laura! Where are you?"

He clawed at the debris giving no thought to the potential dangers of exposed nails, electrical lines, or broken glass. He had only Laura on his mind. He kept digging and kept yelling for her.

"I'm here!" came a soft voice. "I'm here!"

Pastor James ran a few feet to his left and resumed digging. "Thank you, God! Thank you!" he kept repeating as he continued to dig. He uncovered the basement steps and pulled her up. He embraced her and ran his hands all over her to make sure she was in one piece. "Are you all right?"

"I'm fine. I'm fine. Thank you!"

Lori was still frantically searching her home for her children hoping they were playing a practical joke on her. "Michael! Daisy! This isn't funny!" She could hear a roaring sound outside her house. Lightning and thunder partnered together to cut off the electricity to the entire town. Fear set in even deeper for Lori, but she refused to give up her search. She climbed up the stairs to the bedrooms for at least the fourth time to check every closet, hiding place, and corner she could think of when the roof began to break apart directly above her. She felt pushed down the stairs. She landed on the floor in the living room and crawled on her hands and knees into the kitchen to hide under the table. The entire house made a sudden jolt as if the tornado had given it a giant kick. And then silence. Lori waited a few moments to be certain it was over before she slowly crawled out from the table. She opened the front door to complete darkness. Something prevented her from taking a step. She stood there and waited while the rain tried to get past her into the house. As she was about to step out, a flash of lightning showed her the cellar floor seven feet below her. She nearly fell into her own cellar below her front step. Her house was pushed off its foundation and was precariously sitting atop its basement at an angle. She was trapped in her home. She delicately closed the door and searched for her flashlight and another way out.

Officer Helen Schafer was south of town along the highway listening to the warning siren blare. When the sky had turned green shortly before sunset, she knew she should be there to observe. She watched the tornado, lit up by relentless lightning, jump like a pogo stick from place to place, turning as it went, picking up pieces here and depositing them there. It grew and shrank as it wanted. Sometimes completely disappearing in the dark clouds only to reappear in another place. Shaking her head at the ongoing trauma her town was experiencing, she calmly called into dispatch and had them call in the county sheriff's department and the local fire department volunteers. "We're going to need help. There will be lots of damage. Send them now. Remember, we have two missing children. Bring every available body."

Marty was opposite Helen on the north side of town near the grain bins and water tower searching for Michael. The siren blared above his head pulverizing his eardrums. He found shelter in a shed holding equipment for the town maintenance workers. The tornado skipped over him with barely a breeze. Marty left his sanctuary expecting to see minimal damage to the town if any. At first, his expectations were correct. A turn onto Main Street told him otherwise. Two roofs from two different business places were completely blocking the street, one from the cafe in the city center and one from a gift shop across the street from it.

"My God!" was all Marty could say.

Craig was just leaving the park heading away from his bar when he heard a crashing noise behind him. It was so loud he thought it was directly behind him. It was not. A flash of lightning showed him a building being torn apart into kindling. "Oh, no! You've got to be kidding me!" he said out loud and started running towards the building. He stopped in his tracks when a huge piece of metal fell directly in front of him. He shined his flashlight on it. It was a mangled beer neon sign from inside his bar normally on the wall next to the dart board. "Thank God, I sent everybody home," he said. His insides began to shake. He never actually saw the tornado. "I didn't hate the place that much," he said out loud.

Mrs. Benson and Daisy crouched under a potting table in the basement. The wind shook the house. Daisy began to scream. Mrs. Benson gathered the child up close to her and reached out for her rosary. She began to pray for them both. The wind quieted down. Daisy cried in Mrs. Benson's arms.

Pete was blocks from his house. He knew there was trouble, but he was determined to be the one who found those kids. *Maggie will see I am a good man. I can be a hero.* He searched in earnest everywhere putting his flashlight to good use. The wind suddenly changed directions on him making him stop in his tracks. A feeling of fear overcame his spine. He turned around as the wind gave a wild blast. A parked car less than ten feet from him was picked up by an invisible hand and thrown across the street into a tree. Pete turned and ran home. "Maggie! Maggie!" He never ran so fast in his life.

He arrived to find Maggie standing in the front yard with Charlie in her arms glaring at a downed tree in the front yard.

"Can you believe this?" she asked, giving no regard to Pete's safety in the storm. Something made her stop and take another look at Pete. Even in the dark, he looked like a ghost. "Are you okay?"

"Yeah, yeah. I think I am." He sat down on the tree trunk in front of her. "Maggie?"

"Yes?"

"I'm glad you're ok."

"I'm glad you are too."

"I'm going to do what you asked. I will give Lori that new car."

"If it survived the storm."

"If it didn't, I'll get her another." He paused. "Maggie."

"Yes, Pete."

"I'll do whatever you ask if it means you will stay with me."

"Okay, Pete."

They sat in silence staring at each other for a moment. Maggie went over, moved Charlie to one arm, and wrapped her other arm around her husband. She still loved him and was determined to forgive him.

Michael was in the sanctuary. He wanted to have a serious conversation with this ethereal being called God or Jesus depending on who he asked.

"God? Can we talk? I don't know how to pray. I hope this is good enough for you.

"I noticed my mom has been changing a lot lately. I just wanted to say thanks for that. It's been kind of nice to have a mom around. She can't cook at all. She's trying, though. I like that. I like that she talks to me and my sister. She used to ignore us all the time. She sees us now. She loves us. Thank you for that too.

"I also want to say thank you for Marty. I have friends, but Marty is a real friend. You know what I mean? I wish he was my dad. He talks to me like a dad does. Or should. I've seen my friends with their dads. I've never had one before. It's nice.

"My sister, Daisy? I'm sorry I'm not as nice to her as I should be. But she's a sister, you know? I'll try to do better.

"I will try to do better in other ways too, God. I have been kind of bad. I've done things I shouldn't have done. I'm really sorry. Marty has got me thinking about things. Things like how what I do can hurt other people. I never cared about how other people felt before. Why should I? Nobody cared how I felt. You know? I've always been by myself, even when with my friends. They only hung out with me until their families wanted them home. No one ever wanted me around anywhere except when they wanted to do something fun, sometimes bad fun. They would go home to have dinner with their parents. I would go home to find something to eat. A peanut butter sandwich maybe. A bowl of cereal. Spaghettios. My mom tried to make pancakes. They were terrible! I couldn't eat them. But she tried. I like that she tried.

"I'm sorry for all the things I did, God. I'm going to try and be better. I want my mom to be happy. She is trying to make Daisy and me happy. I want to make her happy too.

"Thanks, God, for this talk. I know you don't usually talk back. But thanks for listening."

Fr. Andrew, under the same roof but at the opposite end of the building, sat in his bathroom waiting out the storm, eating a bowl of soup for his dinner and reading a prayer book propped up against the sink as he asked for protection for the people of Pennington's Corner. He didn't hear any noise until his prayer book suddenly fell from the sink onto the floor. *That's odd. That should not have fallen.* As he bent over to pick it up, careful not to spill his soup, he heard a noise like a bookshelf had fallen over. He put down the bowl of soup onto the countertop and left the bathroom to investigate.

Michael started walking towards the candles he had lit with the intention of blowing them out. Before he got near them, the wind began to howl so loud his ears started ringing. The building began to shake, and a loud cracking sound indicated the roof was being peeled off from the back of the church to the front.

At first, Michael froze in his tracks and covered his ears. Fear of the roof coming off sent him running to the basement of the church. He tried making his way down the stairs in the dark, feeling his way while going as fast as he could at the same time. He made it down, found the bathroom, and hid under a sink clutching the pipes. The noise was intense. His eardrums hurt. Fear gripped him, and he let out a scream no one could hear because the tornado above him sucked his very breath out of his lungs and up into its gullet.

17

Hallowed Be Thy Name

Fr. Andrew stepped out of the rectory. He looked up in time to watch the tornado, lit up by lightning, peel the roof off the church. As one entire piece, the roof flew over the rectory. Fr. Andrew spun around to watch it fly like a kite over the railroad tracks where it landed in a corn field. He heard a cracking sound behind him. He didn't have enough time to react. A broken off tree branch from behind hit him in the back of the head leaving him unconscious in the rain. The tornado disappeared not wanting to stick around and take responsibility for the destruction it caused. All was quiet.

Flashlights waved about as the search for the missing and injured was on. Neighbors checked on neighbors. Emergency vehicles gave up driving through town. Roads were blocked from downed trees and other debris. Power lines crackled on a couple of roads. Within minutes the sounds of chainsaws filled the air.

Larry continued to field calls and announce them on air hoping as many citizens as possible were hearing the reports.

"This is KPCN. What have you got?"

"Larry? This is Jim over on 8th Street West. We got the big oak tree out of the way so cars can get through. And, so far, no sign of those missing kids."

"Okay. Thanks. Next caller. Hello. You are on the air."

"Hey, Larry! This is Coach Meir. Sounds like there was damage up at the school. We need some able bodied men up there."

"Okay. You heard him, folks. Anybody who can, head that way." Phone rang again. "Hello. This is Larry on air."

"Excuse me? This is Mrs. Carol Benson."

"Mrs. Benson. Hello, this is Larry with KPCN."

"Hello. Yes. Could someone please inform Ms. Greenfield that her daughter, Daisy, is with me in my house? She is safe."

"Daisy Greenfield is safe with you? Oh! Thank God! Happy news! I will get that reported."

"I attempted to call Ms. Greenfield. There was only a busy signal. I would think a woman searching for her children would keep her phone line open for incoming calls."

"It was busy?"

"Yes. I tried multiple times. I think someone should go check on her."

"I'll report that too. Thank you, Mrs. Benson."

"You're welcome, and God bless you."

"All right, people. You heard Mrs. Benson. Daisy Greenfield has been found safe. Repeat: Daisy Greenfield has been found safe. Michael Greenfield still missing. Lori Greenfield has not been notified. Someone needs to check on Lori Greenfield. Repeat - Michael Greenfield is still missing, and Lori Greenfield has not been notified. Could someone please check on Lori Greenfield?"

Larry began to sweat. He felt this need to leave his post and search for Lori. He fought the urge deciding he was a bigger help keeping communication flowing.

His phone rang. "Larry here on KPCN."

"Larry. It's Marty. I'm with Craig. We are heading over to Lori's house now. We will update you when we know something."

Thank God! Larry thought.

Another call.

"Larry? This is Officer Schafer. I can confirm a sighted tornado. There is damage throughout the town. I ask people to please be cautious as they search for Michael Greenfield. Please stay off the roads so emergency vehicles can get through. And, please stay away from downed lines. Electrical company has been notified and is sending in crews right away."

On the radio, he said, "Here is a news update: The storm has passed by. Confirmed by authorities it was a tornado. Significant damage has occurred in various places around town. The search for Michael Greenfield is still on. Be cautious. Emergency personnel are spreading out through town. If you need help, seek one out. Check on your neighbors. Electricity is out all over town. Streets are blocked. Stay away from downed power lines. Electrical crews are on the way.

"Daisy Greenfield has been located and is safe. Michael Greenfield, age 12, is still missing. Lori Greenfield has not been notified. If anyone has any information on Michael Greenfield or Lori Greenfield, please report to me or to authorities."

Lori was crawling out from a window when Marty and Craig arrived.

"Lori!" yelled Craig. "Lori!"

"I'm here!"

"Where are you?" asked Craig.

"Craig, I can hear her," said Marty. "Listen."

"I'm over here! I'm stuck in the window!"

She saw flashlights shining in her direction. "There she is! Over here!" said Marty.

"Careful, guys. Seems like my house got blown sideways. It's off the foundation. You might fall in the basement." The men stopped and examined the situation in the dark. She was correct. The tornado pushed her entire house approximately eight feet off of its foundation and turned it about sixty degrees, exposing the basement and leaving the house in a precarious position. It could fall over at any moment.

"Whoa!" said Craig. "We'll get you out." Marty pried the window further open which was jammed in place because the house was tilted. Craig grabbed her by the arms and dragged her out. The two of them rolled on the wet ground amid broken glass and debris. "You okay?"

"Yes. I'm okay. Any word on my kids?"

"Yes," said Marty. "Daisy is fine. She is with Mrs. Benson. They hid from the storm together. Mrs. Benson tried to call you, but you didn't answer."

Lori chuckled. "Thank God! And thank you! Nothing is working in my house. Not even my house. What about Michael? Any word on him?"

"Nothing yet," said Craig.

Lori wanted to cry, but she didn't want to waste time when she needed to be searching for her son. "Let's go." The three of them headed off into the darkness calling for Michael.

"Michael!"

"Michael!"

Michael's name could be heard all over town along with the chainsaws. People abandoned their own destroyed homes in search of the young man who caused so much trouble in town. Calls continued to the radio station so people could report where Michael was not found.

"We searched the grain bins."

"We walked all the way to the trestle."

"He wasn't found at the swimming pool."

"No sign of him at the school."

But, two others were found at the school. A certain half-dressed couple were heard and rescued by Coach Meir.

"Well, well, well. What have we here?" he asked the two as he and a couple other men pushed the roof off the car.

Angela began crying from embarrassment and relief. Jake could only stare at the ground. Another neighbor approached with blankets to wrap around them. Angela ran off for home in the dark.

Jake started after her, but Coach Meir stopped him. "Hold on! Let her go. She's only going home where she belongs. We have to get you home." Neither man moved. Coach Meir couldn't hold back. "What were you thinking? You know she is underage. How far did you get?"

"What?"

"Listen, I am not a fan of 'kiss and tell,' but she is jailbait. How far did you get?"

"Not that far."

"Keep it that way."

The night dragged on. Storm clouds gave way to a clear sky filled with stars and a dimming moon. People started giving up from exhaustion and the idea that maybe it was best to wait for sunrise for safety.

Sunrise was coming. The first light of its rays peered over the horizon. As the list of places to search gradually got smaller, people naturally gathered at the scoreboard to decide on the next idea to find the boy.

"There aren't any places left to look," said Maggie. "Is it possible he ran away?"

"Maggie!" scolded Pete. He indicated Lori's hurt face at those words.

"I'm sorry," she said, "but I can't come up with any more ideas."

Some people agreed with her.

Pastor James decided he needed to rally the troops. "We can't give up. I'm sorry to say this, Lori, but for all we know, the tornado may have picked that boy up and deposited him somewhere. He may be hurt." *Or worse.* He didn't dare say those words out loud. Others were nodding as if the same thought was occurring to them as well.

Pastor James was about to continue his rally cry when he realized someone was missing.

"Has anyone seen Fr. Andrew?" No one was paying attention to Pastor James. They were discussing amongst themselves other theories that may have happened to the boy. "Hey!" he yelled to get everyone's attention. That was the only time most of them had ever heard him yell. It was a little shocking. He repeated his question with a great deal of force. "Has anyone seen Fr. Andrew?"

People looked at each other shaking their heads. Concern grew. Pastor James looked in the direction of St. John's Catholic Church, to the East, in the direction of the rising sun. The warm glow was barely starting to peak out over the horizon. Or so he thought.

"That's not the sun," said someone. "It's way too early for sunrise."

Pastor Andrew shined his flashlight on his watch. 4:14 a.m. It was too early. He squinted his eyes to see details in the distance.

The same thought began forming in everyone's minds. "Fire," Marty quietly stated, his voice refusing to work properly in its state of shock and fear. He had to mentally kick himself out of his frozen state to repeat the word. "FIRE!!"

Pastor James started to run along with every other member of the community right behind him. His friend was in danger.

Someone called the dispatch to alert the fire department, but the fire department volunteers had seen the flames and were already making their way there. Another called into the radio station, and Larry immediately reported on it. More people showed up to clear debris, grab hoses, and do anything they could.

Pastor James, Laura, Pete, Maggie, Marty, Craig, and Lori all arrived on scene at about the same time. They found firefighters hard at work on the old brick and wood building that was quickly succumbing to the flames.

Laura looked over to an ambulance that had made its way there. "James! Over there!"

Pastor James ran over to the ambulance where he found his friend being looked at for a very large bump on the back of his head?

"Are you alright?" asked Pastor James.

"I think so. Nasty headache, but I know who I am and where I am, so I should be okay. Ugh! That hurt."

"What happened?" asked Laura.

"I don't know. I saw the roof of the church come off and then something hit me on the back of the head."

"How did the fire start?" asked Pastor James.

"I don't know that either. I know I snuffed out all the candles before the storm hit. Maybe I missed one?"

Lori came running up. "Fr. Andrew, Michael is missing. Have you seen him?"

Fr. Andrew looked up in surprise and worry. He had no idea. He looked at Pastor James. The same idea entered both of their heads.

"Candles," said Pastor James.

"I'm positive I snuffed them all out. Someone may have relit them," said Fr. Andrew.

"Michael was carrying around a book of matches," said Marty. "He showed them to me."

Both men ran to the nearest firefighter and relayed their fear. "There could be a boy in there," yelled Pastor James.

"He may have lit candles as the tornado hit," said Fr. Andrew.

Marty tried to find a way into the church. The flames were too hot.

In seconds, firefighters were running into the flames. Lori began to scream. Craig held her.

The moments that passed were short but agonizing. Finally, a group of firefighters came out. In the lead of the group was a volunteer with his arms filled with the lifeless body of Michael Greenfield.

Once safely away from the flames, they dropped him on the ground and began CPR. There were char marks on areas of his body. They continued to work. Craig held onto Lori as she continued to scream. The ambulance team brought over a gurney blocking everyone's view. His body was lifted to the gurney and rushed over to the ambulance.

Helen was at the ambulance watching. As they closed the ambulance doors, she approached Lori who stopped screaming. "He's breathing. Let's go. We'll follow in my car."

Lori started crying again silently. Helen put her and Craig into her squad car, and they followed the ambulance to the nearest hospital almost thirty miles away.

Everyone else stared after the ambulance in silence while the firefighters continued to battle the flames. At this point, the only thing they could do was keep the fire from spreading. St. John's Catholic Church of Pennington's Corner, Minnesota was a complete loss. And Michael Greenfield's life was hanging by a thread.

18

Thy Kingdom Come

The sun did rise.

No one slept. Everyone got to work putting back together their beloved town. Tarps covered holes in buildings left by trees deposited by the whirling wind where trees did not belong. Streets were cleared. The fire continued to smolder in the blackened remains of a Pennington's Corner landmark.

St. John's Catholic Church was gone. Smoke rose from the black timbers like incense sending prayers to God's ears. Fr. Andrew walked alongside the remnants of his beloved building observing the disintegration still happening as charred wood collapsed into ashes in front of him leaving charred walls of pale brick.

Pastor James walked alongside his friend. "It's a real-life metaphor."

"What is?"

"What's happening there, here, under our feet. Disintegration. Just like the community was disintegrating."

"It was, wasn't it?"

"Until Jesus showed up."

"And a tornado."

"And a fire."

"What's the status of it now? Are we too late?"

"I don't know. I hope not."

"How are you and Laura?"

Pastor James did not want to answer that question. He didn't have an answer for himself. "Why do you ask?"

"I think the status of your marital disintegration will be more indicative of the community than this building."

"Hmph. Interesting theory."

Fr. Andrew noted the dodge of the question but didn't push.

Officer Helen called out to the two gentlemen over to where she was talking to the fire marshal and the county sheriff. "Looks like the fire marshal and the sheriff have a handle on what happened."

They walked towards them. "Well?" asked Pastor James to the fire marshal.

He responded. "It appears the fire started in the sanctuary to the right of the altar, up over there, from a lit candle. Fr. Andrew, you said you were certain you blew out all the candles before going to the rectory to ride out the storm?"

"That's correct. I am certain I put out all those candles. I would have seen if I had missed one."

"I think you would have as well. So, the theory is, Michael Greenfield was in the church and re-lit a candle."

"Why would he do that?" asked Pastor James.

"To pray," responded Fr. Andrew very matter of fact.

"Have you ever known Michael Greenfield to pray?" asked Pastor James.

"No," admitted Fr. Andrew.

"Well, gentlemen," said Laura, "I've noticed a lot of things Michael has been doing lately since that Jesus thing happened at the park that I never would have expected him to do. Prayer would no longer be a surprise to me." She continued with the fire marshal's theory of what happened. "Anyway, it seems he was possibly in prayer when the storm hit. He made his way down the stairs into the basement and made it to the men's bathroom where he hid under a sink when the tornado hit."

"Did the tornado actually hit him directly?" asked Pastor James. His voice quivered a little as he imagined what that child must have gone through.

"Looks like it, yes," responded the marshal. "Like it was directly above him. It threw debris around him and probably straight at him for a few seconds. That sounds like a short period of time…"

"…but not when you're in it," finished Fr. Andrew.

"Right," continued the sheriff. "His little body got beat up pretty badly. He was probably unconscious when the fire slowly started above him in the sanctuary."

"Wouldn't the wind from the tornado have put out the candle?" asked Pastor James. "How could it have started the fire?"

"Look around you," answered the fire marshal as he pointed to the charred remains on the brick walls. "Look at how spotty the damage is. Look at that home right there." He pointed across the street. "See into the living room? The front wall is gone. Half the living room furniture is missing. In fact, I think the recliner in that tree over there matches the sofa still in the house. But look at the throw pillows on the sofa set up for a picture-perfect family room. They didn't move. Tornadoes do crazy shit like that. Oh! Excuse my language."

They chuckled.

"I think we can forgive you on a day like today," said Pastor James. He went back to the subject at hand. "Did the tornado hunt that little boy down?"

"Feels like it," said Fr. Andrew.

"Why?" asked Laura. "Why would God do such a thing? Especially to a child like him? Hasn't he suffered enough in his young life."

Pastor James answered, "I think we are going to get asked that question a lot."

"I'm asking it now, too," admitted Fr. Andrew.

"James," said Laura. She spotted Angela walking towards them wrapped in a blanket. She appeared traumatized. Her eyes wide and red. Signs of hours of tears stained her face along with dirt. Her hair was a mess.

"What happened?" asked her father.

Angela began to cry. "I was in the tornado with Jake."

"You what?" Pastor James looked over at Fr. Andrew and the other two men. They immediately turned away to give the family some privacy. Pastor James directed his wife and daughter a few feet away. "Where were you?"

Angela tried to push out the words between sobs. "I was with Jake in his car by the school. Dad, a roof from a shed or a barn or something landed on the car. It crushed the top. And we were stuck on the floor of the car. Jake started screaming. And I started screaming. It was so scary..." Her voice trailed off.

"How did you get out?"

"Coach Meir and some others got the roof off and pried open the door."

"Is Jake okay?"

"I think so. He tried to walk me home, but, Dad, there's a tree in the house."

"I know," he replied, hugging his daughter. "I saw it. How did you know to come here?"

"People said you were here. I walked here." She burst into tears.

"You're with us now. You're okay." Angela hadn't cried on her father's shoulder since she was a young child.

At the hospital, Lori paced in the waiting room outside of the emergency room. Craig followed her pacing back and forth preparing to catch her if she fainted or something.

"How about I get you some water? Or a coffee?" asked Craig. He needed to feel like he was doing something to help.

"Coffee," she simply replied.

"Okay. I can do that." He darted off to find coffee.

He returned to find her sitting in a chair with her arms tightly crossed over her chest, holding herself, staring at the floor in front of her feet. He looked to see if something was there. There was nothing but a simple pattern on the linoleum floor.

"Here," he tried to hand her the coffee, but she could neither see nor hear him so she could take it from his hand. "Lori, drink something." He again prodded her to take it. She held it briefly and then set it down without taking a sip.

"I wish they would come tell me something."

"Me too."

"Craig."

"Yes?"

He looked at her in silence as she continued to stare at the floor.

Finally, she said, "Was I right not to tell you?"

"I don't know. Maybe."

"I thought you might've gotten scared and left town. I thought it best you were at least nearby even if you weren't being the dad."

"I think you were probably right. I would have left."

"So I did the right thing?"

"Yes."

"How do you feel about it now?"

"I'm glad I know now." He contemplated life with a son. "I'm sorry I was a coward before. So much so that you couldn't tell me."

"You aren't one now."

"I hope not."

"You aren't."

"How do you know?"

"If ever there was a time to run, this is it. You aren't running. You're here." She looked at him. Her eyes, though filled with tears, looked on him with love. It was the first time he ever saw it, and it was beautiful.

The doctor came out. "Ms. Greenfield?"

"Yes?"

"The next hours are going to be critical. We have your son in the ICU. I suggest you go home and try to rest. Come back later."

"Go home? Come back later?" Lori had never felt anger like this before at the idea of being separated from her child. "I can't go home! My baby boy is in there fighting for his life! And, I have no home. The tornado moved it."

"Can't she at least see him for a few moments?" asked Craig.

"I'm afraid she can't. He has third degree burns on about ten percent of his body, and second degree on another twenty percent. We can't risk any infections. Plus, his body was beaten up by flying debris from the storm. He has a broken arm and leg. Pulled muscles on his arms like he was clutching something like a handrail. He's bruised internally and externally. We are monitoring him closely. He is heavily sedated. Please rest while he is sleeping. Come back later."

Lori cried at the idea her son was experiencing so much physical trauma. "What happened to him?" She asked the doctor. He gave no reply. He shrugged his shoulders. "No one can know what Michael experienced."

Craig and Lori gave in and left the hospital leaving specific instructions on where they would be if anything changed. They went and checked into a local hotel just blocks from the hospital.

Craig checked into two rooms. He unlocked the door for Lori's room and led her inside. He stood in the open doorway. He felt odd about the moment. In the past, there wouldn't have been a need for a hotel. Every encounter they had occurred in the backseat of a car or outside someplace else. He never was with her in a bedroom or a hotel room. He felt horrible inside that he had treated her so cheaply. This time, standing there in the doorway of a hotel room with her son, their son, in a hospital four blocks down the road fighting for his life, he felt the weight of the respect he should have been giving her for all those years pressed down on him.

He tried to look at Lori's eyes. He wanted her to see he was there for her in every aspect. She refused to look up at him. Her mind was entirely on Michael. He bent down to give it another try. Still no connection. "If you need me, I'll be just down the hall a few doors. Room 107. Just over there." He pointed, hoping to see her look up at him. She continued with her arms crossed, her head bent down, her eyes on her feet. She nodded as if she understood and turned to enter her room. "Lori…"

She turned back but still didn't look up or say anything.

"I am so sorry about all that's happened." Craig meant throughout their lives. She thought he meant the storm and the fire and Michael. "I'm really sorry."

"Okay." She turned back to her room and closed the door on him.

He turned and went to his room and called in a status report to Larry.

Larry broadcast to the town that Michael Greenfield was still in intensive care at the hospital. Then he did something he had never done before. He got philosophical. "Listeners, let's talk about what happened last night. No. Let's talk about what has happened over the past few days.

"The entire town was having a pleasant day, 4th of July, if you all remember. Jesus himself decided to crash the party. Jesus. The big guy. Son of the big guy. And all hell broke loose. That was - what - four days ago? Four days. Our entire world turned upside down in four days. What is that all about?

"Isn't God supposed to be benevolent? Loving? Aren't we his children?

"Speaking of children, God's children – what about what happened to Michael Greenfield? There he is in the House of the Lord, and God sends a tornado and a fire to take him out. What kind of God does that? Certainly not a benevolent, kind, loving God.

"I only have one phone line. But call me if you have something you want to say on this matter. Look at that! I already have a call. You are with Larry on KPCN. With whom am I speaking?"

"This is Anders from out here along Highway 4, North of town a few miles."

"Hello, Anders. What do you think of our benevolent God who tried to take a kid from us?"

"Well, I gotta say, I was out there playing on the softball team when this all went down. You know? And I think this is not the work of God, or Jesus. I think this is the work of Satan."

"Satan?"

"Yes sir. I think Satan made that blood look like Jesus just so he could set us up for all this. We all got trusting that God was looking down on us with favoritism. You know what I'm saying? He set us up so he could send the tornado and cause the fire so we could all suffer watching this poor kid almost get killed."

Back at the remains of the Catholic Church, Laura came running up to the two men of God who were searching debris for items that could be saved. "James! Fr. Andrew! Come to the car. You both need to hear this!" Both men jumped into the car with her to hear the radio broadcast. Almost all of the town started listening in.

Larry continued. "Okay. Satan. But what about God? If Satan did this, why didn't God help us out?"

"Cause He wasn't here in the first place. He didn't do this. He wasn't here to do it."

"Isn't God supposed to be everywhere?"

"Well, yeah. But He wasn't here for this."

"All right. Thank you, Anders, for that thought. I'm hanging up to see if another call comes in. Yep. Right away. Who is this?"

"Hi. This is Carl from Cedar Ave. and 7th street West."

"Hello, Carl. What is your take on the events?"

"I saw the tornado coming right at us. I saw the face of Jesus in it."

"You saw Jesus in the tornado?"

"That's right."

"And what do you make of that?"

"I don't think Satan did this. I think God did."

"Why do you say that?"

"Cause he was the tornado."

"Okay. But why would he come to destroy us?"

"Well, that I don't know. I guess we weren't getting the message from his face on the scoreboard fast enough, so he decided to take the whole town out?"

"But he didn't take the whole town out. He just took bits and pieces and a little boy."

"Yeah, but that little boy isn't a good kid. You know? He's done some bad stuff. So has his mom."

Larry immediately hung up the phone on Carl. It immediately rang. "Okay. Thanks for your theory, Carl. On to the next caller. Who is this?"

"Wendy. I'm right down the street from the church that burned down."

"Hello, Wendy. What do you have to add to the conversation?"

"I think God came after that little boy not because of him but because of his mom to punish her. We all know what she is..."

Larry hung up even faster. He was now angry with himself that he started this. The phone rang again. He told himself not to answer, but he did. "And you are?"

"Hey, Larry. This is Marty. I live in town near Main. I know Michael Greenfield very well. He is my friend."

Larry let out a sigh of relief. "Hello, Marty! So glad you called! What can you tell us about the young Mr. Michael Greenfield and his relationship to God?"

"Well, probably quite a bit. But I don't think I would be much of a friend if I divulged that. I can tell you this. Michael is a good kid who was lost for a while. We all know he has a history of causing trouble, but he always pulled back before it got really bad. He did that because deep down, he has a heart. A good heart. I've seen his heart lately. He cares about his mom, his little sister, even about his friends.

Marty continued. "I don't know why Jesus came to town. He did. He came. He saw. Did he send the tornado? Did Satan? Was Michael the target? I don't know. I have a hard time believing that because...

He paused for a moment to take a breath. "Well, here's the thing. I saw miracles happening with that boy every day since the 4th of July. Every single day. His heart was buried his whole life. It was opening up. His mom was opening up too. And his sister. I think maybe they, as a family, were the targets, but not of the tornado and the fire. But of God himself. I think God came to Pennington's Corner for them. I'm positive he came for Michael. Not to hurt him. To reach out and help him.

"That young man was starting to see himself as part of a family, as part of this community, as a real friend to others." Marty's voice cracked a little. "He started to see himself as a person of worth. He was starting to have dreams of a real future for himself and his family."

Larry interjected. "Maybe Anders is right. Maybe Satan did send the tornado. If he did, maybe he sent it because he saw Jesus doing so much good in that boy that he decided he needed to stop it."

"Yes, that's what I think," said Marty. "I saw something else happening in this town too the past few days. I saw people being nicer to each other. More considerate. We shouldn't forget that."

"Thank you, Marty. I think that's great insight." The phone rang again. "Hello? And you are…"

"This is Mrs. Carol Benson."

"Mrs. Benson! What's your take…"

She abruptly interrupted him with fire and brimstone in her tone. "How dare you! How dare you question the wisdom of God! How dare all of you! This entire community! We have no idea why God came! The only thing we know for sure is He came! He blessed us, our little town, with His presence! We are nothing to Him! Nothing! He came here anyway. His very presence is reason to believe He loves us."

"Okay. Then, let me ask you this. Didn't you have all the answers why God put Jesus's face on the scoreboard? Are you now saying you don't know why? Did He send the tornado and cause the fire? And why would he do that?"

"We don't know what He did or didn't do. He may have done it as punishment for something. Or, He may not have sent it at all. Here is what I do know. He led me to find that little girl, Daisy Greenfield, Michael Greenfield's little sister. She was out there at the scoreboard looking for her mother, and God led me to her so I could bring her to safety. God did do that."

"If He wanted to punish us, why did He spare her and not her brother? Why? Does that really make any sense to you? It doesn't to me," replied Larry.

"I have been at prayer for years now, since the death of my husband in 1942. I have learned a few things about Him. Even though He loves us, that doesn't mean we aren't meant to suffer at times. Sometimes we have to go through terrible suffering. Why? I don't know why. No one does. Don't you see? He has a wisdom we cannot understand. We have to endure these things so we can know that God is God. Read your bibles. You'll see."

"Thank you, Mrs. Benson. Next caller?"

"This is Valerie. Elm and 3ʳᵈ East. We all know why this happened. It's because of that woman, Lori Greenfield. She is being punished for her years of being a slut. God tried to take her children as punishment for her doings, and we are all suffering from it!"

"Okay! That's all we have time for today, folks." Larry hurriedly hung up the phone on that caller before she could say any more. "Thanks for joining us. Now, how about we lighten the mood with some good old-fashioned polka?"

Larry was sorry he started that. He dropped his head down on his crossed arms on the table in front of all his radio equipment and sobbed. *I did it again, Lori, didn't I? I just hurt you again? Why did I do that? I hurt you. I hurt your kids. I hurt the whole town. I'm sorry. I'm so sorry.*

Two men sitting in a car on the other side of town looked at each other with the same thoughts about suffering going through their heads.

"We're going to need a meeting," said Fr. Andrew.

"Yep," agreed Pastor James.

19

Thy Will Be Done

Craig did not fall asleep right away. His mind was racing. *I should be with Lori. She should not be by herself. I can't believe I have a son. A son. Michael. And he could be dying. I should have taken him fishing. Except I don't fish. I wish I fished. He should be fishing. He needs a dad to take him fishing. I'm going to take him fishing. Will I be able to? Should I marry Lori? Marry! We'd be a family then.*

He turned on the television to try and divert his thoughts and slow down his brain. Eventually, he fell asleep. Once he reached the dream state, he was out. Three short hours later, a persistent knock on the door woke him. He opened it to find Lori there, her eyes red and swollen.

"The hospital called. They want me to come in. Come with me?"

"Of course!"

A nurse took them to the ICU where the doctor was waiting for them outside Michael's room.

"Ms. Greenfield, Michael is still in critical condition. The burns he sustained make him susceptible to infections that could wreak havoc on his system. So, I need you to be very careful and not touch him no matter how strong the urge. However, he is slowly waking up. I thought it would be best if you were the first person he saw."

She nodded her head. A nurse took her to the side to put a gown on her. Craig watched from outside the room as Lori entered. Her first instinct was to hold Michael's hand, but the nurse gently scolded her. She folded her hands carefully on her lap and began softly speaking to Michael so only he could hear, if he was conscious enough.

Craig took note of her mother's instincts kicking in more and more. It excited him. He hoped his father's instincts would someday kick in as well, if Michael would accept him. Craig was so enthralled at what he was witnessing between a drastically changed mother and son that he didn't realize he said those things out loud as a prayer to God until a nurse near him said, "Amen."

"Did I say something?"

"Yes. You asked God to make you a good dad for him."

"I did, didn't I?"

"I heard you loud and clear." She turned to get back to work.

Craig watched with intense anxiety as Michael's eyelids began to flutter. He couldn't see her because her back was to him, but he saw Lori's shoulders move in an expression of excitement as Michael opened his eyes, focused on his mother, and smiled. He heard Lori give out a sound of joy that originated deep in her soul, a soul she didn't know she had until now.

A few moments later, Michael was sedated again as Lori was removed from the room. Doctors and nurses descended on him. Craig was ready to spring through the door to see what was wrong. Lori came out in tears.

"What's wrong? What's wrong with Michael?" Craig yelled out.

"What?" asked Lori, at first confused by what Craig was asking. "Oh, no. No. It's fine. It's good. The doctor said this was a good sign. They just wanted to put him back to sleep to relieve his pain and so he doesn't cause more harm to himself. But, Craig, he woke up. He saw me. He knew me. He was happy to see me there." She put her head on his shoulder to let out all her fear and anguish in one good cry. He embraced her and relished in her reliance on him. Deep down, he always wanted this.

The doctor came back out. "Okay, Ms. Greenfield. Thank you for coming in. After seeing you, his vitals have stabilized more. Still in critical condition, but definite improvement. He's more stable. As I told you in there, I have sedated him again. He will sleep for hours more, so please go back to your hotel and get more rest yourself. Tomorrow is going to be a long day."

"Thank you, doctor," responded Craig. He took Lori by the arm and led her out. She seemed so relieved and worried at the same time, he wasn't sure she knew where she was or what she was doing. She had the look of a mother, and he loved it. "How about a little breakfast before we get back to the hotel?"

She nodded.

A little café provided hot coffee and cinnamon rolls to soothe their down-trodden souls. This time, she ate and she smiled. She was coming around again, acting like herself.

"Better?"

"Yes. Much." She changed the subject. "What am I going to do, Craig? I don't have a home anymore to take my children."

Craig thought about his destroyed business. He didn't know the condition of his own house. He kept that to himself. He decided to focus on one disaster at a time. The rest would have to wait. "We'll figure something out."

"We?"

"We."

Lori visibly relaxed. "He's going to be okay, isn't he? Scarred, but okay."

"I believe so."

"Thank you for breakfast."

"You're welcome."

"For everything."

He didn't know how to respond.

"Take me back to the hotel?" she asked.

"Okay."

They returned to her room. Lori unlocked the door herself. Craig said, "Sleep well," and turned to go to his room.

She reached for his arm and said, "Wait…" He felt the pull to go in with her but resisted it. He stood in the doorway holding it open. He was tired. He wanted to sleep. He wanted more.

She walked into the room and sat on the edge of the bed to make a phone call. Seeing her on the bed made his mind travel to all the men she had sex with over the years including himself. The quickies, the sleazy places, back seats of cars, behind sheds, and around various corners in the school building. Those images he conjured up from his own imagination hurt.

"Good morning, Mrs. Benson. I wanted to check on Daisy. See how she is doing. She is? Good. I am so glad she is able to sleep with all this happening. Yes. Michael is doing better! He is still in critical care, but he…"

Craig quietly closed the door to give her privacy and went to his room. He got ready for bed, an odd thing to do at 10 a.m., and laid down hoping for sleep. No sleep came. His mind continued on its imaginative journey putting her in different positions with different men. He started obsessing. He became angry at every man in Pennington's Corner. He realized that was why he hated the bar. He was catering to the very men who were repeatedly with the woman he loved, touching her, taking advantage of her, assaulting her, maybe even raping her, sometimes right in front of him. Anger created a slow burn inside him. This was why he was avoiding her as much as possible all these years. Deep down he knew he was Michael's father, but he couldn't get past her sexual exploits to be a husband, father, provider for her and her children.

And what about Daisy? Who was her father? Where did he fit in this equation?

He forced his eyes closed attempting to sleep. His mind went round and round in circles. Thinking about the children again brought his thoughts back to Lori and other men. His thoughts were circular, spiraling downward. Most of those men he knew. He sold them beer and burgers. Many of them considered him their friend. He played pool with them. He wanted to kill them. His mind wandered where it did not belong. After all, he had no claim to her. He never told her he loved her. She owed him nothing and could do as she pleased. Could he ever get past those images in his head?

He heard a soft tapping at his door. He got up from the bed and abruptly opened the door without looking at who was there. He knew it was her. He didn't hold the door for her. He deliberately let it swing back against her. She caught it and entered the room gently closing the door behind her.

"I wasn't sure if you were awake or not. I thought I should check on you."

"Why?"

"I asked you to come in. You left."

"I didn't think I should stay." He sat on the foot of the bed with his feet touching the floor and laid the rest of himself on it. He closed his eyes. Out of his own shame and guilt, he couldn't look at her.

"Why not?"

"Why did you want me to stay?"

"I wanted to thank you for everything you've been doing for me and for Michael. Staying with me through all this. The hotel room. Being my friend. Everything."

She crouched down in front of him at the foot of the bed, her knees on the floor. She positioned herself between his knees and ran her hands from his knees part way up his thighs. She looked at his face while his eyes remained shut. He let her hands do what they were doing enjoying the sensation, but either his conscience or his anger got the better of him. He suddenly sat straight up grabbing her hands and pulled them both up to a standing position. She gave out a little yelp at the unexpected movement.

"What are you doing?" he asked in an accusatory voice. "Is this how you show appreciation?"

"What?"

"A man does something for you, so you have to have sex with him to show him gratitude?"

"I guess..."

"You guess?"

"This is all I know how to do it. To say thank you. I... I don't know any other way. I've been doing it like this my whole life."

"Really?"

"Yes. Really. My mother always had men in the house. They gave her things. She gave in return. I learned to do the same thing. Somebody helped me with a homework assignment..."

"That was me."

"Or showed me some attention when I was lonely..."

"Also me."

"And others."

He winced.

"If we are going to talk about this, we have to be honest. You weren't the only guy I was with in high school."

"Marty..."

"And others."

"What others?"

"What does it matter?"

He stayed silent waiting for her to answer his question.

She continued. "And then there was Larry…"

"Larry? After high school?"

"When Michael was a baby."

"What did Larry do?"

"He helped me gain independence from my mother so I could raise Michael on my own."

"I could kill Larry."

"Why?"

Craig didn't answer.

She continued. "Cause he turned me into a prostitute? You had already done that. What difference is there in exchanging sex for baby formula versus exchanging sex for an English essay? It's still sex for a favor."

"He made it your career."

"He helped me make a career as a hairdresser."

"So, you're saying he's a good guy?"

"Kind of."

Craig winced again. "Larry is the good guy and I am the bad guy?"

"No! You're a good guy too."

"Neither of us are good guys. Not after what we did to you."

"It's not a competition. One has to be good. The other has to be bad. No! That's like an old western movie where the good guy wears a white hat and the bad guy wears a black hat. You each have two hats. Sometimes you're good. Sometimes you're bad."

"And you?"

"I've been bad long enough. It's time I try on a white hat for a change."

"We made you that way."

"No. I didn't know I had choices, but I did. I made them. I have to suffer the consequences for them. Maybe that's why Michael is where he is now."

"What? No. I refuse to accept Michael almost died as punishment for you. Or me." Inside, he was thinking it was punishment for himself, for not being a responsible father to him.

"Mrs. Benson would say it is."

"I don't care what Mrs. Benson says."

"Me neither," she whispered.

He liked how he felt when she whispered. It changed the atmosphere in the room. He tried to shake off the feeling. He didn't want to go there. Not today. She did.

She approached him again slowly, cautiously. "Is there anything I can do to show you my gratitude?"

"You can stop showing me gratitude."

She put her hands on his chest. "Why?"

He side-stepped around her and approached the window, keeping his back to her. "I don't want you feeling like you have to sell yourself anymore. Not even as a thank you."

"I don't."

"Then what is this?"

She came up behind and ran her hands up his back. "This is me recognizing that you love me, and me trying to tell you that I love you too."

He spun around to face her. He grabbed her wrists again and put them down. "You are making it very hard for me to be the good guy."

"I told you. You already are. There's nothing to prove."

She moved in closer. He bent down and kissed her. He intended to make it a short kiss. He failed. She pressed herself against him. He pulled her in, wanting her to melt into him. Visions entered his mind again. Visions of her in various positions with other men he knew. Friends. He stopped abruptly. "No!" He pushed her back and held her firmly by the arms so she could not move close to him again. "I need to be sure this is right."

"Why wouldn't this be right?" She honestly did not understand.

"Because..."

"Because?"

"There is so much history here, most of it not good."

"I don't agree. Most of it is good."

"Like when?"

"How many times would you and I spend hours just talking? Nothing else. Just sharing our lives with each other. No touching. No sex. The good times. The bad times. Sitting at the bar. Sitting in the car. Talking. We did lots of that over the years."

"Yes, we did."

"Those were my favorite times in my life. Being with my best friend. Not doing anything but sharing myself. And you shared with me."

"Not enough. I need to know I am doing right by you."

"How could this not be right?"

"Sex? How could sex not be right? Because it's all you know about relationships."

"What do you know that's so different? You think I don't know your dating history?"

Craig's head felt a little knocked to the side. "What do you mean?"

"What do I mean? How many other women have you been out with all these years? Hm? It's a small town, Craig. People don't just gossip about me. They gossip to me, too. I know."

"What do you think you know?"

"I know about Stacy. And Rebecca. And Janice. I know about your one-night stands. Your very few one-night stands. I know that you have hardly dated anyone because you've wanted to be with me. But you avoided me. You didn't have to, but you did. I know that you have been out on no more than a handful of dates in your entire life. I know that once you had sex with each of them one time, that you never called them again, and wouldn't go out on another date for years after. I know the only woman you've had sex with more than once in your life is me. And I know why."

He knew why too.

"It's because I am the only one you've ever really loved. Thing is, Craig, you're the only guy I've loved too. We love each other. Our histories don't matter."

"Don't matter? They do matter. What if you need something from another man? What then? Are you going to have sex with another man to get something you need?"

"Why can't I get what I need from you from now on?"

"What if I can't give it to you?"

"Is that what you're worried about? That you aren't adequate? That you can't provide for me? That's not what this is about. This is about what I am. I am a prostitute in your eyes. It's true. I was. I'm not anymore. I'm done with that. If I can't get what I want for myself or from you, then I will have to go without."

"Can you do that?"

"Yes. I can do that. The real question is can you let go of my past and leave it there?"

He contemplated. "I don't know."

"But you do love me?"

"Yes. Yes, I do."

"And I love you. Is love not enough for you?"

"Maybe not." He thought more about what he did want. "Maybe I need proof of loyalty."

"I don't know how to give that."

"Lie down with me."

"I'm here to do that."

"Without sex."

She paused. "I can do that."

"Can you? Can I?"

"Let's find out."

Lori pulled the bedclothes back and turned toward Craig. She stood in front of him and removed her clothes. She wasn't trying to be provocative, but Craig was suffering. He wanted her very badly.

"Craig, teach me how to love without sex."

She finished undressing and got into the bed covering herself with the sheet. She turned to face the wall so she wouldn't be able to watch Craig undress.

It helped. He removed his clothing as quickly as he could, climbed in next to her, laid on his back, and covered himself with the sheet. He tried to keep space between them. It was difficult. He could see her breathing out of the corner of his eye.

"Okay," she said towards the wall. "Let's sleep."

They remained in those positions for at least twenty minutes before exhaustion took over and they both fell asleep. A couple of hours later, both completely out, without any thought, Craig rolled over and put his arm around Lori, and she cuddled up to him.

20

Jesus! Where'd You Go?

Larry put out the word over KPCN radio shortly before noon. "I have an announcement from Pastor James of St. Paul's Lutheran Church and Fr. Andrew of St. John's Catholic Church. They are holding an emergency tent revival at the softball field in the park at 4 p.m. this afternoon. That's right. You heard me. A tent revival. Has anyone ever heard of either a Lutheran pastor or a Catholic priest holding a tent revival, much less together? Me neither. This should be interesting. See you all there!"

"A tent revival?" Maggie asked Pete as she entered the kitchen after walking Charlie. The sound of chainsaws making it diffi-cult to communicate as locals hired by Pete were busy removing the tree outside the front door. Pete was enjoying his last and only cup of coffee for the day. Maggie restricted him to one cup in the morning. Without a word about it, she removed the cup from his hand and dumped the remains in the sink. She could tell he would lie if she asked him how many cups he drank while she was out walking, but she knew it was at least his third by the looks of the coffee pot sitting out in the open. *How did he get away with sleeping around? He's not good at lying.*

He did respond to her inquiry about the revival. "I heard they rented a huge tent together. They've got something planned."

"Is it Sunday again already?"

"No. It's Thursday."

"Only Thursday? What a week. Are we having services together on a Thursday because of the fire? It will be odd worshiping alongside the Catholics. I mean, I can see letting them use the building so they can have their services, but to have them together? Is that allowed? Isn't that what the Catholics would call sacrilegious or something?"

"I don't know. I don't care." *The only thing I care about is you took away my coffee like I'm a child.*

Mrs. Benson wasn't any happier about it. As she taught Daisy how to clean up breakfast dishes, she complained out loud to nobody in particular because she knew the child wasn't listening. "A tent revival? Well, we can't go to that. That isn't the Catholic way to do things. That's sacrilegious. And at the shrine to Jesus too. I'll have to go. I'll have to make sure they don't disturb Him in any way. I work very hard to keep it clean. The ants keep wanting to crawl on Him. It's an ongoing battle. I guess I will have another battle to contend with: making sure no one takes advantage of Him and harms the sanctity and the holiness of it. I will stand guard and monitor."

By the time 4pm rolled around, a large white tent covered an area beginning from directly behind the scoreboard, almost touching it, outwards towards Main Street. There was a dais with a table on it and a few chairs. Out from the dais were a few more chairs, as many as they could find, and the rest of the tented area and the open park behind needed to suffice for people to stand.

Laura placed the tablecloth over the folded table for the altar. Pastor James put large candles on it to keep the wind from blowing it off. "I love how you told Larry to call it a tent revival," said Laura trying to start a conversation with her husband.

"Well," responded Pastor James, "I thought that would get everyone's attention."

Laura had a moment of hope. *Does he even realize he is talking to me?*

"Not long now," said Fr. Andrew as he looked at his watch. "People should start gathering soon."

"You think most people will come?" asked Laura.

"Out of curiosity if not for religious reasons," responded Pastor James. Another response. More hope for Laura.

Fr. Andrew nodded in agreement.

Mrs. Benson arrived with Daisy in tow. "Fr. Andrew! What do you think you are doing? This is not the Catholic way!"

"I didn't think about dealing with her," whispered Fr. Andrew to the other two as he turned to calm down Mrs. Benson, the beads of her rosary clinking together as she waved her hand in disapproval. "Don't worry, Mrs. Benson. This is not in place of Mass. This is more of a meeting than a service."

"Really?" She did not sound convinced.

"I promise. We will still have Mass as normal on Sunday. I just don't know where yet." He turned to Pastor James and grinned in an effort to persuade the Lutheran minister to share his worship space. Pastor James glared back at him without any response. Fr. Andrew continued his conversation with Mrs. Benson unheeded. "This event is to address all the chaos the community has been dealing with. That is all."

"Well. I would hope so. Things have been chaotic."

"I'm glad we agree on that. Maybe you can help?"

"How?"

"This started with you right here at the scoreboard. The arrival of Jesus made you an important figure in the community. Would you and Daisy be willing to sit up here with us? Your visible presence might help people stay calm."

"I have been the only one trying to maintain the shrine."

"Exactly. See? You are important to this entire endeavor. You are a central figure."

"Okay. I will help in any way I can."

"Thank you, Mrs. Benson, for joining us," said Laura as she led both Mrs. Benson and Daisy to sit in chairs up front.

"I haven't had an opportunity to clean the area yet this morning. Would you like me to do it now before we get started?" asked Mrs. Benson pointing to the area of the scoreboard under the tarp still covering it from the storm.

"I don't think that will be necessary," responded Fr. Andrew.

"Ope. Here we go," said Pastor James as cars started lining up in the parking lot.

Pete and Maggie were one of the first to arrive. They had their puppy, Charlie, in tow. Larry was there ready to broadcast it live to the listeners at home. Marty came with Officer Helen in her squad car. Dozens and dozens of others from in and out of town came to hear what the two men of God had to say about the situation.

Larry arrived with a microphone and broadcasting box slung over his shoulder weighing him down. He positioned himself in the front and held out the microphone. "We are live," he whispered to the two religious leaders of the community.

"Welcome! Welcome, everyone!" Fr. Andrew got started with a group prayer. "Let's bow our heads and pray for guidance and wisdom from the events we experienced together these past few days. Dear Jesus, we ask you to be with us, to guide us, and to teach us your ways. You have wisdom, purpose beyond our understanding. Help us to be patient to bear our burdens joyfully. In Jesus's name we pray. Amen."

Amens were scattered among the crowd. About half the attendees made the Sign of the Cross.

Pastor James spoke next. "This is not meant to be a worship service to fulfill our Sunday services. This is an opportunity to give all of you a chance to ask your questions, voice your concerns about the events of the past week, and for Fr. Andrew and I to help you sort through them as best as we can. Before we start, I would like to remind all of you that he and I are both human beings. We do not have a privileged two-way conversation with the Big Man behind that tarp there to understand his purposes for nearly destroying our town. We will do our best, but, please, extend a little grace to us as we also have questions of our own. Thank you."

"Why don't we start there, with some questions?" asked Fr. Andrew. One hand immediately went up. "Mark?"

"I don't understand all this."

"All what?"

"Why did He," indicating the covered image on the front of the scoreboard, "come here in the first place? Was he trying to warn us about the destruction coming? Is that why he came in blood?"

"I don't think any of us knows the answer to that," responded Pastor James.

Another hand. "Yes?"

"If God supposedly loves us, all of us, why did he try to kill that boy?"

Fr. Andrew attempted to tackle that very important question. "Us Catholics and Lutherans, we have slightly different views on suffering. These differences are small but significant. However, there are some things we agree on."

"Such as?"

"Such as the fact that we do suffer. It is part of human existence. It is required. We are here; therefore, we shall experience suffering."

"So, life sucks," said Jake from somewhere in the middle of the crowd.

"At times, but not all the time," interjected Pastor James. "Life is still beautiful. It's still worth living and sharing with each other." He found himself looking over at his wife as he said that.

She smiled at him. He felt a stirring in his heart. He continued. "Have you ever heard the phrase, 'You don't know what you have until it's gone?' Well, I think, as a community, we didn't realize how special we have it here. We were, all of us, taking things for granted – taking each other for granted."

Fr. Andrew stepped forward. "Everyone, take a moment and look at the people around you: your wife or husband, your child, your parents, your friend, your neighbor. Think for a moment if that person you care about had been where Michael Greenfield was during the tornado and fire and was the one in the hospital fighting for life now instead of him. Or, worse yet, that person's life was gone. How would you feel? Would you be standing here now wishing you had told that person one more time how you felt? How do you cherish your relationship with each other? How important is that person to you? Would you want that opportunity to express how you feel one last time? You have that opportunity now."

Pastor James continued, "We don't know God's perspective in all of this. We don't know why he caused blood to pour forth from Mrs. Benson's hand and create that image on that board. What we do know is that given the events of the past few days, we have the gift of opportunity to look at each other, to look at what we have done and have not done, to take this chance to give voice to what's in our hearts, to tell someone how we really feel about them deep down. Take this opportunity to express to someone how important he or she is to you. I will start." He looked at Laura, took her hand, and pulled her up to stand next to him in front of everyone.

"Laura," he continued, "I want to tell you that what you have done hurt me to the core. It shook my foundation as a human, as a husband, and as a pastor. However, as a Christian husband who serves God, this is also my opportunity to practice what I preach. I forgive you. I love you. I am not okay with what you did, but I accept it happened. I want us to move past it. I want us to continue working on our marriage. I believe, in the end, this trial we are experiencing will make me a better man, better equipped to serve you as a husband and better equipped to serve God by ministering to hurting people. Will you explore with me where we both went wrong and where we can make things right?"

Laura was unable to speak. Tears poured out. She embraced him.

Mrs. Benson looked at Fr. Andrew. "Father, I want to apologize to Lori Greenfield when she comes back to town with her son. I have judged her very harshly all these years. This time with her daughter has shown me that she needed help and that it was up to us in the community to give her that help. We didn't. I didn't. God called me to, but I ignored it."

"You are forgiven," Fr. Andrew. "God has forgiven you of your sin."

She continued, "We should organize an event to raise money to help her get her home rebuilt. I would like to help with that."

"I tell you what," said Fr. Andrew. "We'll organize another softball game." Fr. Andrew turned to the crowd. "I want to confess to God above and to all of you my sin of pride. I reveled in the numbers of people I brought to Him through the church, through the confessional. I lacked the humility I needed to understand that God was the one saving those souls, not me. My sin is the sin of pride, and I will work on that."

"Better say ten Hail Marys, Father!" yelled Coach Meir. A laugh traveled through the crowd.

Marty turned to Helen. "I love you. I want to marry you. Today. Right now."

Helen beamed. "Not now, my love. I have to keep an eye on this crowd. But tomorrow? I say yes!"

More mumbling filled the crowd as people hugged, shook hands, and some even cried. Long-standing proverbial hatchets were buried. Arguments settled. Friendships reborn.

Pete and Maggie sat in the front row not looking at each other.

Charlie wanted to get down off her lap. She let him go.

Pete saw the dog get down and took the opportunity to turn and face his wife. "Maggie, I don't think I can do what Pastor James just did."

"What did he do? He wasn't the one who had the affair."

"No, but he was the one who extended the olive branch to his wife and promised to try and make things better. I don't think I can do that."

"Why not? Not man enough?" she scoffed with contempt.

"Yes. That's why."

She looked bewildered. She expected anger in return, not agreement. "I don't understand."

"Because I'm not man enough for you."

"You're right. You're not." Maggie slowly took in what he was saying and found herself agreeing.

"I'll give you the house and alimony. You have your own business too. I'll even give Lori Greenfield the car I promised her."

"Yes, you will. I will see to it."

"You won't have to. This is a promise I will keep." He looked more deeply at her than ever.

Tears fell from Maggie's eyes. "I will use our attorney. I'll call him later today."

"That's fine. I can find another."

They both stood up and shook hands.

Pete started to walk away. He stopped and turned to his wife. "I really did love you. Every year. Every day. I forgot. But I did."

"Maybe one day we will love each other again."

"Maybe. Not today."

"Not today."

Pete walked away.

Other people were deep in conversations much the same. Some were crying and embracing each other. A couple of arguments occurred. A fight broke out but was quickly subdued by others around them. Some were laughing with each other like they hadn't laughed in years. Emotions were running high.

The pastor and the priest looked around at all the human connections, good and bad, taking place and decided all was becoming right with the world again.

"Fr. Andrew, my wife and I will be in need of some counseling sessions. Think you'll be available?"

"I think I can find time in my schedule."

"Good. I'll call you tomorrow." He looked around at the crowd and saw good things happening everywhere. "Should we say a word of appreciation to Jesus on the other side of the scoreboard?" asked Pastor James.

"Yes. I think we should."

The two men walked around to the other side of the scoreboard followed by Laura, Larry, and Mrs. Benson. Charlie had his nose to the ground right with them, and Daisy was on his trail along with Maggie yelling at him as usual. "Charlie, stop eating things off the ground." Most of the rest of the crowd walked through the opening of the fence and poured into center field to watch the tarp being pulled back from the face of Jesus.

The two men, smiling, almost ceremoniously removed the tarp, and the group peered at the red face of Jesus to show some appreciation for the time He took to affect their beloved town of Pennington's Corner. They were greeted with quite the sight.

Ants. It was covered with ants.

A moving stream of ants followed up from the ground and back down again to an ant hill that had grown up rather large over the past day. Mrs. Benson's constant cleaning of the area had kept them at bay until now.

Mrs. Benson let out a scream of shock at the condition of her place of worship which brought Officer Helen pushing through the crowd to reach the scoreboard closely followed by Marty. Those close enough to see let out expressions of shock. Those who could not see were informed of the latest event through murmurs that rapidly extended throughout the throng.

Charlie followed his nose which followed the ants to the red blotch. He gave it a good sniff and then a solid lick thereby removing a significant portion of it. Mrs. Benson screamed again and nearly fainted. Fr. Andrew caught her. Everyone was frozen in shock.

Maggie gathered up her dog. "Charlie! No! Bad dog!"

Everyone stared at the now half-eaten face of Jesus.

Officer Helen decided it was time to investigate. She approached the blotch, took her finger, and attempted to remove a piece of it. It had grown hard and turned a very dark brownish maroon color. She sniffed it and gave it a delicate taste. She turned to look at everyone.

"It's ketchup."

"It's what?" asked Pastor James.

"It's ketchup." She looked around at everyone. Everyone started looking around at each other. "Didn't anyone bother to check and make sure it was blood?"

They all looked at Mrs. Benson. "Well," she stammered. "It looked like blood. It felt like blood."

"It's not blood," reminded Helen. "It's ketchup."

The entire crowd continued to stand still in complete silence. No one knew what to say or how to react.

"So, all those things that happened…" started Marty.

"…had nothing to do with God?" finished Larry.

"How did it get there?" asked Laura.

The two men of God looked at each other. Neither had anything to say. There was no offer of explanation.

Daisy, standing in the middle watching and listening to all the grown-ups, shrugged her little shoulders and said, "I don't know."

Without words, one by one, and two by two, people walked away. They went home to examine their own behaviors over the past few days, and throughout the years. They went home to rethink all their religious beliefs, behaviors, and traditions. No one had any answers. Confusion reigned so intensely that all questions stopped.

All the spiritual confusion, questioning, crises of faith that developed over the past few days due to a ketchup stain on a scoreboard during a small town softball game was enough to pull a town apart and put it all back together again.

One question on everyone's mind was never answered. Did God do it on purpose? Was this a part of His plan? Was it some sort of heavenly cosmic joke? Or was it simply a ketchup stain?

The ants resumed their walk to and from the ketchup uninterrupted, breaking it apart, taking it to their underground bunker, and using it cooperatively to feed their own community nourishment so it could grow and prosper from this relatively inconsequential ketchup stain. Except it was not inconsequential. It was manna from heaven. From it, the ant community continued to thrive. Much could be said about the humans above ground in Pennington's Corner.

The End

About the Author:

Sarah Hauer was raised in the little town of Hector, Minnesota, a community still near and dear to her heart. Sarah is a Lupus warrior and an advocate for awareness of the lifelong effects of sexual assault and abuse. Along with painting, writing has become her way of dealing with the stresses of disease and helping to make the general public more comfortable with conversations around difficult subjects. Sarah currently lives in Southern California.

Synopsis

In the small town of Pennington's Corner, Minnesota, where two competing churches are holding their annual ultra competitive albeit comical softball game,what should be an insignificant event leads the townspeople to reevaluate their lives and their relationships. Six year old Daisy is attempting to eat her hotdog loaded with way too much ketchup and unintentionally smudges the ketchup onto the bottom of the scoreboard creating a fuzzy likeness of the face of Jesus in what appears to be blood. This creates an uproar among players and townspeople who debate whether or not this is a miracle from God telling the citizens of Pennington's Corner to repent. Chaos erupts as townspeople begin individual soul searches leading the town's Lutheran pastor and Catholic priest with the task of helping their community come to grips with multiple crises of faith including their own. The competing leaders of the two churches discover they must come together if they are going to bring the town to a peaceful settlement, but chaos reigns again as tragedy strikes the already burdened town.

BOOKS BY THIS AUTHOR

Shattered Crystal

Crystal is a fighter. A single mother and paralegal from Southern California, she is fighting crime, abuse, and, most of all, Lupus. Through it all, she finds reasons to keep on fighting. Witness to the horrific murder of a new friend, Crys becomes more engaged in her own life even as it is in danger of ending. Family, friendship, and love create the moments of joy that keep her pressing forward.

Between Layers Of Earth

The Honorable Veronica Marshall has returned to her hometown of Hector, Minnesota to attend the funeral of her favorite teacher, Mrs. Jane Mitchell, a poor widow with no living relatives. While balancing a busy court schedule, supporting her wife as she recovers from a serious accident, and enduring the judgments of a small community; Ronnie discovers Mrs. Mitchell's life was much more complicated than anyone believed.

Made in the USA
Las Vegas, NV
23 July 2021